'Sweeping powers of description transport her readers
to another place and time'
Rosanna Ley, bestselling author of
Return to Mandalay and *The Villa*

'A most engaging story . . . the past always catches up with
the future' *Image Magazine*

'Oh, lucky reader, here is a really super book . . . riveting,
moving and utterly feel-good'
Daily Mail

'Marcia's writing is, as always, lyrical and immensely
readable . . . An excellent and uplifting read'
Western Morning News

'Willett portrays the pleasures of life and the joy of simple
things, while remembering the sadness that comes with
ageing and the complex nature of family relationships'.
Good Book Guide

'Echoes of carefree childhood summers resonate throughout
Marcia Willett's beguiling story of family relationships'
Yorkshire Evening Post

'Willett captures the sights, sounds and smells of Devon
superbly . . . A must for women's fiction readers'
Booklist

www.penguin.co.uk

Marcia Willett's early life was devoted to the ballet, but her dreams of becoming a ballerina ended when she grew out of the classical proportions required. She had always loved books, and a family crisis made her take up a new career as a novelist – a decision she has never regretted. She lives in a beautiful and wild part of Devon.

Find out more about Marcia Willett and her novels at www.marciawillett.co.uk

By Marcia Willett

Forgotten Laughter
A Week in Winter
Winning Through
Holding On
Looking Forward
Second Time Around
Starting Over
Hattie's Mill
The Courtyard
Thea's Parrot
Those Who Serve
The Dipper
The Children's Hour
The Birdcage
The Golden Cup
Echoes of the Dance
Memories of the Storm
The Way We Were
The Prodigal Wife
The Summer House
The Christmas Angel
The Sea Garden
Postcards from the Past
Indian Summer
Summer on the River
The Songbird
Seven Days in Summer
Homecomings
Reflections
The Garden House

REFLECTIONS

MARCIA WILLETT

CORGI BOOKS

TRANSWORLD PUBLISHERS
61–63 Uxbridge Road, London W5 5SA
www.penguin.co.uk

Transworld is part of the Penguin Random House group of companies
whose addresses can be found at global.penguinrandomhouse.com

First published in Great Britain in 2019 by Bantam Press
an imprint of Transworld Publishers
Corgi edition published 2020

A CIP catalogue record for this book
is available from the British Library

ISBN 9780552175074

Typeset in 11.53/13.48pt Fournier
by Integra Software Services Pvt. Ltd, Pondicherry.

Printed and bound in Great Britain by Clays Ltd, Elcograf S.p.A.

Penguin Random House is committed to a sustainable
future for our business, our readers and our planet. This book
is made from Forest Stewardship Council® certified paper.

1 3 5 7 9 10 8 6 4 2

To Vivien

PART ONE

CHAPTER ONE

The town is waking and stretching, gearing up for the day ahead. No traffic moving. No tourists. It's a warm, golden September morning: shreds of mist lying along the estuary, white wings skimming low over the water; the trees' canopies touched to flame with early sunlight. Outside the house in Buckley Street, Cara closes the front door quietly behind her, crosses the road and goes quickly down the flight of stone steps beside the Fortescue Inn. Pausing for a moment on the quay, she gazes across the harbour to the smooth sands and wooded coves on the further shore, and then, impulsively, turns and makes her way along Fore Street. At the bottom of the Ferry Steps the small passenger ferry is already waiting and Cara boards, pays her fare and goes forward to sit in the bows. Several more locals join her on their commute to work, the engine throttles up, and the boat heads out across the harbour to East Portlemouth.

It's odd, she thinks, how being only a few feet away from land seems to bring a sense of freedom, of detachment from reality.

She glances towards the mouth of the estuary where the silvery, silken skin of the sea stretches towards the misty, indistinct horizon. A small boat is heading for harbour, hugging the deeper channel as it crosses the hazardous spit of sand called The Bar.

The ferry's engine cuts to a purr as it slides alongside the wooden pontoon and Cara waits her turn to climb ashore. No sooner has she stepped down on to the sand than she pauses to slip off one shoe, then the other. The tide is making, but above the high-water mark the sand is soft between her toes. Carrying her shoes, she walks along the beach and then perches on a rocky outcrop. In all the thirty years since her older brother, Max, bought the house in Buckley Street, it seems to Cara that Salcombe never changes. Time is irrelevant. Sitting here she is able to imagine that she is not alone, that Philip might come strolling along the beach, that she has not sold their house in London and that she still has somewhere to live.

The waves ripple along the sand and, on her second impulse of the morning, Cara bends forward, rolls up her jeans and gets to her feet. She walks down the beach and treads cautiously into the water. It is warm on her bare skin and she stands, feeling it ebb and flow around her ankles, watching a dinghy being rowed out to one of the yachts at anchor further up the river.

Presently she will put on her shoes and catch the ferry back to Salcombe, to Buckley Street; back to Max and breakfast. Just for this moment, however, she will remain caught up in her memories; listening to the cry of the sea birds, the hush of the sea, and the sounds of Salcombe waking up across the river.

Cosmo Trent drives slowly in these steep, narrow lanes behind Salcombe. This is not because he is nervous, but because he has discovered that through nearly every farm gateway, or round an unexpected bend in a lane, a photographic opportunity might be revealed. Here is one. A miracle of composition. Cosmo brakes and reverses to find the exact perspective. Between high banks of alder, thorn and hazel, the brackish waters of a narrow creek flow right up to the lane's edge. On the bank above the creek a house is almost hidden by the trees but a flight of steps leads down to a landing stage. A wooden footbridge spans the stream and on the far bank, amongst the reeds, a sign has been thrust into the mud: 'Private. No fishing'. A small dinghy, which has floated upstream of its mooring, is now wedged by the rising tide beneath the rickety footbridge. Beyond this scene, downstream, a swan is sailing gracefully towards the wider reaches of the estuary.

As he sits, turned sideways to look through the passenger window, Cosmo is aware of a movement in the back of the car. He glances round to see Reggie watching him. Framed by his long, floppy ears, his brown spaniel's eyes manage to look both patient and reproachful.

'Sorry, old boy,' Cosmo murmurs, putting his camera back on the seat. 'You've got to remember that this is all new to me. It's OK for you. You're used to it.'

If Reggie could sigh and roll his eyes he'd be doing it now.

Cosmo laughs. 'I can take a hint,' he says cheerfully. 'Home it is.'

Home. His home for the next few months is a contemporary miracle of stone, wood and glass. The converted barn is set near the head of the creek and Cosmo loves the barn's light and space, its heavy wooden crossbeams high in the roof, and the floor-to-ceiling windows. He drives on, thinking about the circumstances that have brought him here: the decision to take a few months' sabbatical from his job as a risk assessment analyst with an investment bank in London; his colleague Alistair telling him that his parents were trying to find a house-and-dog-sitter.

'They had someone lined up,' Al said, 'but she's cried off and they've got the cruise booked and everything. You'd love it down there.'

He and Al have been friends for the last five years, ever since they both joined the bank as graduates. When his parents invited Cosmo to Salcombe for a taster weekend, Al drove them both down from London. His parents, newly retired to their dream home, were delightful, Reggie was well behaved and benign, and even the problem that Cosmo doesn't own a car was quickly set aside.

'Mum's old Suzuki is insured for the dog-sitter,' Al told him. 'And Dad has an account with the local wine merchant.' He laughed. 'Three months' paid holiday in a dream location, mate. What's not to like?'

There is nothing, yet, not to like. Two weeks in and London has become unreal. As Cosmo descends the wooden staircase each morning, seeing from those huge windows the ever-changing creek, it's almost impossible to imagine the rush and bustle of the city, the noise and clamour of the Tube. At low tide the mud shines, smooth and soft as toffee, an egret paces at the margins and gulls bicker; at high tide the reflections are breath-taking. On fine mornings Cosmo makes coffee and carries it out on to the apron of lawn with Reggie at his heels. Sometimes it's so early that the whole scene is in monochrome. Then the sun rises slowly out of huge grey pillows of cloud and the creek is transformed.

Now, as he drives, Cosmo is aware of the last crowns of pale honeysuckle trailing in the hedgerows, the rosy flush of hawthorn berries and the ripening blackberries. Four small fields, neatly divided by hedges, are spread like a flag on the side of a hill. Each field is a different colour: rich red earth, pale gold stubble, brilliant green grass, and dull brown mud. Cosmo brakes and leans from the window to take another photograph.

'Whatever do you do all day?' Rebecca asks each time they speak. Her voice is a calculated mix of incredulity and sarcastic amusement. The subtext reads: 'What person in his right mind could stand the boredom?' He won't allow himself to be influenced by her distant attempts to control. If he's honest he's rather surprised at how little he's missing Becks, and at the extent of his relief that she has no desire to travel west to visit him.

'Much too busy,' she says when he invites her for a weekend. 'You know what it's like at the moment.'

Her slightly impatient response implies that he should know better than to imagine she could possibly get away. Rebecca is a junior barrister and is tied up with a complicated case that she hopes will result in plaudits and consolidation in her career. Though she has made it clear that he could move in permanently with her, Cosmo still maintains his small flat in Hackney. They have fun together, she's attractive and clever, yet some instinct keeps him from making the final commitment. He's hoping that the sabbatical will help him to clear his mind.

Cosmo swings the Suzuki on to the track that leads past the farmhouse and down to the barn. A small part of one of the fields has been sold with the barn, and shrubs and saplings have been planted to form a new hedge. He drives through the gateway, into the lean-to shed, which also houses a big pile of logs, and climbs out. Reggie jumps down and goes to check his territory. Cosmo watches him, enjoying the sunshine and the

peace. Here at the head of the creek there are a few houses clus-
tered above the lane, which winds away, round the point and
on into Salcombe, but there is no one about. The morning is
clear and hot. Cosmo knows that these remnants of summer
will not last long. Perhaps, when the evenings draw in and the
westerlies bring rain, he might find it lonely and depressing,
but meanwhile he'll fetch Reggie's lead and they'll walk into
Salcombe. He'll sit in the sun outside the pub with a beer and a
sandwich and watch the boats. Cosmo thinks of Al, and he
smiles: what's not to like?

He and Reggie climb down the steps from the garden, out into
the lane, and set off round the head of the creek. Dinghies
swing at their moorings as the tide begins to turn and a swan
rears up, beating the surface of the water into a flurry of spray
with its powerful wings so that the scattered drops flash in the
sunlight. Reggie potters ahead, glancing back from time to
time to check that Cosmo is keeping up, pausing to wait for him.

'Sorry,' says Cosmo, hurrying to catch up, putting his phone
back in his pocket and regretting that he hasn't brought
his camera.

As they pass the boatyard Cosmo clips Reggie's lead to his
collar and they walk on together, turning into Island Street.
Cosmo is fascinated by the old boatyards and sail lofts, the
smell of salt and varnish and tar, and the unusual shops and
cafés. Most of the summer visitors have vanished away but
there are still people around, enjoying the sunshine, eating pas-
ties on the waterfront, idling in Fore Street.

It's early for lunch and Cosmo decides to have a double
espresso in the Coffee Shop in Fore Street. The tables outside
are occupied but there's room inside so he settles Reggie and

goes to the counter to order his drink. The staff are friendly, seeming to recognize him, and an elderly man smiles and pauses on his way out to make a fuss of Reggie, so that Cosmo feels as if he is already becoming a local.

As he sits down, Cosmo reflects on this atmosphere of friendliness, the way strangers smile and say 'Good morning', or comment on the weather. He is not used to eye contact and brief exchanges, and he likes this easy-going cheerfulness. The words '*Dolce far Niente*' chalked up on a board above his head make him smile, too. 'The sweetness of doing nothing' suits the mood perfectly. He gazes out through the open doorway, at the sunny street and the people moving in and out of his line of vision, and wonders whether Becks would like it here. She would be restless until she had an itinerary: her phone showing her places to go, things to see, galleries to visit. Not for Becks the sweetness of doing nothing.

The sunshine is suddenly blocked as a figure comes in, just a silhouette at first against the brightness outside and then clearer as the girl comes right into the café. Her long dark curly hair is caught up in a series of clips and she is wearing white dungarees splashed with paint. Someone behind the counter calls a greeting to her and she smiles back, glancing around her and briefly catching Cosmo's gaze. Cosmo bends to stroke Reggie, not wanting to look as if he is staring. His espresso arrives, there is a little flurry of new arrivals, and the girl leaves with her takeaway coffee. Feeling irrationally disappointed, Cosmo sips his own coffee, ruffles Reggie's ears and settles back to enjoy the moment.

From the next table Cara watches him. The little thump of shock she experienced when she first saw him come in has made her heart beat fast. How strange that this thin, elegant, young stranger should bring Giovanni so forcibly to her mind after nearly forty years. He has Joe's dark, Italian colouring, that oddly familiar energy; his grace of movement, and the wide mouth ready to smile.

Cara lifts her cup to drink, holding it with both hands to steady it and resting her elbows on the table. Nevertheless, her hands tremble a little and she sets the cup down again very gently. She remembers Joe's little Fiat rushing them through the traffic from Fiumicino Airport, the heat, sex in the high bedroom looking over the city . . . Her mind clamps down on these memories and she sees that the young man, who is not Joe, has glanced towards her. The discipline of years kicks in and she relaxes, dropping her shoulders, lifting her chin and smiles politely at him.

His answering smile is friendly, humorous, and he gestures to the message chalked on the beam above their heads.

'*Dolce far Niente*,' he quotes. 'I love it.'

That his first words should be in Italian is another shock, but Cara continues to hold on to her self-possession and nods.

'It says it all,' she agrees. 'From which I gather that you're on holiday here.'

'Sort of,' he answers, and indicates the dog lying at his feet. 'House-and-dog-sitting for a couple of months. What about you? Are you on holiday here?'

'Sort of,' she answers, deliberately mimicking him. 'I'm staying with my brother, Max. He and his wife have owned a house in Salcombe for years and now they've retired to it.'

'It's just great here, isn't it?' he says almost wistfully. 'I mean, it's not a bit like London.'

'No,' she agrees, amused. 'Salcombe is definitely not like London. You'll notice that especially when the winter kicks in. But by then you'll probably be heading back to the bright lights.'

The dog is struggling to sit up, encouraged by this interchange, and Cara reaches to fondle the brown silky ears.

'His name is Reggie,' volunteers the young man. 'And mine is Cosmo.'

Cara keeps her head lowered, stroking Reggie, not wanting to reveal her own name but knowing she must return his friendly gesture.

'And mine is Cara,' she tells him.

'Cara.' He laughs delightedly. 'We're having quite an Italian morning, aren't we?' he exclaims. 'How odd, although there is an Italian connection on my father's side of the family.'

She experiences a swift stab of panic but luckily Reggie is standing up now, encouraged by Cara's attention, wagging his tail and causing a disturbance amongst the tables. Cosmo gets to his feet.

'Better be moving,' he says. 'I expect we'll meet again.'

'I expect we shall,' Cara answers.

She watches him go out and then picks up her cup again. Her coffee is almost cold but she sips it anyway, willing down the symptoms of a full-on panic attack. During these last few months, since Philip died, she has become subject to these episodes. He was her refuge, her rock, her co-conspirator; for nearly forty years he held the mirror that reflected her life. 'We need to be seen by others to be convinced of our existence.' She can't remember where she has read the words but she believes them to be true. Who will hold the mirror for her now?

Cara finishes her coffee. She remembers Giovanni, the way he used to call her 'Cara, Cara' — 'darling, darling' — and she always called him 'Joe'. She met him at a party in a friend's house in Kensington. She was nearly twenty and he was four or five years older. His friends, like his own family, were wine exporters and they were sophisticated, well travelled and great fun. He spoke English fluently and when she tried out her small stock of Italian words, he laughed at her and said the most important one was her name. How attractive he was: how easy to fall in love with him.

Cara pushes her cup aside. These thoughts, so long denied, are unnerving her. They've caught her with her guard down. She's still not used to being alone, to having nobody else to consult or consider, and it seems so strange: so lonely. The café is busy now and Cara reaches for her bag and stands up. She'll buy some bread and then go home to Max.

Max is standing just outside the doorway that leads out from the kitchen on to the small balcony, arguing with his wife.

'It's just for a few weeks, Judith, whilst she finds somewhere to live. Good grief, surely it's the least we can do.'

'Such an irresponsible offer,' his wife answers sharply. 'What would she do if you weren't there?'

'But I *am* here.'

'Nevertheless, I dislike these open-ended arrangements. So typical of Cara. And it will probably be a great deal longer than a few weeks, mark my words.'

Her voice is assured, irritated, and he sighs silently, watching Cara climbing up the steps beside the Fortescue Inn just below him.

'I agree that in an ideal world she should have had something lined up,' he agrees pacifically, withdrawing further into the kitchen so that Cara can't hear him, 'but the house sold so quickly. Philip hasn't been dead a year and she's not firing on all cylinders yet. Cut her some slack, for God's sake. How's everything your end?'

The distraction works. Judith's voice quacks on as she reports on the situation in Oxford where their pregnant daughter-in-law has broken her ankle. Their son Paul is lecturing abroad and Judith has rushed away to look after Freya and their two-year-old granddaughter. Max's suggestion that he should accompany Judith was refused. *She* must be the good fairy; the practical, capable one. He is a helpless male who will only be in the way. And, besides, there is Oscar, the black Lab, who is presently stretched out on the kitchen floor fast asleep. Oscar would not be welcome in the small terraced house in Jericho. Max is used to Judith's reminders of her ability to cope, of managing without him all those years as a naval wife, moving house, making decisions, coping with the boys. Now that he is retired he is careful to respect this. Much though he would like to see his family, especially small Poppy, he understands that he will be *de trop* on this occasion, but he feels guilty at a fleeting awareness of relief, of gratitude to Oscar, and his pleasure at the idea of spending quality time with Cara. However old they both get she will always be his little sister, eight years his junior; the small girl who was there to welcome him home from boarding school, to be rescued from scrapes. Each week their father hurried away from the big old house in Sussex to his work in the City, and to his mistress, whilst their reclusive, dysfunctional mother worked out her frustration on the gin bottle. Away at school, Max worried about Cara, neglected, exposed to their mother's crying jags and fits of temper. She died when Cara was nearly fourteen and Max was twenty-one and a midshipman at Royal Britannia Naval

College in Dartmouth. Philip Grey was his closest friend and, even after he moved on to Cambridge and then to the Foreign Office, Philip was always ready to spend a part of his holidays in Sussex. It amused them both to visit Cara at school and take her out to tea, and, when she was older, to vet her boyfriends; take her to the theatre when she was in London. Max had just been made up to lieutenant commander, the engineer officer on a nuclear submarine, and Judith was pregnant with their second son, when Cara and Philip decided to get married. Philip was First Secretary in the British Embassy in Rome and Cara was barely twenty-one. Max was now spending a great deal of time at sea, and he felt a huge sense of relief knowing that Cara would be looked after and also that his friendship with Philip would remain a close one. He's going to miss Philip.

'Well, give them all my love,' Max says to Judith when he gets a chance to speak. 'Freya must be very glad to have you there. I can come up if you need me.'

He hears the door open below him and Cara shout, 'Hi, I'm back,' and he finishes his call, waiting for her to come upstairs. She is using one of the bedrooms on the ground floor. The house, which is on three levels, has the sitting-room on the top floor to take advantage of the views across the estuary; the kitchen and master bedroom are on the first floor, and there are two bedrooms, a bathroom and a utility room on the ground floor. The stairs rise up directly into the big kitchen and Max waits for Cara to appear.

'Did you have coffee?' he asks. 'Did you remember the bread?'

'Yes to both of those,' she answers as she climbs the stairs. 'It's good to be in Salcombe again, Max. Thanks for letting me stay.'

It's the first time they've spent any decent length of time together since Philip died and now, suddenly, Max feels slightly ill at ease. He hadn't realized how almost any remark can be freighted with either insensitivity or mawkishness.

'It's great to have you here,' he tells her. 'Gives you a breathing space to decide where you might want to live. Obviously you didn't want to stay in London and I don't really blame you.'

Cara puts the bag with the bread in it on the table and stoops to pat Oscar, who lifts his head briefly whilst his tail beats a little tattoo of welcome on the floor. She wanders across to the doorway that leads out on to the balcony and leans against the door jamb. It occurs to Max that Cara never goes right out on to the balcony and he watches her curiously. She seems pre-occupied; jumpy.

'No,' she answers him, after a moment. 'The house was an investment and it was very useful when we did that home tour. And when Philip retired. He was so passionate about the theatre and the opera, and he loved London, but somehow it never felt like home to me. Perhaps at heart I'm a country girl, though I'm not quite sure where I really want to be. It was crazy to sell so quickly but it was too good an opportunity to miss.'

She still looks rather distant, as if she is untethered from the world about her, and he hastens to bring her back to some kind of reality.

'You could afford to rent for a while,' he suggests, 'while you think about it. No need to dash into anything. You could get a winter let round here somewhere.'

She turns to look at him then, her eyes alight with amusement.

'Judith would love that,' she says.

'Stop it,' he says at once. 'She'd be fine with it.'

But he's pleased to see the familiar wicked glint in Cara's eyes, to see the sadness dispelled. She's wearing jeans with a long blue denim overshirt, and deckies on her feet, and because she is so small and slight, her short fair hair barely touched with grey, she looks incredibly young.

'Well, of course she does,' snapped Judith when he commented on this to her. 'She's had a great life as a diplomat's wife, living in embassies all over the world, and she's had no children to worry about. No wonder she doesn't look her age. She doesn't act it either. More's the pity.'

It's such a nuisance, thinks Max, that Judith and Cara have never hit it off. It's going to make life very difficult now.

'Renting is a good idea, though,' Cara is saying thoughtfully. 'I might be able to find something quite quickly and get out of your hair.'

'I wish you wouldn't talk like that,' he says irritably. 'It's great to spend time with you, especially now that Philip . . .'

He flounders, not quite knowing where this is taking him, and Cara begins to laugh.

'Darling Max,' she says. 'You are the best brother in the world and I'm just so glad you are here, and yes, I'm going to say it. I am so glad that Judith isn't. Two's company and three is definitely a crowd. Now, for this moment, I'm glad it's just you and me. But I don't intend to milk it. Let's go online and look at rented properties around here. Not necessarily Salcombe. Maybe Dartmouth.'

Her earlier preoccupation seems to have vanished. Max heaves a silent sigh of relief and goes to get his laptop.

Cara watches him. As Max sits down at the kitchen table and opens his laptop, she wonders how it is that this young man,

Cosmo, has managed to rip the lid from memories she's hidden away for years. Was it just that extraordinary resemblance: the way he moved, his energy, his smile? That Italian phrase he used? And is she especially vulnerable now that Philip is dead? He stood between her and the past, protective and reassuring. They'd kept each other's secrets for so many years. Now she is alone, although she has Max. She studies her brother as he Googles properties, lips pursed in a silent whistle.

'There are a couple of interesting ones,' he says. 'Come and have a look.'

She goes to stand beside him, wondering how she will react if she sees Cosmo again, as she almost certainly will in such a small town. At least next time she will be ready for the encounter. She leans forward, trying to concentrate on the properties Max is showing her, but she is still thinking about Cosmo. And remembering Joe: how they'd danced at night-clubs and parties, shared intimate suppers in a small Italian restaurant where Joe was treated like a prince, and made exciting, passionate love in his friend's flat. How quickly she fell in love, so ready to believe that this was going to be the biggest thing in her life. How devastated she was when he went back to Italy.

'Are you OK?'

Max is staring up at her, frowning a little with concern.

'Yes,' she answers, pulling herself together. 'Yes, of course I am.' She points randomly at the screen. 'That one looks nice. Are there any more details?'

CHAPTER TWO

Cosmo is sitting on a bench on the waterfront, watching the boats and eating a crab sandwich he's bought from The Salcombe Yawl. Reggie sits attentively beside him, one eye covetously on the sandwich, but Cosmo is thinking about the girl he saw in the Coffee Shop: her paint-stained dungarees worn over a T-shirt, the way her hair was twisted up. She looked workmanlike, confident, happy. He knows that he shouldn't want to see her again but he does. It's probably because she's the antithesis of Becks, whose short black hair is always cut into neat sharp angles, whose business suits are smart, her high heels clack along busily and her iPhone is always clamped to her hand. She is ambitious, driven, successful. He admires that, finds it sexy. At the same time it's leaving less and less time for fun, for chilling, for seeing their friends. It's why he's kept his little pad in Hackney – so that he can take time out from the rarefied atmosphere that surrounds Becks; from her expectations of him. It's why he loves it here: the slower pace, the boats bobbing at anchor, the rise and ebb of the tides.

As he turns to share with Reggie the last piece of crust he sees the girl again. She is swinging along towards him and even as he looks at her, his fingers still outstretched to Reggie, she sees him and begins to laugh.

'I saw that,' she says. 'Very bad habit.'

He laughs too, delighted by this friendliness. He drags his handkerchief from his pocket and wipes his fingers.

'I couldn't resist, he looked so pathetic,' he tells her. 'Don't tell anyone.'

'I shan't have to,' she answers. 'He'll be begging now every chance he has. Is he yours?'

Cosmo shakes his head, making a face, guying guilt.

'Thought I'd seen him around before,' she says. 'You're in big trouble.'

He gets to his feet, seizing this opportunity. 'I'm dog-sitting him,' he tells her. 'His owners live just round the head of the creek. I'm looking after the house and Reggie whilst they're away for a couple of months. My name's Cosmo.'

He holds out his hand and she takes it briefly with a firm clasp.

'I'm Amy,' she says. 'I'm a local. I work with my dad. I'm a painter and decorator.'

He's slightly taken aback but doesn't show it.

'So that's like interior design? Must be fascinating.'

She smiles at his effort to reclassify her work, to make it sound more upmarket, but shakes her head, rejecting it.

'No,' she says. 'Just painting and decorating. I like working with light and space and colour. That's all.'

'Sounds good,' he says, trying to make right his well-intentioned blunder. 'You must be pretty busy round here with all the holiday letting.'

'We are.' She bends to stroke Reggie. 'What did you say his name is?'

'Reggie,' Cosmo reminds her. 'He's such a good dog. So obedient and well behaved.'

'You'll soon change that,' she says, and nods to him. 'See you around, then.'

'Yes.' He's reluctant to leave it so casually. 'I saw you earlier in the Coffee Shop. Perhaps we could have a coffee sometime?'

'Perhaps we could.' She smiles, and then relents a little. 'I'm in most mornings around ten thirtyish. I'll look out for you.'

She turns away, walking with that easy graceful stride, and he watches her out of sight and then looks down at Reggie. It seems that there is a look of reproach in Reggie's brown eyes: disapproval, even.

'Oh, come on!' says Cosmo defensively. 'It's just coffee, OK? It's not like a proper date or anything.'

He grabs the end of Reggie's lead and they set off towards Island Street, heading back to the creek, past the quirky galleries and cafés, the Salcombe Distilling Company. Cosmo has promised himself a visit to the Distillery and Gin School. They have a tasting bar but he hasn't quite liked to go on his own. He thinks it might make him look a bit of a loser. Briefly he wonders if Amy likes gin and, almost as a knee-jerk reaction, he pulls out his phone and pauses to send a text to Becks. Reggie stands patiently watching him. His tail wags gently as if with approval and Cosmo begins to laugh.

'What are you?' he demands. 'My conscience or something? Tell you what. How about we go up on Dartmoor? Explore a bit? OK. I know you've done it all before but I haven't. I'm on holiday.'

He puts the phone back in his pocket, gives Reggie a pat and they set off again. Cosmo feels light-hearted, excited, happy. He knows why but he doesn't want to admit it even to himself. Instead, he plans what he must take on his jaunt to the moor: his camera, the Ordnance Survey map, water for Reggie. He remembers the woman in the Coffee Shop, Cara, and he laughs and repeats the words to himself: *Dolce far niente.*

As she drives out of the car park, Amy sees him striding along with Reggie. She likes the look of him: the short spiky black hair, those dark brown eyes, and his ready smile. She wishes now that she'd asked him where he lived when he wasn't dog-sitting, what he did for a living, but it seemed all a bit too quick: too keen. She might go into the Coffee Shop tomorrow or she might wait a day or two. Amy drives away in the opposite direction, up Shadycombe Road and into the residential part of the town. She parks outside a semi-detached Victorian villa and gets out. Collecting some tins of paint from the back of the car, she walks up the drive, opens the front door of the house and shouts: 'It's me, Dad.'

There is an answering call, and she carries the cans inside, puts them on the doormat and shuts the door behind her. Her father appears in a doorway just up the hall and nods at her.

'Perfect timing. Thought they were in the van. Thanks, sweetheart. Bring anything else?'

She grins at him. 'If you mean, did I bring you something to eat, the answer's yes.'

'Come into the kitchen,' he says. 'I can take ten minutes. How're you doing down in Courtenay Street?'

She nods, following him into the big kitchen. 'Pretty good. It's a nice space to work in and they're lovely people.' She glances round. 'I like it better than this. And it's really cool that it's only just a few doors up from us.'

'Bigger, though,' he says, taking a flask out of a large canvas holdall. 'Much posher than we are in our little cottage.'

'I like our little cottage,' she says. 'And talking of posh, I've just met this guy called Cosmo.'

He raises his eyebrows. 'Seriously? Cosmo? Very posh. What is he, a grockle?'

She shakes her head and passes him a pasty. 'No. He's dog-sitting for some locals for a couple of months, he says. Nice dog.'

Her father bites into his pasty. 'What's the dog's name?'

'Reggie.' Amy laughs. 'Cosmo was feeding him a bit of his sandwich so I told him off.'

Her father nods. 'Sounds familiar. Interfering as usual.' He pours tea from his flask into a mug. 'So are you seeing him again?'

She shrugs, feigning indifference. 'Dunno. I expect so. Salcombe's a small place. Well, I'd better get back.'

'OK. Thanks for bringing the paint and the pasty. Don't forget it's quiz night at the pub.'

She gathers up the wrappers and crumbs, gives him a quick kiss. 'I'm off to Kingsbridge. Had a call from a lady who wants me to create a nursery for her new baby. I'm just going over to check it out. Should be a nice little job. See you later.'

Jack hears the front door close but stays where he is for a while, finishing his tea. He feels his luck at having such a bright, lively daughter living with him, working with him, but it hasn't been all roses. He can still hardly believe that it's been nearly ten years now since Sally died from that bloody awful cancer. Amy was thirteen. She'd been three when he and Sally bought the little cottage in Courtenay Street, raising every penny they'd saved towards a fearsome mortgage but determined to stay in the town. No way they could do it now, given how property prices have gone through the roof, but they'd managed it back then. Sally worked with him, took any odd jobs that came her way, helped him do up the cottage, which was a wreck. How she loved that little cottage. They'd grafted, and they'd been so happy . . .

Jack puts the mug down with a bang. The disease had eaten her up so quick and he'd felt so helpless, so angry. It was only having Amy that kept him going. He couldn't believe his luck when, after she'd finished her art course at Falmouth, she told him she wanted to join him, work with him, stay here in Salcombe.

'I love it here,' she told him. 'And I love this work, making things fresh and clean and bright. I like going sailing and going to the pub and walking on the cliffs. If you're happy with it then that's what I'd like to do.'

He could barely answer her without blubbing.

'I'll take that as a "yes" then,' she said.

And that's how it's been for the last couple of years. Amy's like her mum: she grafts, she's cheerful, likes a bit of fun.

Jack washes his mug under the tap, wraps it in a tea towel, puts it back in his holdall, and wonders about Cosmo. There was a certain note in Amy's voice, a little sparkle in her eyes, but he's glad now he didn't tease her about it. There have been a few young fellows about, quite a serious relationship while she was at college, but nothing too serious. He's learned to give her space and independence, and together they've learned to manage the pain of losing Sally. It will be very difficult when Amy decides to leave home but he knows it will happen and he hopes that he will be able to make it easy for her.

Not with Cosmo, though. He couldn't cope with a son-in-law called Cosmo. Grinning to himself he prepares to start work again, fetching the tins of paint from the hall, prising off a lid with a screwdriver. Suddenly he has a thought, takes out his phone and sends a text. Then he picks up his paintbrush, plugs in his earphones and switches on his music. Bill Withers. 'Lovely Day'. That'll do nicely.

The text comes in just as Cara and Max are finishing lunch. They sit at the big kitchen table, the doors open to the balcony and to the sunshine. Max takes his phone from his pocket and reads the message.

'Jack,' he says. 'Reminding me that it's quiz night at the pub. I had a senior moment a couple of weeks ago and missed it. He doesn't let me forget it now.'

'Jack?' she queries.

'Jack Hannaford,' he answers, tapping a reply. 'He did all that work here when we moved the kitchen upstairs. He's good news, is Jack. If you come along tonight you'll meet him, but don't underestimate him. He's a very intelligent man who gave up a career as a teacher in favour of being his own man. He's a free spirit.'

'Sounds like fun,' she agrees. 'You're so lucky to have all this, Max. Very clever of you to buy way back and to have this to retire to, and your little boat. I envy you.'

Max gets up, collects their plates, not knowing how to answer. He feels his good luck in the face of Cara's situation but the right words are so difficult to find. As he puts the plates into the dishwasher he has a sudden recollection: a flashback to childhood.

He was twelve years old, just home from prep school for half term. He was looking for Cara, calling her name, but she was nowhere to be found. He climbed the narrow stairs to the attics, pushed open one of the doors and then stopped, staring. At the end of the small room a huge, gilt-framed mirror was propped against the wall, taking up almost the whole space. Standing before it was four-year-old Cara. She was gazing into the mirror, talking and gesticulating eagerly to her reflection. She laughed, twirled round and pointed her toe. He watched, fascinated, yet something prevented him from going to join her. He retreated on to the landing, backing down the steps, and then he called her name again. She came running out, hurrying down the stairs to him, delighted as always to see him home.

'Come and see, Max,' she cried, hugging his knees, then taking his hands and pulling him up the steps. 'I've got a friend, Max. Come and see.'

He followed her, touched and almost frightened by the intensity of her excitement as she gestured at her reflection. She laughed, and twirled and then suddenly leaned forward and kissed her mirror image. Then she stopped and stared in delight.

'And look, Max,' she said. 'You have a friend, too.'

He knew that he must take it seriously, but that he must also try to diffuse the intensity, so he stepped forward and bowed to his reflection.

'Good day, sir,' he said solemnly.

Cara clapped her hands together. She stood for a moment and then bowed to her own reflection.

'Good,' he said. 'But now it's time for tea and I'm starving. Come on.'

She allowed him to lead her away, downstairs, but he still felt disturbed by the depth of his small sister's passion.

Remembering, he realizes how lonely she must have been, the late mistake in a loveless marriage. How much was her gaiety a shield against the silence and bitterness that existed between their parents; their mother's unpredictable behaviour? And now the wheel has come full circle and Cara is alone again.

She is watching him, puzzled by his preoccupation, and he pulls himself together.

'Yes, we've been lucky,' he agrees, 'but there's no reason why you shouldn't find somewhere to live here, too.'

'The trouble with moving around so much,' she says, 'is that there's been no real chance to put down roots. The house in Fulham was the nearest we ever came to it.'

'It's early days,' he says. 'Look, I need to get Oscar out for a walk. Do you feel like a yomp over Bolberry Down?'

'Love to,' she answers promptly.

'Good,' he says. 'Let's get going.'

Oscar is already clattering down the wooden staircase, and Cara pushes back her chair.

'Give me a moment,' she says, 'and I'll be with you.'

Max feels an awkward corner has been successfully negotiated. Tomorrow they'll check out a couple of rentals in the town. He shrugs away Judith's probable annoyance and follows Oscar down the stairs, whistling just below his breath. After a moment he realizes that he's whistling the opening bars from 'Let's Face the Music and Dance'. He shrugs. There might well be trouble ahead but he can't give up on Cara now.

CHAPTER THREE

O n the next few mornings Cosmo walks round the head of
the creek and into the town. He goes into the Coffee
Shop and orders a double espresso, but there is no sign of Amy.
He waits as long as he can without looking conspicuous and
then gives up and goes down to sit by the harbour and watch
the traffic of small boats and the passenger ferry heading up
the estuary to Kingsbridge. He's working on a new idea for a
blog and looking for a theme he can use with accompanying
photographs. Water seems to be an obvious choice here – the
sea, rivers, moorland streams – but he's hoping for something
unusual. Everybody these days is a photographer so it needs to
be really good. Today the town is being battered by strong
westerlies. The water is choppy, slapping against the quayside,
flags smack and the boats dance on their moorings. He sets up
his camera and takes a video, wishing that there might be some
sort of emergency that would bring the RNLI crew dashing
out, clambering on to the boat, heading out to sea, but he must
content himself with sight of the local ferry beating its way
through the spray to Portlemouth, and the cry of the gulls as
they are blown about like feathery rags above it.

'So you're a photographer?' says a voice behind him.

And here she is, standing watching him with a smile, as if she knows that he's been hoping to see her for the last few days. He can't understand this feeling of happy anticipation that seizes him at the sight of her. The amusement in her eyes, the quirk of her lips, put him on his mettle, but in a fun, exciting way. Becks challenges him to be as clever as she is, to be as quick, as successful, and he enjoys it, but Amy's is a different kind of challenge. This is a challenge to amuse, to entertain, to be worthy of keeping her company.

'I wish I were,' he says, putting his camera back in its case. 'It's just trying to find something different. What is it? That genius that sets the great apart?'

She nods, getting it, agreeing with him.

'It's a way of seeing, I guess. Of having an instinct for an angle, for a shape, for a composition, that's never quite been done before.'

He is delighted that she is immediately on his wavelength. Becks regards his passion for photography as a kind of childish game that bores her.

'I shan't give up,' he tells Amy. 'I'll get there one day. It'll be the perfect storm.'

'So have you had your coffee this morning?' she asks. 'I'm going for some breakfast. Want to join me? Where's the dog?'

'We went for a very early walk around Snapes Point,' he tells her, as they head for the Coffee Shop. He doesn't mention that he's already been in for his coffee. 'Poor old Reggie was knackered so he stayed at home.'

He follows her inside, glances around and waves to Cara, who is sitting by the window, whilst Amy goes to the counter to order.

'I'm having scrambled eggs and bacon,' she says. 'D'you want some?'

'Just coffee,' he answers. 'I'll get mine.'

They sit down together and she begins to talk about her work, the renovation of the cottage, planning the colours for a nursery, decorating a converted sail loft.

'So if you're not a photographer,' she says, 'what do you do when you're not minding Reggie and house-sitting?'

He tries to explain his work in London as a risk assessment analyst and she opens her eyes wide at him.

'Sounds very clever,' she says. 'I'm full of admiration for anyone who works in IT.'

'Are you?' He's taken aback but pleased. 'It's great to have time off, though. It was amazing luck that my friend's parents needed a dog-and-house-sitter just now. I love it here.'

'Not missing London?' Her breakfast arrives and she picks up her knife and fork. 'Not bored yet?'

He laughs. 'You have to be kidding,' but he feels another little stab of guilt. He should be missing Becks, or at least telling Amy about her. But he doesn't. It's as if he's in a different dimension, an alternative universe that has nothing to do with his work or London or Becks. Out of sight, out of mind. And anyway, what harm is there in sitting in a café talking to a girl? This time Reggie isn't here to act as his conscience and Cosmo relaxes, picks up his coffee and sits back in his chair. Out of the corner of his eye he sees the words chalked on the board above his head: *Dolce far Niente*. And he smiles to himself.

From her table, Cara watches them. It might be she and Joe sitting there, happy, excited, enjoying each other, and she is filled with foreboding. She can find no reason for it, no explanation, apart from that odd resemblance between Cosmo and Joe. There is no reason why two attractive young people shouldn't enjoy being together, except that she can tell from their body language that this is no casual meeting. Cosmo may think that he's looking relaxed, at ease, but there is a tenseness in his frame, a constant tapping of one foot; he is fizzing with energy. The girl seems calmer – she is able to be busy with her knife and fork – but she is aware of him, totally focused on him. There is no sign of intimacy – no display of affection – only an obvious physical attraction. Cara tries to be detached, yet she has this odd sense of impending trouble.

Before she can analyse it further, the door opens and Max comes in. To Cara's surprise he smiles at the girl, who waves and calls a greeting to him, before he goes to order at the counter and then comes to sit at Cara's table.

'So who is she?' she asks him. 'The pretty girl with Cosmo.'

'With whom?' Max glances back over his shoulder.

'That's Cosmo,' Cara says lightly, hoping to rid herself of her fears by talking naturally about him. 'He's dog-sitting, apparently. He's only been here a few weeks but he seems to have made a friend.'

'Well, the girl is Amy. She's Jack Hannaford's daughter. You met him at quiz night. They work together, painting and decorating.'

Cara rather liked Jack Hannaford. There was a positivity about him: good humour, confidence. He'd headed his team, they'd beaten the visitors and his delight was palpable. Cara was amused by his unashamed pleasure in victory and said so when he joined her and Max for a drink afterwards.

'Ah, they're old foes of ours,' he said, picking up his pint. 'Can't afford to give 'em an inch.'

Cara looks again at Amy. 'She's not like her father,' she says, thinking of the tall, fair man, blue-eyed, tanned, tough-looking.

'Amy's like her mum,' says Max. 'She died when Amy was a teenager. I told you.'

'Yes,' answers Cara, remembering the sad story. 'How awful for them all.' She watches Amy responding to Cosmo's charm and once again she feels that little *frisson* of apprehension. Then Max's coffee arrives and he's leaning forward, talking again.

'I've had a call from Sam,' he's saying. 'He's asking if he can come and stay for a few days and I'm wondering how you'd feel about that.'

'Sam?' she queries, frowning in puzzlement. 'Sorry. Who's Sam?'

'Sam Chadwick. Actually, you might not remember him. He's my godson. His father and I were oppos way back.'

'I'm not sure I've ever met him,' says Cara. 'You've got so many godchildren, Max.'

He laughs. 'Can't think why, but I try to keep up with them all. The thing is that young Sam has passed his Admiralty Interview Board and he'll be off to Dartmouth after Christmas. Perhaps he needs a bit of encouragement.'

'And is his father pleased that he's following in his foot-steps?' she asks.

Max's smile fades. 'Well, that's the thing. His father was killed. An IRA bomb back in the nineties. He never knew Sam.'

'My God,' says Cara, shocked. 'How terrible.'

Max gives a snort. 'And then, would you believe, the boy's mother died in a skiing accident when he was three.' He sighs. 'Why is it that some people just get all the shit?'

'Poor Sam. Poor little boy.' Cara still looks shocked.

'Sam was brought up by his aunt Fliss and her husband, Hal Chadwick, over near Dartington. They're a good old naval family, the Chadwicks. Hal rose to great heights, actually. He's now Admiral Sir Henry Chadwick but he doesn't take it too seriously. He asked me to stand godfather because Mole and I had served together and Hal was an old naval mate, too, though not a submariner like me and Mole.'

'Mole?'

'Sam's father. It was his family nickname. No idea why. His proper name was Sam and I suppose the child was named for him. Anyway, that's the background. How d'you feel about him coming for a day or two? He's a good lad.'

'How old is he?' asks Cara. 'Is he joining the navy straight from school?'

'No, no. He's been to uni. Durham. He's twenty-two but he's a very mature twenty-two. Hal and Fliss were in their fifties when Sam went to live with them and the military background at home, plus boarding school, has its effect. He's very self-contained but great fun. We see him a bit more since we've retired. I think you'd like him.'

'Well, of course he must come,' she says. 'Did you say he lives near Dartington?'

'Yes. They've got a big old family place there. The Keep. Hal can drive him over or I can pick him up. Or he can catch the bus. He's got a little car but the parking here is usually so dire that he often makes his own way. It would be good to see the boy, if you're happy with it.'

'I'd love to meet him,' she says firmly. 'If he's asking to see you there must be some reason for it.'

'Probably needs some money and he's afraid to ask Hal,' says Max. 'No, no, I'm joking. He likes to talk about old Mole from time to time. He looks just like him, too. Gives me quite a jolt when I see him these days.'

Cosmo and Amy are standing up, preparing to leave. Amy lifts a hand to Max and Cosmo turns to see whom it is she's smiling at. He smiles at Cara, his face alight with friendliness, and that resemblance, so like Joe's smile, strikes afresh at her heart. She raises her hand to him, glad that Max is with her to discourage any further communication, and feels relief when the door closes behind them. She is beginning to feel the danger of keeping secrets, of being in denial, for so many years. Only she knows the truth now, and without Philip she feels a kind of instability, like a long dormant volcano about to erupt. She smiles quickly at Max, who is watching her thoughtfully.

'So when is he coming?' she asks, trying to sound excited. 'Should we do some shopping? Make the other bedroom ready? What would Judith do?'

'Judith would be fussing,' he answers, 'but I don't intend to get in a state about it. If we run out of food we'll go to the pub. Let's get home and I'll phone him and make a plan.'

Cosmo and Amy walk together down Fore Street and into Island Street. She has to pick up her car and drive to Kingsbridge. Her latest client wants to see some new paint charts Amy has found and to discuss the nursery in more detail.

'You could come with me if you like,' she suggests casually, and Cosmo stares at her in amazement and delight.

She doesn't quite know what has made her say the words – they seemed to come from nowhere – but she really likes being with him. He's stimulating, fun. She knows he likes her and she's enjoying the sensation.

'I'd love it,' he begins, and then his face falls. 'But there's old Reggie. I've been out quite a while and I'm not sure I should leave him much longer. He might start eating the furniture or something.'

'Bring him too,' she says recklessly, surprising herself further. 'You and he can explore Kingsbridge while I do my thing and then we could take him for a walk on the cliffs on the way home. He'll have to squash up a bit in the back of my car but the back seats are down anyway to get my stuff in. He's not that big.'

She's amused by Cosmo's expression. Clearly he's not used to acting on a sudden whim but he's enchanted by it.

'OK then,' he says. 'Let's go for it. Where are you parked?'

'We've got a special parking permit down in the boatyard,' she answers. 'Dad's got a boat so we're really lucky. Parking's terrible here, especially in the summer.'

They walk together past the car park, along to the boatyard and Amy indicates her car.

'Dad's got the van today,' she tells him. 'We share the car. It works very well in the main. Now you'll have to direct me. OK?'

'It's a barn conversion round the head of the creek,' he tells her. 'There are steps up to the garden but I have to take the car in from the lane at the back.'

'Yes, I know what you mean,' she says. 'There are quite a few of those around here.'

'I could go in and bring him down the steps,' suggests Cosmo, 'but perhaps you'd like to see the barn?'

'Yes, I would,' she answers. 'It's always interesting to see how they've been converted. It might have been one Dad worked on. I deal mainly with the holiday flats and cottages in the town but Dad sometimes works on bigger projects.'

She drives away from the creek, up the lane, and turns when he tells her into the track leading down to the barn. Amy sits for a moment looking at the scene.

'It must be wonderful,' she says with a sigh, 'to have a place like this. Imagine waking up every morning to that view.'

Cosmo nods. 'It's amazing each time. I have this little flat in Hackney and it's great to have my own space, even such a small one, but this . . . Well, it's another world. I'm really going to miss it when I go back. Not just the view but all of it. I love it here.'

It's on the tip of her tongue to say, 'Well, stay here then. Find some work, a place to live,' but she swallows the words down. He gets out, fishing in his jeans pocket for a key, and she waits while he opens the door and then looks around for her. Suddenly her confidence deserts her and she wonders whatever she's doing with this guy that she hardly knows, but he's gone in ahead of her. Now Reggie comes wagging out, delighted to see her, and she's able to regain her poise as she makes a fuss of him. She crosses the grassy space and steps inside, glancing about her at the space and the light, and the fusion of stone and glass and wood.

'The architect's done a really good job,' she says appreciatively. 'It's beautiful. But, look, I hadn't realized how late it's getting. I must get a move on, so if you're coming . . . I'll just make room for Reggie in the back of the car.'

She goes back outside while Cosmo collects a few things together and comes out again with Reggie. She's cleared a space for him, and Cosmo throws Reggie's rug in, arranges it and encourages him to jump up. He seems quite happy and, once he's settled, Cosmo gives him one of his treats and closes the door on him.

'This is great,' he says, climbing in beside her. 'Thanks, Amy.'

'You're welcome,' she says lightly. 'Now don't forget to keep your eyes open for a subject for your blog. Or for a really good photograph.'

He's told her about his new idea for starting a blog while they were having coffee and she's rather touched by his enthusiasm. As she turns the car and bumps slowly back up the track she wonders how her dad might react to Cosmo. She knows that she'll come in for a good bit of teasing: London boy called Cosmo; risk assessment analyst. Dad will do his local yokel act and she'll be embarrassed. Amy refuses to be daunted by the prospect, though. She hasn't met anyone she likes so much since she was at Falmouth. Briefly she wonders if Cosmo has a girlfriend in London but she guesses that it's unlikely that he'd come away for three months if there was anyone serious. It's rather good for her ego to be singled out by this very attractive man who is probably four or five years older than she is and who is so confident and amusing. She can tell that he's enjoying himself and she begins to smile as she pulls out into the lane and heads towards Kingsbridge.

CHAPTER FOUR

S am Chadwick walks through the lanes, away from The
Keep towards the bus stop at Shinners Bridge. When Hal
and Fliss heard of his plan to visit his godfather in Salcombe
there was the usual discussion about how he should get there.
He's decided not to take his own car this time, nor to accept
Hal's offer of a lift, but to catch the bus. As he strides along,
shouldering his backpack, he considers his motives for visiting
Salcombe. Since finishing uni he's been battling a sense of confusion and a real anxiety about his future. Once, way back
when he was little, a small friend said to him: 'You're an
orphan.' Even now he can recall his sense of surprise. After all,
he had Hal and Fliss, and, most importantly, Lizzie. When he
came to live at The Keep he was three years old and Lizzie was
the closest, dearest person in his life. His father was dead – he'd
died a few months before Sam was born – and if he's completely
honest with himself he can't really remember his mother. He
knows that in his early years Lizzie helped his mum to bring
him up and that it was Lizzie who decided that he should come
to his nearest relations at The Keep after his mother died. In
the years that followed, Lizzie almost replaced her, almost

became his mother. Of course, there was Fliss, his dad's older sister, and Hal, and they were very happy to welcome Sam into the family, but Lizzie stayed on, too, so that there would be that necessary continuity for the small Sam. It's been Lizzie who has gradually revealed his own story: how his mum and Mole weren't married, although marriage was a probability. How, after Mole was murdered, she hadn't had the courage to turn up at The Keep with his baby. It was only after his mother died that the three-year-old Sam finally met his family at The Keep.

Eighteen years on, Sam can see how lucky he was that Lizzie was prepared to stay on with him in his new home. She was his link back to his mother and to his past. Also, importantly, she was young. When she took him to the little village school, and picked him up, she looked like all the other young mums at the school gate. It was hard to be called an orphan but somehow Lizzie bridged the gap and gave him security and he didn't *feel* like an orphan. The Chadwicks were a large, close-knit clan, and very soon he began to be a part of it.

Sam pauses to watch a flock of long-tailed tits flittering in the hedge, and then strides on again. He misses Lizzie now that she is no longer there at The Keep – now that she's met David, married him and gone to live in Bristol – but he really likes David. He's glad that Lizzie is happy. Of course, they stay in touch – he's been to stay with them – but things have changed and he wonders sometimes what it might be like to have a mother and a father. Hal and Fliss have often talked to him about his father, who had the odd nickname of 'Mole'.

'It was because he was always under tables or chairs, burrowing behind things when he was little,' Fliss told him. 'It seemed very natural, when he joined the navy, that he would become a submariner.'

It was a shock to Sam to find out that his father was murdered by an IRA bomb when he was working at the MoD. Clearly there was some secret here. Hal hinted at Naval Intelligence, but refused to be drawn further about Mole's career. It was another shock when Sam learned that his grandfather and uncle, Mole and Fliss's elder brother and their parents, had been murdered in Kenya when Mole was only four and that he'd come back home to The Keep at almost the same age that Sam was when Lizzie brought him to meet his family. To hear this was extraordinarily upsetting: history repeating itself. Although he's known these things for a long while, it's only very recently that they've crystallized and come to the fore. During this last year Sam has become subtly aware of his own mortality. Worse, there's an inescapable and decidedly uncomfortable feeling that there's a curse on the males in his lineage. It is as if there is an ill-defined shadow lying across his future.

He tells himself that it's crazy to feel like this, way too dramatic, that Mole would be proud of him. He's passed the Admiralty Interview Board and might be following in his father's footsteps. But, instead, he feels this strange confusion, the sense of terrible loss as if, after all these years, he's mourning for his parents and for his grandparents.

At a crossroads where the lanes intersect and a small stone bridge crosses a tiny stream, Sam pauses in the sunshine, absorbing the sounds and smells of the surrounding countryside. He leans over the bridge, looking down into the peaty brown water, watching a wagtail hopping between the rocks, and unexpectedly he remembers another bridge in Shanghai. He thinks of its modern design compared with this ramshackle stone, and of the neat cultured landscape contrasted with this, his native countryside. He remembers days of heat and humidity, and of Ying-Yue's hand in his, and then shakes his head irritably as if to dispel the memory. Yet it has reminded him of the other idea, the other path that might be open to him. He recalls again the school in Shanghai, the ordered, well-disciplined classes of children. The chorus of: 'Good morning, Mr Sam.'

Why was he so happy then? Was it the teaching? The lure of being needed, of feeling welcome? Or was it Ying-Yue?

At Durham University he'd read Modern Languages, specializing in Mandarin. It was a four-year course and he spent the third year at the Shanghai Normal University. It was the most formative and exciting year of his life. He was good at languages, good at teaching: should he be contemplating abandoning something that made him so happy for a career in the navy?

A tractor rumbles by. The driver raises a hand and Sam returns his salute, then walks on. He can remember the shock when he returned to England from China, gazing out of the window of the train on its way to Devon, marvelling at the greenness of his homeland. He isn't sure why he feels this need to head for Salcombe, except that he's always felt close to Max and he needs to be away from The Keep just for the moment in case he betrays his fears, expresses his doubts. He loves Fliss and Hal and he doesn't want to worry them or hurt them.

As he reaches the Totnes road at Dartington, and waits to cross it, Sam feels irritated that Max's sister will be there. It would have been good to be alone with his godfather; to try to discover more about Mole from an outsider's point of view. Max and his father worked together in the navy and were good friends, which was one of the reasons Hal asked Max to be Sam's godfather. He knows from Hal that Max was one of the few people that Mole liked and trusted, and Sam's hoping that Max might help to clarify the past so that he feels less disturbed and more confident about the future. The bus arrives minutes after Sam reaches the bus stop. He swings himself aboard and settles down for the journey.

'What sort of boy is he?' Cara is asking Max.

Max thinks about it. 'He's very like his father. Mole wasn't unfriendly or standoffish but there was a solitariness about him. He was a first-rate officer, his men loved him, but there was just this air he carried with him, as if he had some secret.' He shakes his head. 'I can't explain it. Sam's a bit the same. Self-contained.'

'I'm not surprised after what you've just told me about his family history,' says Cara. 'It's so strange that they should both be orphaned in such a terrible way and both brought home to The Keep as infants. Awful.'

'At least Mole had his sisters,' says Max, 'although Susanna was not quite two so she really didn't know what was happening. And Fliss and Mole knew their grandmother. Sam had nobody except Lizzie.'

'So Lizzie stayed with him as a kind of nanny? And now she's got married?'

Max nods. 'David's a really nice guy and I think it's great for her. She's been so important in Sam's life and now it's good that she's going to have a whole new adventure whilst Sam starts his own new career in the navy. The time is right for them both.'

There's a little silence.

'Remember when Mother died,' Cara says, 'and then Father sold up in Sussex and moved us into the flat?'

'Yes, of course I do. I was at Dartmouth at the time but it must have been harder for you. Very tough.'

Cara raises her eyebrows at him. 'Seriously? You think it was tough to be living in swinging London after years of childhood with a reclusive, unapproachable and unpredictable mother and a mostly absent father?' She begins to laugh. 'Do you remember Harmony?'

He smiles too, albeit reluctantly at the foolish name. 'Hermione? Yes, of course I do. It's not exactly run of the mill to be introduced to one's father's mistress when you're twenty-one. I'm not likely to forget it.'

Cara gives a sigh of happy remembrance. 'She was utter heaven,' she says. 'That's why I called her Harmony. After all those years of bitter silences, chilly atmospheres, the bliss of being with someone who talked and laughed and took me to the theatre, to the ballet, to see *Peter Pan*. We went to art galleries, met her chums for lunch. I thought I'd died and gone to heaven. And she and Father were so happy together even though she was much younger than he was. He was like a different person.'

Max is silent. At twenty-one he'd found it embarrassing to see his father so unashamedly happy with a young woman who was not his wife. It was a relief to be away at sea. Not long afterwards he'd met Judith and he was even more relieved to have his own future to plan for, though he was glad that Cara and Hermione got on so well together.

'She had a boutique in the King's Road,' Cara is saying, 'and she gave me some gorgeous clothes. She used to come and visit me at school and the other girls were simply green with envy. I loved her so much.'

Max knows that Cara loves anyone who will allow her to love them and it worries him, especially now that she is alone again.

'I'm glad,' he says rather awkwardly. 'I didn't see as much of her as you did. But I'm glad she was there for you.'

He was going to add, 'And then there was Philip,' but once again he is hindered by his anxiety of being tactless, reminding her of what she's lost.

'So what time is Sam going to be getting here?' she asks.

He glances at his watch. 'Any time now,' he says, and he forgets about Philip and begins to think about his godson and to prepare for his arrival.

As soon as Sam sees Cara he realizes that all his preconceptions were wrong. He's been preparing to meet a slightly forbidding if pleasant woman. A woman who has lived in different cities all over Europe: sensible, confident, even judgemental.

This stereotype fades as he and Max walk into the sitting-room and Cara, sitting on the sofa with her bare feet tucked under her, and wearing an oversized shirt over jeans, waves to him informally.

'Hi, Sam,' she says. 'Sorry I can't get up but poor old Oscar is exhausted.'

She indicates the dog, who is stretched beside her with his head on her thigh. His tail thumps lethargically and Sam laughs.

'Don't get up, Oscar,' he says. 'I'll take it that you're pleased to see me.'

He crosses the room and shakes Cara's outstretched hand while Max makes the introductions.

'I can't believe we've never met,' she says, smiling at Sam.

Her smile is delightful and he feels at ease, welcome. He gives a silent sigh of relief and pleasure. Perhaps this was the right decision: to get away for a few days in an attempt to try to sort out his feelings. Max has gone back downstairs to the kitchen to make tea and Sam perches on a nearby armchair.

'Poor Oscar is feeling his age,' Cara is saying, 'and all these stairs aren't helping. It would have been sensible for him to stay downstairs after his walk but he can't bear to be left out of anything.' She grins. 'But I so get that, don't you? I can't bear to be left out of things either so I can't blame the poor old boy.'

Sam smiles back at her. 'Max will have to put in a stairlift.'

'Actually, that's not a bad idea,' says Cara, considering it. 'He and Judith might need one before too long. It's a long way up.'

'When I come up those stairs straight into the kitchen I always feel I'm climbing a gangplank,' he tells her. 'I half expect somebody to be waiting at the top to pipe me aboard.'

'Oh,' exclaims Cara, 'and that reminds me that I have to congratulate you on passing the Admiralty Interview Board. Well done!'

He feels pleased but faintly embarrassed. 'Thanks,' he says.

He wonders how she might react if he were to tell her of this weird confusion about his future, his thoughts about his father, but then he remembers that Cara's husband died earlier in the year. She knows all about real loss and bereavement. He hears Max coming up the stairs and turns, getting up to clear a space on the low, long table for the tray Max is carrying.

'Tea,' announces Max, putting a large pot on the table. 'Ordinary builders' tea. No fancy stuff, I'm afraid. And there's some lemon drizzle cake.'

He begins to pour the tea into the mugs and Sam glances around, at the view of the beaches across the estuary, and up at the skylight windows.

'This room is fantastic,' he says. 'So much light. And the view is amazing.'

'Not many people have their sitting-rooms in the attic,' Max agrees, 'but it seemed a pity to waste all this space and those views on a bedroom.'

'Sam thinks you should install a stairlift,' says Cara, drawing her mug towards her, 'now that you and Judith are getting senile.'

She bursts out laughing at Sam's protest and Max's indignant expression, and Sam begins to laugh too.

'I didn't say that. Well, I did, but for Oscar, not for you.'

'Poor old fellow.' Max sits at the other end of the sofa, shifting Oscar slightly and patting him. 'It's not the best house for an elderly dog. You might have a point, actually. Well, it's good to see you, Sam. I thought we might do some sailing while you're here if you're up for it. I'll be taking the boat out of the water for the winter soon but we might get a few more weeks in if we're lucky.'

'I'd like that.' Sam accepts a slice of lemon drizzle cake. He enjoys going out in Max's Vivacity 24. 'Are you a sailor, Cara?'

She considers the question. 'Not so's you'd notice,' she answers at last. 'I get muddled with sheets and jibs and all that "ready about" stuff. I like to be on the water but I'm not useful.'

'You said it,' agrees Max, ruefully.

'I shall stay with Oscar,' says Cara, patting the old dog's head. 'We'll walk out to Snapes Point and wave as you sail past.'

Sam drinks his tea. He feels relaxed with these two people. There aren't the usual questions about what he's doing that he generally gets from older people. A text comes in for Max from Judith, and Sam remembers to ask after Freya.

'Judith is rather worried about her,' Max tells him. 'It was quite a nasty break and the baby's due in a couple of weeks. Paul's on a lecture tour at Harvard. Judith's wondering if she should stay on in Oxford, just in case.'

Just briefly, on Cara's face, Sam notices an expression of hopefulness. It's gone in a flash but he wonders how well these two women get along and he's amused by the possibility that Cara finds Judith as tiresome as he does. He feels guilty about it but Judith is so managing, so controlling. Fleetingly Sam meets Cara's gaze and he knows that she's thinking exactly the same. He has to smother a smile but she sees it and her mouth twitches in sympathy. In the small silence that follows, Sam feels that some message has passed between them; something important, special. It's as if he has unexpectedly found a friend and an ally.

'Poor Judith,' Cara says to Max. 'Such a worry. It will be a great comfort for Freya to have her there.'

'Mmm,' says Max, non-committally, tapping out a reply.

As Sam finishes his cake, Oscar climbs down from the sofa and comes across to him. He licks Sam's fingers, his tail wagging with pleasure. Sam pulls his ears gently.

'You're just after my cake,' he tells Oscar. 'You don't fool me.'

Max and Cara laugh and the conversation turns to the dogs at The Keep. Sam tells them that Hal and Fliss are considering a rescue dog: a Labrador. Then Max suggests they all have supper at the pub and Sam agrees. He feels happier than he's been for weeks.

CHAPTER FIVE

'Seems we've got a settled spell of weather coming in,' Jack says, switching off the local news and weather programme and getting to his feet. 'Makes a nice change. Think I'll go for a pint. Want to come?'

Amy looks up from her tablet. 'I can't, Dad. I'm going out with Cosmo this evening. I'm taking him over to Prawle, to the Pigs Nose.'

Jack stands looking down at her, smiling a little, unable to resist the tease.

'Cosmo, eh?'

'Yes,' she says. 'That's right. Cosmo. That's his name. Get over it, Dad.'

'Get over what?' he says, pretending indignation. 'So when am I going to meet him?'

Amy shrugs. 'When I know you'll behave yourself and stop pretending that you think he's posh. It's no big deal, OK? He's just doing this house-and-dog-sitting thing up in Batson Creek. He's only here for a couple of months and then he's going back to London.'

Jack watches her. He knows his girl and he can see that she's not quite as casual as she makes out. He wants to protect her – to make sure she's happy – and he knows that this is quite out of his power. Still, he'd like to meet this Cosmo and get his measure.

'Well, perhaps we can all meet up for a drink sometime,' he says casually. 'Or bring him here for supper.'

She looks up at him again. 'Perhaps,' she agrees. 'I'll mention it when I see him.'

'See you later then,' he says, and lets himself out into the dusk.

Mist drifts in from the sea, slicking the streets, obscuring the harbour, diffusing lamplight. There is the hint of autumn in the soft air and he is glad to go down the steps and into the bar, to the light and warmth and the clink of glasses and the sound of laughter. He's even more pleased to see Max and Cara standing at the bar with a lad of about twenty-two or -three, and he remembers Max mentioning something about his godson visiting. Jack raises a hand to them. He likes Cara, though he's met her only twice. There's no side to her and she has an unexpected sense of humour. He can empathize with the pain of bereavement, with what it means to lose your own special person, and he can sense her struggle and respect her courage. As for Max: he's done quite a bit of work for Max but they also sail together and enjoy a pint on quiz evenings. Max is an old mate. He joins them, smiling at Cara, shaking Sam's hand as Max introduces them.

'Max tells me that you're going into the navy,' he says. 'Not another engineer, I hope?'

Sam shakes his head. 'No, not me. Much too complicated. I'm useless at anything mechanical.'

Jack claps him on the shoulder. He likes the look of this young fellow: quiet, self-contained, but not awkward or shy — and at least he's not called Cosmo. An idea begins to form in his mind. The barman pushes Jack's pint across the bar and he lifts it in the direction of the other three and then takes a pull at it.

'We're having supper here,' Max is saying. 'Want to join us?'

Jack looks quickly at Cara — Max has never made this suggestion when he's been with Judith — but she's smiling at him, nodding as if seconding the invitation. Sam is watching him with that same inscrutable look, unusual in one so young.

'I'd like that,' Jack says. 'Thanks very much.'

As they sit down at the table with their drinks, looking at menus, Cara experiences a swift, terrible longing for Philip. These moments come so unexpectedly, lacerating her heart and leaving her feeling achingly lonely. She breathes deeply, reads the menu again, and then smiles at Jack.

'How is Amy?' she asks. 'Max and I saw her in the Coffee Shop. Such a pretty girl.'

'Oh, she's abandoned me tonight,' he replies. 'I've been deserted for a guy called Cosmo.' He rolls his eyes humorously. 'I mean, come on. Cosmo? What kind of name is that?'

Max is grinning. 'Not being a snob, are we?'

Sam looks up from his menu, his face serious. 'We had a Cosmo in my house at school. He was in the first fifteen,' he says, as if this should put Jack's mind at rest.

Cara sees a whole variety of expressions pass over the older man's face as he sums up Sam's background, his education, his social position, and she sees a smile steal into Jack's eyes. He gives a little shrug.

'I rest my case,' he says ironically.

Cara shakes her head at him, wondering if Sam knows he is being teased, and Jack winks back at her.

'Who is Amy?' asks Sam calmly.

'She's my daughter,' answers Jack. 'She's about your age, I would guess. She's a painter and decorator like me. The ladders and overalls kind.'

Cara can see that he's waiting for Sam's reaction but Sam simply nods.

'I'm impressed,' he answers. 'I'm useless with a paintbrush or anything practical. There must be lots of work for her here with all the holiday cottages and summer lets.'

It's clear that this isn't quite the response Jack is expecting and Cara gives Sam a silent cheer.

'So,' says Jack, 'if you're no good at anything mechanical, and you can't hold a paintbrush or do anything practical, how did you get into the navy?'

Sam looks at him as if he's surprised at the question. 'Surely you've heard the saying, haven't you?' he asks. '"The navy only takes half-wits. It supplies the other half in its own way and in its own time."' He shrugs. 'Clearly we were destined for each other.'

Max bursts out laughing and Cara wants to give another little cheer but Jack is already raising his glass to Sam.

'You win,' he says to him.

Sam raises his eyebrows and pulls down the corners of his mouth, as if denying that he's been aware of a contest, but he lifts his pint to Jack.

'We're going sailing tomorrow,' Max tells Jack. 'Any chance of joining us?'

The talk turns to the weather, tides, and Cara sits back and picks up her glass. She glances at Sam.

'So how would you feel about helping me with a spot of house-hunting?' she asks him. 'I sold my house in London rather unexpectedly quickly to some Foreign Office friends and I haven't got anywhere to live.'

'I'd be happy to,' he answers enthusiastically. 'I rather envy people who move about. You must have done a great deal of it.'

'Can't argue with that,' she agrees. 'The trouble is, because of that, there's nowhere I really feel is home. That's why I'm here. But I can't stay with Max for ever, so you see my problem? I'm looking for places to rent or buy but I need some help. You're a local. Where would you live if you weren't at The Keep?'

Sam frowns, thinking about it. 'I'd really need to think about that,' he says at last. 'It depends on what you like to do and how you live. I mean, are you a country person or a town person?'

She laughs. 'Good question. If only I knew the answer to that.'

'Well then, you should look at both,' he says. 'Have you got any details yet?'

'Max and I had a look online,' she answers, 'but not seriously. I need to make a plan. Let's get our order in and you can tell me where I should start looking.'

Jack is listening with half an ear to this conversation whilst Max talks about bringing his boat ashore for the winter.

It must be hard, thinks Jack, to lose your husband and have no home that you've shared together. And no children.

At least he has Amy. He longs to intervene, to tell Cara about several properties in the town that will soon be available as winter lets, which she could rent whilst she looks around, but he sees that this is Sam's show. He suspects that Cara has deliberately involved Sam in this to include him and to show that he's not just a young man amongst three much older people but someone who might be useful and necessary to her. Sam has already taken his phone from his pocket and is flicking through various sites whilst Cara looks on, leaning forward, so that she can see what he's doing.

Jack is aware of a vulnerability only just masked by her cheerfulness. It was good to have that moment of connection with her when he was teasing Sam, and he was pleased at her delight when Sam scored his point, and then he wonders what Amy might make of Sam and how an introduction might be achieved without it looking too obvious.

'Have you been to The Keep?' Sam is asking Cara. 'It's beautiful around Staverton and Dartington. Totnes is great too. And the moor is really close. Fliss loves going to Dartington Hall. There's the gardens and a café, and a pub and a cinema.'

Max has finished talking and is sipping his beer so Jack feels that he can intervene quite naturally in the conversation now.

'Sam's right. It's beautiful. You should get him to take you over and show you around. There's a great little cinema in the Barn Theatre. They stream productions live from the Met and the Royal Opera House and the National Theatre. Do you go much, Sam?'

Sam hesitates. 'I do when I'm home. Films, mainly. Fliss goes quite a lot to the ballet. Hal's not that keen.'

Even whilst Jack is talking he can tell that the positions are now reversed. Cara is surprised that he should talk so naturally about the opera and he looks at her, smiling almost challengingly, as if to say, 'Who's being a snob now?'

She picks up his challenge at once. 'Are you an opera buff?' she asks.

'Oh, I wouldn't call myself a buff,' he answers. 'But I love opera. I was lucky enough to have a very enlightened music teacher. She took our whole class to London on several occasions, and to Plymouth, too, to see the opera.'

He can see that Cara is struggling to come to terms with this but Max is more direct.

'Seriously?' he asks. 'Schoolchildren? But opera is always so gloomy. So dramatic. And you can't understand a word they're saying!'

'They have subtitles now,' Jack tells him soothingly. 'Specially for people like me and you who don't understand Italian. Or German.'

He sees Cara's involuntary smile and he looks at her. 'And what about you?'

'Philip loved opera,' she tells him. 'So I learned to love it, too. Some more than others, I admit, but in the end I got it.'

'Favourite?' he asks her.

'*Eugene Onegin*,' she answers at once, and he laughs, nodding agreement.

'Well, you might be pleased to know that they stream a lot of it live at Dartington and the season's just beginning. I'm about to book to see *The Magic Flute*. Perhaps you'd like to join me?'

There's a tiny silence, as if nobody knows quite how to deal with this direct approach but Cara rises quickly to the challenge.

'I'd love to,' she says. 'Thank you.'

Jack glances at Sam and Max, eyebrows raised, extending the invitation to them, but they shake their heads.

'I think I'll give it a miss,' says Max, 'thanks all the same.'

'OK,' says Jack. 'It's next week sometime. I'll let you know the date, Cara.'

She nods, smiles at him and looks at Sam. 'Sure you can't be persuaded?'

'You mustn't forget,' interposes Jack gently, 'that we have it on his own authority that he's a half-wit.'

Sam shrugs regretfully. 'There you have it. People bursting into song at the least encouragement, murdering each other, committing suicide, dying of consumption. And all in a foreign language.' He sighs. 'I guess I just don't have what it takes to get it.'

Max laughs. 'I couldn't have put it better myself. Good man, Sam. We Philistines must stick together.'

'Just you and me then,' Jack says to Cara. 'I'm looking forward to it already.'

'Can't get over old Jack being an opera buff,' Max says later when they're back at home.

'But it was you who told me I shouldn't underestimate him,' laughs Cara.

She sits at the kitchen table beside Sam, who has borrowed Max's computer and is working through property sites.

'Well, he likes to do what Amy calls his local yokel thing,' says Max.

'You mean he chose what he wanted to do, gave up teaching so that he could do it, but still has a slight chip on his shoulder when snobby people treat him as a tradesman?'

'Something like that. He's a real craftsman, though. He just likes to wrong-foot people. To have a laugh.'

'Well, I hope the opera wasn't a joke,' says Cara. 'I'd like to go.'

Max is checking his phone. 'Will you excuse me?' he says. 'Judith is asking me to call her. Everything's OK,' he adds, 'but it looks like she's decided to stay on in case the baby comes early. Freya's mum can't get over from Denmark yet.'

He goes into the small study, pushing the door closed behind him, and the other two sit in silence for a moment, staring at the computer screen.

'Maybe she'll want him to go to Oxford,' says Cara.

Sam frowns at the screen. 'If it becomes difficult,' he ventures at last, 'you could always come and stay at The Keep. There's loads of room and Fliss wouldn't mind a bit. She was saying she'd like to meet you.'

Cara is touched by this kindness.

'That's very sweet of you,' she says, 'but I'm not sure where Oscar would fit in. In fact, I might be more useful if I stay here to look after him.'

'He could come, too,' says Sam. 'We all love dogs.'

Cara laughs. 'Well, that's very comforting. Thank you. Let's see what the outcome is before we make a plan. Perhaps you could stay on here to help me cope with Oscar and house-hunting?'

She watches his serious face break into a delighted smile.

'I'd like that,' he says. 'Look. There's a rather nice flat to rent in Dartmouth. Amazing views. Do you know Dartmouth?'

'Not very well,' she says. 'Philip brought me down to Max's Passing Out Parade but that was light years ago. It was wonderful. You'll have to show me round.'

Sam talks about Dartmouth, about how he'll be going to the College in January, and Cara jokes about taking the flat so that he can visit her. He's grappling with this sudden whole new take on his situation. He arrived slightly resenting Max's sister's presence, thinking he needed Max to himself, and now here he is, feeling quite elated by the prospect of introducing Cara to the South Hams and not particularly worried about Max going to Oxford.

He's really enjoyed the evening: meeting Jack, who was great fun; being co-opted to sort out Cara's housing problems. It isn't at all as he's envisaged it, but somehow his own problems have drawn back and cheerfulness is breaking in. So when Max appears looking rather serious Sam doesn't feel quite as anxious as he might have done.

'How's Freya?' he asks. 'Is everything OK?'

Max grimaces. 'She's OK but Judith's not very happy about leaving her. She's having difficulty getting about, what with the ankle and the baby, and Poppy's pretty full on. The thing is, Judith wasn't prepared for quite such a long stay. She went on the train, so she didn't take too much. She's made a list of things and asked if I could drive them up.' He looks at Sam. 'I'm really sorry about this, Sam, but it'll only be a few days.'

'We were just talking about it,' Cara says before Sam can answer. 'We could stay here and look after Oscar, if you like.'

Max's face lightens. 'That would be great. If you're sure?'

'It's fine with me,' says Sam, trying not to look too enthusiastic. 'We could do some house-hunting.'

Max sighs with relief. 'That's great, then. It seems a bit rude to invite people to stay and then walk out on them but if you're both happy then I can go with a clear mind. I didn't really want to take Oscar. The house isn't very big and he's just another complication. I'll only be away three nights, four at the most, I should think.'

'When will you go?' asks Cara.

'Monday morning. Sorry, Sam.'

'It's not a problem,' Sam assures him. 'If you're OK with me staying . . .?'

'Of course I am. You'll be company for Cara and I shan't have to worry about Oscar. Thanks.' He holds up the list. 'I'd better go and find some of this stuff.'

Sam hesitates for a moment and then decides to take the initiative.

'We need an itinerary,' he tells Cara. 'It makes it a bit difficult when you don't know the area but I think we might start in Kingsbridge, then Dartmouth and then Totnes, and check out some of the villages as we go along. I'm assuming that you have a car?'

He looks at her, wondering if he's being too bossy, but she's smiling at him.

'Yes, I have a car. Even big enough to squeeze Oscar into, if we need to.'

'That's good,' he says. 'There will be plenty of places to walk him as we go along. The important thing is to get a feel of the area and see if there's anywhere that you specially like. Then we can expand the search a bit. Does that sound right?'

'I can see that I'm in safe hands,' she says. 'And it's a great relief. I'd hate to be doing this alone.'

Sam feels pleased. He takes the laptop into the study and prints off some of the house details Cara has approved. He likes to be organized; to plan ahead. Sitting at Max's desk, listening to the printer, he begins to draw up an itinerary. It's good to feel useful.

When he gets home Jack goes straight to his cluttered, untidy desk in the cubbyhole that he calls his study and begins to search for the programme showing the events at the Barn Theatre at Dartington.

Amy calls to him from the big kitchen-living-room: 'Hi, Dad. Had a good evening?'

He goes to find her, bringing the programme with him. 'Yes, I did. Max was in the pub with Cara and that godson of his. Have you been back long?'

She shakes her head. 'Just got in.'

He looks at her, checking for signs that might indicate that it's been an unusual evening but she looks quite calm, not like a girl who's falling in love. Though he's not absolutely sure that he'd recognize the signs.

'Did Cosmo approve of the Pigs Nose?' he asks lightly.

'Mmm.' She nods almost indifferently and then grins at him as if she knows exactly what he's up to. 'What are you doing?'

'I'm checking the dates for *The Magic Flute* next week. It seems that Max's sister, Cara, is keen on it so I've offered to take her.'

'Ooh,' says Amy, 'that was quick. Nice, is she?'

It's as if suddenly the boot is on the other foot and Jack begins to laugh.

'Very nice,' he says. 'But I thought you'd met. She said she'd seen you in the Coffee Shop?'

Amy frowns, shakes her head. 'I don't think so. Oh, except that Max came in one morning and I think he went and sat with someone. Might have been her.'

'Well, she said that you were a very pretty girl.'

'Trying to get in with you, is she?' She grins at him. 'And now you're going to the opera together. Quick work.'

He sees that he's been completely deflected from any attempts to find out about her evening and gives in gracefully.

He studies the film guide. He needs to get a move on and book the seats. He glances at his watch. The booking office will be closed now so he'll have to do it first thing in the morning.

'It's Thursday evening,' he tells her.

They always let each other know when they have a date planned.

'Sounds good,' says Amy, uncurling herself from the sofa. 'Actually, I might ask you for a lift. I've had a text from Charley suggesting a catch-up. You could drop me off in Totnes and pick me up after.'

For some reason Jack feels slightly put out – it won't be quite the same with Amy in the car – but it's tough having only one car and the van between them, and there's no reason to refuse.

'Of course,' he says. 'How's Charley?'

He likes Charley. Amy met her at uni in Falmouth when they were both studying graphic art and despite the age gap – he guesses Charley must be in her late thirties – she and Amy became good friends. Charley grafts, and has a very laid-back outlook on life.

'She's OK,' answers Amy. 'Only she and Simon have broken up again. She calls it a trial separation but I think she's gutted, actually.'

'They're always breaking up,' Jack says impatiently. 'Simon goes off and does another course on something, or some land-scape gardening, and then the next minute they're back together again. And then Charley gets an idea in her head and rushes off. They're simply incapable of commitment.'

'I know. It's the way they are, but it sounds a bit more serious this time. Shall I say I can go over on Thursday evening, then?'

'Of course,' he says. 'It'll be good to see Charley again.'

'And I can meet Cara,' says Amy. 'What about the godson? What's he like?'

'Sam? He's a very nice lad. He's joining the navy. Going to Dartmouth after Christmas. I was wondering whether to invite them all over for a drink. What d'you think?'

She looks surprised. 'Why not? Max is always good value, though Judith's hard work.'

'Judith's away. I just thought it might be friendly. Cara's husband died earlier this year and she's looking for somewhere to live. You might know a few places coming up for grabs. Anyway,' he shrugs, as if it's not that important, 'it was just an idea. I'm off to bed.'

'OK,' she says, beginning to text. 'We'll make a plan. 'Night, Dad.'

He bends to kiss her, wondering if he should suggest that Cosmo be invited to the party, but decides against it. The presence of a complete stranger might throw the balance and Jack wants it to be fun. He's surprised at how much he's looking forward to it.

CHAPTER SIX

Cosmo walks by the estuary, Reggie a little way ahead, the late morning sun warm on his back. There have been two days of south-westerlies, bringing rain and shrouding the hills in clouds, but this morning the skies are clear and the countryside is sparkling in the autumn sunshine. With his camera slung around his neck, Cosmo is continually amazed by the jewel-like colours in the landscape all around him: crimson new-ploughed earth, green meadows, dark blue seas, gold and orange beech leaves. As he walks, he studies angles and shapes, pausing to take photographs and mentally writing small headings to accompany them. His new blog isn't attracting much attention yet – everyone is a photographer these days – but he still hopes that he will come across that once-in-a-lifetime picture that might set him on a different path.

As he walks, he thinks about Amy. She is like nobody he has ever known: so quick, so amusing, so ready to seize the moment. He loves the way she drives him around in her car, clearly enjoying herself: competent but always ready to stop, in a gateway or on a bridge, to say, 'Look. Isn't that amazing? Want to take a picture?' He's very attracted to her but he is in denial. After all, there is Becks. He still hasn't mentioned her to Amy. He's allowed her to believe he's a free agent. He has mentioned his small pad in Hackney, bigging it up a tiny bit, but not much.

Cosmo stands for a moment, watching the passenger ferry chugging down the estuary from Kingsbridge. The point is, he tells himself, nobody is being hurt. There is no evidence that Amy is getting too serious. Despite the fact that she's obviously attracted to him she has a casual way about her that indicates she can look after herself. Last night when they got home, she waited, engine running, while he got out of the car. Something made it difficult for him to kiss her, even lightly on the cheek, and though he invited her in for a coffee or a nightcap she shook her head.

'Nothing more for me,' she said, 'or I shan't sleep. See you around.'

She drove away, leaving him to stand staring after the car, and then he went in to check on Reggie feeling let down; disappointed. Yet there were moments earlier during that evening when they were almost intimate together. They leaned, heads close, laughing, and once he put his hand on hers on the table to emphasize something he was saying, and held it for a moment. She turned her fingers so that they were clasping his and he knows that they were both aware of that little jolt, like a pulse of electricity between them.

Cosmo gives a tiny shrug. Perhaps she's used to men coming down on holiday, chatting her up, hoping for something more, going away again. And isn't that exactly what he's doing?

He walks on swiftly, feeling confused. He can't get Amy out of his mind; she's a part of all this magic that's around him. London and Becks aren't on his radar here and he doesn't want to think about his life there. Just for now he wants to live in the moment: walking on the cliffs and in the lanes, looking forward to another evening at one of the local pubs, going into the Coffee Shop and waiting for Amy to come swinging in. He feels more alive than he can remember and when the text pings in he takes out his phone hopefully. Amy has his number now and has promised to tell him when she is free for another meeting. The text is from Becks.

Sounds good down there. Missing you. Thinking of coming for a weekend to recharge my batteries. xxx

As he stares at the text he feels as if he has had a blow to the solar plexus. It's the last thing he's been expecting: Becks here, critical, expectant, curious. It simply mustn't happen – but how can he deflect her? He puts his phone in his pocket and walks on, his mind doubling and twisting and seeking for a solution. And after a while an idea occurs to him. He takes his phone out again and sends a text to Al.

Help. We need to speak.

Amy puts away her stencils and her paints and glances around the small bedroom. Storybook characters and cartoon creatures have been carefully worked into the wall spaces and cupboard doors, and the effect is good. But even as she looks critically at her handiwork, Amy is thinking about Cosmo. As she packs up for the morning she knows that she's never felt like this before: not this madness, this fizzing in the blood when she's close to him. She's almost certain that he's feeling the same way but she's too afraid to test it. It's been such a short time and he's older, more sophisticated. She doesn't want to seem a naïve, foolish girl.

On an impulse she takes her phone from her pocket and dials Charley's number.

'Hi, Ames,' says Charley. 'How are you doing?'

At the sound of her voice Amy takes a deep, relieved breath. She feels calmer already.

'I'm OK,' she says, 'but it would be great to see you before next Thursday. I'm just finishing a job in Kingsbridge. Could we get a sandwich together? I can be in Totnes in about twenty minutes.'

'Not a problem. I'm working at the Potting Shed this morning and I'm going to lunch in about fifteen minutes, so suppose we meet in the Terrace Coffee Shop? Take it carefully, hon.'

'Thanks,' says Amy. 'Honestly, that's just great. See you there.'

She puts her phone away, still feeling this weird kind of madness, as if the world is in a sharper relief, that she is more aware of everything and everyone around her. Charley is the one person Amy can talk to right now. Charley's such a kind, happy, good person. She used to listen for hours when Amy talked about what it was like to lose her mum, what it was like never to have that kind of support and maternal love. Charley listened, made endless cups of coffee, and put the world into some kind of perspective for Amy. And the really good thing was that Charley was never pious or critical because she, in her turn, had problems of her own and was always ready to talk about them, so that Amy felt it really was a friendship and she didn't have to feel grateful, or foolish because she was younger.

As she says goodbye, gets into the car and drives away towards Totnes she is wondering how she could manage a meeting between Cosmo and Charley, to see her reaction and hear what she thinks about him. It's impossible to imagine introducing him to Dad; not yet, anyway. She needs to feel more confident. Perhaps, once she's talked to Charley, she might be more ready to move forward.

Charley comes out of the Potting Shed and walks the few yards to the Terrace Coffee Shop. She enjoys her part-time job, likes chatting to the customers buying bulbs and plants, or garden equipment or bird food, likes sharing a joke with Matt and Jane. She's also enjoying her two days a week as a classroom assistant at the local primary school. Since Simon's been working in Gloucestershire she's been lonely, confused as to where she should be directing her life, and it's good to have work, to have a purpose.

She goes into the café, smiles at the owners, Rob and Andy, who always greet her so warmly, and glances around. Amy hasn't arrived yet but this isn't surprising. She tells the boys she's waiting for someone and goes to sit at one of the window tables looking down on to the path that runs between the High Street and the car park. From this vantage point she'll see Amy approaching. She wonders what is so urgent that it can't wait until their Thursday meeting and hopes that it isn't a serious problem. Amy's voice sounded tense, excited. Thinking about it, Charley reflects that there was nothing that implied bad news in that voice. It was more that Amy was bubbling over with something that simply had to be shared, something exciting, extraordinary.

Charley hopes it's something good. Perhaps Amy has fallen in love. There was a boy at Falmouth that she went around with but it was a pretty calm kind of romance, not the world-shattering, earth-moving kind of passion that makes you identify with all the love songs ever written. Charley gives a reminiscent sigh and looks out of the window.

Amy is hurrying into view, her bag clutched over her shoulder, curls escaping from their combs and, as Charley watches, she knows that her suspicions are confirmed. There is something indefinable in Amy's expression, the upward curve of the lips, the glancing brightness of her eyes, that sets her apart. A man passing in the other direction turns to glance back appreciatively at her, and Charley begins to laugh.

'Pheromones, darling,' she says to herself. 'Good old pheromones.'

And, as Amy hurries into the café, Charley gets to her feet and stretches out her arms to her. Amy hugs her tightly and then inexplicably begins to laugh.

'This is so crazy,' she says. 'But I just needed to see you. Now. Before Thursday.'

Charley releases herself and sits down again. 'I think I'd grasped that.'

Amy sits opposite, takes a deep breath as if she's been running. She glances up at Rob, who gives her a menu, smiles at him and sits staring at it. Charley watches her for a moment and decides to take control of the situation.

'Veggie lasagne,' she says to Rob. 'OK with you, Amy? You know you love that.'

'Whatever,' says Amy randomly. 'Yes. Vegetable lasagne would be great.'

Charley smiles up at Rob. 'And two elderflower pressés? Thanks.'

She sits back and studies Amy, who beams at her. 'Is Jack OK? Work flowing in? All good in Salcombe?'

'Yes,' answers Amy, visibly pulling herself together. 'Yes, everything's fine. Dad's in great form.'

Charley waits. The pressés and the cutlery arrive. Amy fiddles with a fork.

'The thing is,' she says slowly. 'Well, the thing is, Charley, I've met this man . . .'

CHAPTER SEVEN

On the morning of Max's departure for Oxford, Sam suddenly raises concerns about using Cara's car for their house-hunting expedition.

'After all,' he says as they sit at breakfast, 'you don't know your way around this area and you need to be getting a good idea of where you might like to live. How can you do that if you're driving? I suggest I go home and pick up my car. I didn't drive it over because parking is difficult in Salcombe, but now I can use Max's space in the boatyard.'

There is a short silence. She glances at Max, who is considering this plan but without any kind of alarm and anxiety. Cara is relieved. She has no idea what kind of driver Sam might be, or what kind of car he might own.

'I think that sounds very sensible,' Max says to him. 'These lanes can be pretty scary for anyone who hasn't grown up around them, and Cara won't get much idea of the country whilst she's trying to follow directions and avoiding tractors. Tell you what, why don't I drop you off at The Keep on my way upcountry? After all, it's hardly any distance off my road, is it? Then you can drive back? Is that a plan?'

'It's a very good plan,' says Sam enthusiastically. 'And Cara can come with us and meet Fliss and Hal.'

Just for a moment Cara experiences a little flick of panic.

'But if you're leaving in the next hour, Max, I think that's a bit unfair to Fliss and Hal, don't you?' she suggests. 'They'll have hardly finished breakfast.'

'You won't faze them,' answers Sam confidently. 'I'll call them now and give them a heads-up.'

He pushes his chair back from the table and disappears downstairs. Max grins at Cara.

'Definitely a leader of men,' he says. 'Are you OK with this?'

'If you're sure they won't mind,' she replies, still trying to subdue the foolish panic. Suddenly she feels fearful at the thought of Max going. The now familiar sense of being untethered, of being utterly alone, assails her. 'It just seems a bit impolite.'

'Honestly,' he tells her, 'there won't be a problem. Sam will handle it.'

'Yes,' she says. 'Yes, I'm beginning to think you're right.'

Soon they are travelling out of the town, heading for Dartington and The Keep. Cara tries to get her bearings, gazing out at the countryside, questioning Sam about the little villages, and before too long they are climbing the hill and driving in beneath the arch of a gatehouse, into the courtyard of The Keep. Sam told her that it was built in the 1840s from the ruins of an old hill fort. Cara stares at it in delight: a central castellated tower three storeys high, two wings, set back a little and obviously added at a later date, high stone walls encircling the courtyard.

Sam jumps out and dashes in to announce their arrival, and almost at once Hal and Fliss come hurrying out. Max remains only long enough to say 'hello' before driving away again and, whilst Sam goes to get his car from the garages built into the gate-house, Fliss and Hal take Cara into the house, through the great hall with a huge granite fireplace, along a slate-floored passage to the warm kitchen with its Aga. She looks around at the pretty patchwork curtains, and at the built-in dresser bearing delicate survivors – rose, blue, gold-leaf – from long-forgotten dinner and tea services. There are two windows set in the far wall and Cara is drawn towards them. Looking out, she gives a little gasp of delight. The hill slopes away so steeply that the kitchen seems poised high up in the air. She can see birds circling below her, and the great sweep of multicoloured fields and small rounded hills unfold, distance upon distance, into a misty blue infinity.

Hal and Fliss brew coffee and make her feel welcome, batting away her apologies, sympathizing with the problems of house-hunting, reassuring her that Sam will love showing her the South Hams. She suggests that they must be very proud of him, passing the AIB, and they agree that they are. They are an attractive couple. Hal, tall and grey-haired, wears an old Guernsey with his faded cords whilst Fliss, small, fine-featured, is dressed in jeans, a shirt, and a gilet.

'Neither my children nor Hal's went into the navy,' Fliss says, as they sit around the long refectory table, 'so it's rather nice that Sam will be following the family tradition. And in Mole's footsteps, too, of course.'

She looks at Cara enquiringly, wondering if she understands this, and Cara says cautiously that Max has told her something of Sam's history.

'With Mole,' says Fliss, 'it was a passion from childhood upwards. He wanted to be a submariner more than anything else in the world.'

Cara glances at Hal. 'And was it a passion for you, too?' she asks.

Hal shakes his head. 'Too long ago to remember,' he says ruefully. 'Probably. Not submarines. That was never my idea of fun. But yes, I suppose it was the only thing I wanted to do back then. Sam must have been pretty convincing, too, or the Board would never have passed him. You've really got to want it. It's a pity he couldn't go straight in. I think he's feeling a sense of anticlimax after the excitement of passing so it's good that he's able to be of use to you with your house-hunting.'

Cara begins to talk about some of the properties she and Sam have looked at on Max's laptop.

'So are you going to be looking at any today?' Hal asks, reaching to pour some coffee as Sam comes in and drops some letters on to the table.

'Postman's been,' he says. 'No. We won't be viewing anything today because there hasn't been time to make appointments.' He sits down and takes his mug. 'Thanks. Though we might do a few external recces. But I do think it's an opportunity to show Cara some of the area. We might go back through Dartmouth and along to Torcross.'

Cara smiles at Fliss and shrugs. 'He's the boss.'

'I envy you,' Fliss answers. 'How wonderful to be seeing the South Hams for the very first time.'

'And are you a town mouse or a country mouse?' asks Hal.

Cara laughs, remembering the Beatrix Potter book. 'Sam asked me that question and I know it sounds crazy but I really don't know. I suppose it all depends on the town and on the type of country. We stayed with Max and Judith in Salcombe on the occasions when our leaves matched up, which wasn't often, but it seems odd to imagine myself living there. But then it's odd to imagine myself living anywhere for any length of time.'

'Service life syndrome,' observes Hal. 'I know lots of friends who still feel that they should move house every two years.'

'Apart from which,' adds Sam, 'Salcombe has some of the most expensive real estate in the country.'

'Yes, Max did well to buy when he did,' agrees Hal. 'It's been a great investment.'

'We need to get moving,' says Sam, finishing his coffee. 'We've got a lot of ground to cover.'

'And if you need a change from Salcombe,' Fliss says, as they all walk out across the courtyard, 'you would be welcome to come and stay with us. The important thing is that you don't rush into buying something that doesn't suit you.'

Cara climbs into Sam's blue Mini feeling warmed by Fliss's kindness.

'How sweet they are,' she says to Sam as they drive away through winding lanes towards the main road. 'And what an amazing house. It's like a little castle.'

'Well, when Judith gets back you can come over and stay,' he answers.

She hears the amusement in his voice, as if he guesses that she and Judith don't hit it off too well, and she glances at him sharply.

'I might just do that,' she says, and then settles back to look around her.

'You'll only get a glimpse of Totnes,' he says, 'because I want to get on. But we'll come back and do a proper recce.'

'Fine by me,' she says. 'But when you say you want to get on, do you have a particular destination in mind?'

He nods, smiling. 'My favourite place in all the world,' he says.

She laughs, hearing all of his childhood in those words.

'Not the Naval College?' she queries teasingly, and watches with interest as his smile turns into surprise, almost as if he has forgotten such a place existed.

'No,' he says, giving a little shake of the head. 'Not the College, though you'll see that, too. Or as much as you can from the road.'

She looks around her as they skirt Totnes, glimpsing the castle crouching on the hill, and then they are out into the countryside once more. He gives a little running commentary as he drives along but she can feel that he is intent upon his destination. They turn on to the road to Dartmouth and he begins to tell her a little of the history of the town. Suddenly, away across the farmland, there is a dazzle of silver, brilliant in the autumn sunshine. She gives a little gasp, and there it is again, as if a mirror were reflecting the sunlight.

'The sea,' she cries. 'Look at the sea!'

He glances briefly, nodding, acknowledging it.

'You just wait,' he says, driving on. 'We're nearly into Dartmouth now and then you'll see the College, on your left as we go down the hill.'

She sees the great wrought-iron gates first, with the words 'Britannia Royal Naval College' arched above them, glimpses of the imposing building half hidden behind the trees. Suddenly she remembers Philip bringing her to the Passing Out Parade, the proud young men in their uniforms, and the band of the Royal Marines playing on the quarter deck. Afterwards she and Max and Philip went out on a boat on the river. It was a little motor boat and Max and Philip joked and laughed, and argued as to who should steer. Somewhere upriver they berthed it by a pontoon and went ashore to have tea in the pub. She hasn't thought about it for years but she has a little vision of tiny creeks, wooded banks, and reflections on the water.

As they drive down the hill and along the embankment, Sam continues his running commentary, and Cara exclaims in delight at the sight of the river with the castle guarding the entrance to the harbour, and another little town perched on the opposite hill. More memories come flooding back to her. She thinks about Philip, how he picked her up in London in his mother's Hillman Imp and drove her down to this delightful town. How happy she was to be with him. He was so dear, so familiar. He organized everything and she was so excited. Back then he still seemed to be like Max: a kind, elder brother.

Now, she peers around, trying to remember where they stayed.

'Aren't we going to stop?' she asks, disappointed, as they turn into roads that lead away from the river and out of the town.

'Not today,' Sam says. 'But we'll come back, I promise.'

She is amused by his single-mindedness, touched that she is to see this place that is so special to him. And then her breath is taken away by the scene ahead of them: the sea, vast, infinite, rolling as far as she can see and, inland at its nearest shores, coves and beaches curving away to a distant headland where she can just make out the tiny shape of a lighthouse.

'Start Bay,' says Sam with satisfaction.

In steep-sided meadows that plunge to the sea, sheep cling toe to toe with their long shadows, small villages perched high above them, and Cara leans from her window, gazing down at the half-hidden, rock-sheltered coves, at the tall pines and deep-clefted valleys.

'Oh, this is amazing,' she says. 'However do you get to those beaches? Only by boat, I suppose?'

And even as she asks the question, Sam swings the car off the road on to a metalled track that runs between some tall shrubs, and into an almost deserted car park. He parks, switches off the engine and smiles at her.

'Come and see,' he says.

They sit at one of the wooden tables outside the Venus Café, waiting for their breakfasts to arrive. Sam watches Cara, delighted with her reaction to this very special place, happy to be sitting here in the warm early October sunshine. He looks around him, at the two cliffs that enclose the cove, the stretch of golden shingle, the tall pines that lend an almost Mediterranean feel to this enchanting beach. He tries to imagine seeing it through her eyes for the first time, watching the sea curling round the rocks, the little pools, the way the stream that runs down from the valley carves a runnel across the sands to the sea.

'It's perfect,' Cara says. 'And I can see now why you wanted to get here.'

'Well, that's just so that we were in time for breakfast,' he says. 'They stop serving it at eleven thirty. We were in such a hurry this morning that I'm starving.'

She laughs at him. 'I don't believe a word of it. Fliss would have given you breakfast. But I don't blame you. It's beautiful here. I love it. I'd want to share it, too.'

She turns in her seat to watch a dog racing across the beach to retrieve a stick its owner has thrown and, though her delight is evident, he's aware of a sadness and he remembers that she is newly widowed, that her sense of loss must be sharp, fresh. After so many years of marriage he imagines that she must miss her husband terribly and he feels guilty that he's briefly forgotten it.

Sam knows deep down that it is right to bring her here. This is a good place to be: it's a healing place. Here, his own loneliness recedes, the sense of emptiness draws back. Some instinct told him to bring Cara here and he can see by her face that the magic is working. He's been to Blackpool Sands often in the last few weeks, when this new sense of confusion and the pressing in of the past has weighed upon him. He's walked on the beach, watching families having fun, and tried to imagine what it must be like to have parents, people to call 'Mummy' and 'Daddy'. He's wondered what kind of shot he might make at being a parent and he suspects that part of the attraction of teaching is bound up in his own sense of loss.

It was here that he came last year after his incredible experience in Shanghai; to find the privacy he needed to come to terms with his unhappiness. The pain has faded, the world restabilized. He no longer yearns to see her, to feel her in his arms. He can even say her name – Ying-Yue, 'reflection of the moon' – without the spasm of pain that used to assail him. Here, on this beach, he is not the Gwailou, the Ghost Man. The foreign devil so despised by Ying-Yue's parents. There was never any possibility of bringing Ying-Yue home, of showing her this precious place. They were irrevocably separated by culture and distance, but he loved her with a passion.

Sam realizes that Cara is looking at him and he flushes slightly, uncomfortable under her scrutiny. He's relieved when the waitress arrives so that he can cover his lapse of concentration with the organization of the table, sharing out the cutlery, and with the process of eating.

'Lizzie used to bring me here,' he tells Cara, 'when I was very small. Me and Rufus.'

'Rufus?' queries Cara, buttering some toast.

'He was our dog back then. He used to love it here, chasing stones, rushing in and out of the water. I would hide my eyes and Lizzie would hide chocolates in the sand. Those round chocolates wrapped in gold paper. We pretended they were doubloons. Treasure trove. I had to find them.'

'Just you and Lizzie? And Rufus?'

He nodded. 'Mostly. Fliss would come sometimes. Her children, my cousins, were all grown up by the time I arrived. Jamie and Bess are in their forties now.'

'I hope you realize,' Cara says, 'that everything after this is going to be an anticlimax. Unless you're suggesting that I live here on the beach. Didn't I see a little cottage way over there? A pink one? And one further up the valley?'

He smiles, shaking his head. 'No, no. This is just to get you into the mood. To give you an idea of what the South Hams can offer. The Salcombe estuary is only the beginning.'

'So where next?' she asks, finishing her bacon and eggs, pushing her plate to one side and picking up her coffee cup. 'What's the agenda for the rest of the day? I still feel that after this everything is going to be a let-down.'

'I think we'll drive back into Dartmouth,' he says, 'and have a walk around the town. You can get the feel of the place and we can look at some of those properties we printed off.'

'I hope you've got a map,' she says. 'It's a long time since we stayed with Max and did some sightseeing, and I've lost my bearings completely. I mean, where are we in relation to

Salcombe? I feel as if I've gone through the looking-glass at some point this morning and I'm in another country.'

Sam picks up the little satchel he brought with him from the car and opens it. He draws out an Ordnance Survey map and the print-outs of the properties in Dartmouth.

'Have a look at these before we go,' he says. 'Here's the map. You see we're not very far round the coast from Salcombe.'

He spreads out the map and Cara leans over it.

'Will we come back here?' she asks almost wistfully.

He grins at her and decides to try a little tease. 'Probably. On the way home we'll drive along to Slapton Sands and if you're good I'll buy you an ice cream.'

She bursts out laughing. 'One with a chocolate flake in it?'

He laughs, too, relieved that she isn't offended. 'Only if you're very, very good. Come on. Let's get going.'

After Sam and Cara have gone, Fliss and Hal wander back across the courtyard. Fliss pauses to fix back some trailing stems of the clematis that grows against the old stone wall, stepping carefully into the border beneath it, reaching up to weave the stems on to the wires that support it. Hal watches her, thinking about the past. It was their grandmother who was firm with him when he wanted to marry Fliss all those years ago when they were both very young. Freddy Chadwick didn't approve of first cousins marrying, and Hal's mother agreed with her. Reluctantly he was prevailed upon to establish his career, to see the wider world – and then he met Maria, pretty, sexy, and he fell in lust. He sighs, thinking back over the drama that was his marriage to Maria. How long ago it all seems.

Fliss steps out of the border, scrapes her muddy shoe on the grass and smiles at him. He smiles back at her, grateful for these last twenty years they've spent together.

'I liked Cara,' Fliss says. 'Did you? Not what I expected at all. I hope you didn't mind me inviting her out of the blue like that. I just felt she must be feeling pretty vulnerable and buying a house is such a big decision.'

'I like her, too,' says Hal. 'And of course I don't mind. She's good value. Sam must bring her over for lunch. She'll be good for him. He still seems to have something on his mind.'

'I know.' Fliss catches his arm as they stroll, frowning. 'I thought it was to do with Lizzie going but I'm beginning to think it's more than that. The trouble is, it's difficult actually to confront him. He's so like Mole. So self-sufficient.'

'Of course, it might just be that he's slightly daunted about going to Dartmouth. He's had too long to think about it. It was better in the old days when you just left school in July and started in September.'

Hal stands back to allow her to go into the hall but once inside she pauses to look around her, and he wonders if she is remembering past times.

'What's up?' he asks. 'Seeing ghosts?'

She looks surprised at his perceptiveness, and gives a little laugh.

'I still can't get over it being only us,' she admits. 'There were always so many people. Grandmother and Uncle Theo. Ellen bustling about, managing everything. Caroline looking after me and Mole and Susanna.'

'And don't forget old Fox living in the gatehouse.'

She shakes her head, sighs. 'And now it's just you and me and Sam, and he'll be gone soon. Perhaps we should start a B and B.'

'Give me a break,' he protests. 'The problem is, when all the family come home we need the space. You'd hate it if we had to say "no" to any of them. There were sixteen of us last Christmas.'

'Yes, I would,' she admits. 'I love it when they come.' She chuckles. 'And I love it when they go! Even so, we're really going to miss Sam.'

'So what's the plan for the rest of the day?' asks Hal. 'I'm going to get some logs in.'

'I shall do a bit in the garden,' Fliss tells him. 'Don't forget that they're bringing the dog to meet us this afternoon.'

'How could I forget?' asks Hal.

He's looking forward to having another dog at The Keep. It's been too long without one – more than a year – and the house needs a dog. As he walks along the slate-flagged passage to the garden room his thoughts slip back to Sam and he remembers Cara's question: *And was it a passion for you, too?*

Hal still can't find an answer to that question. His grandfather was killed at the Battle of Jutland and his own father's destroyer was torpedoed with no survivors in the Second World War. Uncle Theo was a naval chaplain. Somehow joining the navy seemed the obvious thing to do and Hal's never regretted it.

As he kicks off his shoes and thrusts his feet into his boots, he wonders, just briefly, whether Sam has ever thought that it's somehow obligatory to follow in Mole's footsteps; that it will help him come to terms with his father's death. He knows what Fliss means about it being difficult to know what the lad is thinking, or to ask him a direct question. There's something about Sam that makes you hold off, as if you're invading his privacy. In some ways, just as Fliss reflects her grandmother's personality, Sam reflects Mole's. There's strength there, but also a vulnerability.

Hal sighs. He wishes he were better at this: better at drawing Sam out and helping him when times were hard. He remembers how pleased he and Fliss were last year to have Sam home from China; how delighted they were to see him again after his year away, and how they knew at once that all was not well, that something was deeply troubling him. They could do nothing to help. Fliss was sure that it was about a girl and Hal trusted her instincts. Sam returned to Durham a few weeks later but though he talked about Shanghai, about how he loved teaching the children English, he never once spoke to them about the thing that seemed to be diminishing him, weighing him down. They both ached with the need to comfort him.

But at least, thinks Hal, he seems OK now.

He pulls on his jacket and looks around him. The garden room is almost unchanged since his grandmother's time: the big deal table with small pots of plants needing attention; the small sink with a cold tap plumbed in by Fox, who also built in shelves to hold reference books, jars containing labels, seed packets and spools of string. Hal is comforted by the sense of continuity, grateful for the small unexpected joys that reveal themselves, and he goes out to move logs.

Fliss puts the mugs into the dishwasher, washes out the cafetière, and mentally reviews the options for lunch. Hal's right about the ghosts. Some days they seem more than usually present all around her: benign, comforting, bringing so many memories. Here, in this kitchen, so many dramas have been played out under the watchful eyes of Ellen, the housekeeper, who nurtured and loved them all: tutting when Fox came in from his outdoor labours without removing his boots; rolling her eyes when Kit, Hal's twin sister, sat in the dog basket with whichever dog was in residence. Ellen's comment, always muttered just below her breath, 'Whatever next, I wonder', had become a catchphrase with them all.

The dog basket is still there, unoccupied except for its clean rug waiting for the next occupant. Honey, a golden Labrador, is needing a home since her elderly owner died. She's well trained, wonderful with children, the rescue lady tells them, but the younger members of the family are too busy to be able to look after her so she has to be rehomed. Fliss thinks that Honey sounds ideal and she's hoping that she'll approve of The Keep. The whole Chadwick family, children and grandchildren, are waiting with expectation.

Fliss can hear Hal bringing the logs into the hall ready for the winter ahead, piling them into the inglenook. She's glad that Sam will be with them until after Christmas. She just wishes she knew what is behind his preoccupation. Perhaps he will talk to Max about it, or even to Cara. He seems to have taken to Cara, to be enjoying this new role of chauffeur and guide. Fliss glances at her watch and sees that it's nearly lunchtime, and she has an idea. Hal has nearly finished piling up the logs and he glances round as she comes into the hall, giving a groan as he straightens up.

'I should have left this for Sam,' he remarks. 'I must be a masochist.'

'Keeps you fit,' she says. 'You need the exercise. But I've had an idea. Why don't we go to The Cott for lunch?'

'Now you're talking,' he says appreciatively. 'Give me a few minutes to tidy up and I'll be with you.'

'As long as we're back by three for Honey,' she reminds him.

'And is there Honey still for tea?' he murmurs, and she laughs at him.

Suddenly she feels cheerful again, more confident that things will work out for the best for Sam: for them all.

CHAPTER EIGHT

'You're behaving like a child,' says Alistair.

Cosmo knows that he is but he can't help himself. He paces up and down, staring across Batson Creek, clutching the phone to his ear, willing Al to understand.

'It's just so different here, Al,' he says, hearing the pleading note in his voice and despising himself for it. 'It's not Becks' kind of place anyway. Not really.'

Even that isn't entirely true. It would be a novelty to her, though she'd become bored quickly. It would be impossible not to bump into people he is beginning to get to know; people who are already linking him with Amy.

'What's that screeching noise?' asks Al.

'Seagulls,' answers Cosmo. 'The signal's not great in the house. Texting is OK but I have to make calls from the end of the garden.'

'So you want to tell Becks that you were already planning to come to London next weekend. What reason would you give?'

Cosmo has given this a lot of thought. Becks will know that he can download any music or books he might want and that he can buy himself some clothes if he needs some. At last he hit on the one thing she doesn't really understand or have any interest in. He tests this on Al.

'It's some of my camera stuff,' he says. 'I never thought it would be so amazing here. I've got a blog now and someone's put me on to Newsflare. They'll buy videos and things if they're really good. I was talking to a guy about it in the Coffee Shop.'

'Yeah, OK,' says Al.

Cosmo sighs with relief. Al isn't into the photography thing either.

'I really need your help here, mate,' he says, using the voice that he's always used when he needs Al to bail him out. 'I did you a favour coming down here so your mum and dad could go away. You owe me.'

'So what have you told this girl?' asks Al. 'What did you say her name is?'

Cosmo wishes now that he'd never mentioned Amy, although he hasn't actually told Al her name. For some reason, keeping it a secret helps her to seem less real, as if it's a kind of game and all part of this other world he's living in now.

'I haven't told her about Becks,' he answers rather sulkily, 'but she knows I've got my own flat in London. Look, it's no great deal. Do we have to have the third degree?'

'OK,' says Al reluctantly. 'I guess I can come down for a weekend. I'll come down on Friday evening. I'll check train times but it'll probably be quite late. When were you thinking of travelling?'

'I'll check train times for Saturday morning,' Cosmo says. 'Could you give me a lift to the station?'

Al begins to laugh. 'Why not?' he says. 'But only if you introduce me to this girl before you go. And you still haven't told me her name.'

Cosmo laughs, too, feeling quite weak with relief. He's surprised at how important this is: this need to prevent Becks from crashing into the new life he's making whilst he's still holding on to everything he has in London.

'Her name's Amy,' he tells Al. 'You might even know her.'

'Unlikely,' Al tells him. 'The parents only bought the house six months ago when Dad retired. I've hardly been there. OK. I'll do it this once.'

'Thanks, mate. I'll tell Becks then. 'Bye.'

He ends the call but continues to stand looking at the creek, watching an egret patrolling the shallows by the old lime kiln, listening to the cry of the seagulls. Part of his mind is wondering if he can make a good photograph of the elegant white bird against the dark stones, the other is phrasing sentences that will prevent Becks from travelling west. He knows that if they have a conversation she might yet win; she's so quick, so determined. The best way, he decides, will be to email her. He can explain that he needs to get his camera equipment, and that he's been looking forward to them both doing a film and some supper somewhere. Or a show, if they can get tickets. She'll understand that he has to make arrangements for Reggie but that Al has made plans to come down. He'll present it as a *fait accompli*.

Cosmo walks back up to the house wondering why Al was quite so pompous about it all. After all, he and Becks have never hit it off. Al thinks Becks is too controlling and lacks humour. Becks thinks Al is immature and a bad influence. Cosmo tries to keep the peace, refusing to allow slagging matches.

As he goes inside to compose his email to Becks, Cosmo wonders if Al might bump into Amy and what would happen if he does. When he mentioned to her that he must make the dash to London she slightly hinted that she's been thinking of a trip to the capital. He managed to turn it aside by asking her if she'd been before, and the conversation moved on to an exhibition she saw at the Hayward. Now, he must have something ready for that eventuality: a birthday of a relative, perhaps.

Reggie comes to greet him, tail wagging, and Cosmo bends to stroke him.

'Nearly time for walks,' he tells him. 'Let me just get this sorted and we'll be off. Round the creek and then a cup of coffee. You're going to be seeing Al at the weekend. You'll like that, won't you?'

Amy comes into the Coffee Shop, waves to Lydia behind the counter, and glances around for Cosmo. There is no sight of him and she debates with herself as to whether she should simply order a takeaway or sit down and hope that he might show up. Even as she thinks about it, he comes in behind her. His smile, the look in his eyes, threatens to unsettle her, but she manages to stay calm and bends to stroke Reggie.

'I was going to grab a takeaway,' she says, 'but now that you're here . . .'

'I'll order,' he says, 'if you just hang on to Reggie.'

Amy sits down at a table, pulling Reggie in beside her, encouraging him to sit close to her, and looks at Cosmo standing in the little queue. It's odd, that sense of vitality he has; the ability to appear twice as alive as anybody else. As he turns she glances quickly away and he comes to sit with her, carrying a plate of honeycomb tiffin.

'Do you like these?' he asks. 'Shall we share? I've brought two forks.'

She laughs. 'I love it. Thanks.'

He begins to tell her about something called Newsflare; that they're interested in some of his photographic work. They pay for videos and would be interested if he could get clips that could be used on local television news. Anything that would be of interest like special events, severe weather, accidents. He is enthusiastic and she listens and watches him, wondering what will happen when his house-sitting in Batson Creek finishes. He doesn't talk much about London and she's beginning to wonder, to hope, that he might think of relocating down here. Perhaps this photography opportunity might be a way of encouraging him.

'I'm going to have to dash up to London this weekend,' he's saying. 'It's a family celebration that I must go to, and I can pick up a few things whilst I'm there.'

A family celebration. Amy thinks about it. She can see that it's much too early to be included in that so she gives up the idea of suggesting she should go with him. Anyway, it's all a bit tricky: she doesn't really know him well enough yet.

'What about Reggie?' she asks.

She notices a little flash of something in his eyes: relief? Is he glad that he hasn't got to explain why he's not inviting her? A tremor of pride stiffens her and she hopes she hasn't been looking too keen.

'His owners' son is coming to keep an eye,' Cosmo says. 'He's a friend of mine. That's why I'm here, really. I think I told you their house-sitter had some last-minute disaster. Anyway, it's only one night. I'll travel up on Saturday morning and hope to come back on Sunday.'

'Maybe I'll see him around,' she says casually. 'What's his name?'

An odd expression crosses Cosmo's face, as if he doesn't want to tell her his friend's name, and she wonders if he's afraid that she might like him.

'It's Alistair,' he says. 'But you wouldn't know him if you saw him anyway.'

'But I'd know Reggie,' she says. She's amused by this little show of possessiveness. 'Perhaps he'll bring him in here for coffee.'

'His parents only moved down six months ago,' Cosmo says, 'so I'm not sure if Al knows his way around yet.'

'Not an old hand like you, then.'

He grins at her. 'You've got to admit I'm a quick study. Speaking of which, I rather like the look of the Salcombe Gin School. I pass it every time I walk in and I wondered if you'd like to show me round. The Tasting Bar looks like it could be fun.'

Amy relaxes, they make a plan, then she gets up, gives Reggie a pat and hurries back to work.

CHAPTER NINE

Jack is getting ready for his evening at the opera. When he warned Cara that nobody dresses up to go to the Barn Cinema she pretended disappointment.

'You mean it's not black tie?' she asked. 'And I was really looking forward to seeing you in that.'

'Deal with it,' he said. 'It's nice and casual. But I'll treat you to a glass of wine in the Roundhouse during the interval.'

Now he pulls on his moleskin jacket over his checked cotton shirt and jeans and peers at himself in the glass over the chest of drawers. He wonders if he should put on a tie – he doesn't usually wear one – and resists the feeling that he should be making a special effort. For starters he knows that Amy will pull his leg if he does. When she asked for a lift over to Totnes to see Charley he was surprised at the slight disappointment he felt at being deprived of the journey alone with Cara. He's been really looking forward to this evening but Amy's presence will put a different slant on it.

'You don't mind, do you?' she asked him earlier. 'It's just a good opportunity to spend some time with Charley and it'll be nice to see Cara again.'

'What d'you mean "again"?' he asked, surprised.

'I met her in the Coffee Shop,' Amy answered casually. 'She was with a friend, Sam. She came over and introduced herself. Apparently Max had pointed me out to her. I really like her.'

Now, as he picks up his wallet, checks for a handkerchief and his keys, Amy shouts from the bottom of the stairs.

'Get a move on, Dad. You'll be late if you don't hurry up.'

As he comes down the stairs she looks him over critically and he's glad he didn't put the tie on.

'Come on, then,' he says. 'We're picking up Cara on the way to the boatyard.'

It's crazy to feel nervous, as if he's a boy on his first date, but he can't help himself. Maybe Amy will help to keep it all normal. They see Cara, waiting in Buckley Street by the steps that lead down to the Fortescue, and she waves to them. He's pleased to see that she's dressed as usual in jeans but with a long velvet tunic, nothing fussy but still managing to look chic, and they walk along companionably whilst Amy tells Cara about Charley.

As they drive, Jack is relieved that the conversation is easy and he begins to relax. It's foolish to feel anxious but, after all, he doesn't know Cara very well.

At the same time he is aware of some sense of insecurity in her. It might simply be that she is so newly widowed, added to the fact that she has nowhere to live, but something tells him that it's more than that. It intrigues him and, although he responds to her surface bantering and good humour, he finds that he wants to know more about her.

'You remember meeting Sam?' she's saying to Amy. 'He's Max's godson. He's been driving me about, showing me all these amazing places in the hope I might find somewhere I want to live. It's all so beautiful that I'm not sure I could begin to choose.'

'You should think about renting,' Amy tells her. 'Give yourself time. There are a few things coming up in Salcombe that will be let out for the winter.'

'You're certain you want to stay around here?' asks Jack. 'You won't miss the bright lights?'

'I don't know,' answers Cara honestly. 'I feel totally at sea, actually. I didn't want to live in London. After all, I have no friends there. We've been too peripatetic to make real friends. That's why I fled to Max, I suppose. But I don't want to impose myself on them. I must be independent.'

Jack feels another upsurge of compassion for her, remembering those early, lonely days. At least he had Amy to keep him focused, he thinks again, forever thankful for her.

'Of course you do,' he agrees, 'but it's still wise to be cautious about buying. Amy's right, there's almost certain to be something you can rent for a few months.'

He drops Amy off in Bridgetown, refusing her suggestion to go in and say hello to Charley.

'Maybe when we pick you up,' he says. 'We don't want to be late.'

It's beginning to get dark as they turn into the lower drive that leads on to the Dartington Hall estate. Cara is enchanted by the beautiful medieval hall and its courtyard, and by the theatre with the café built into the gatehouse and surrounding walls.

'Let's order our drinks,' says Jack, 'and then they'll be ready for us at the interval.'

He's pleased by Cara's delight in everything, glad that he invited her to come with him. They go into the small cinema, find their seats, and he hands her the single sheet that takes the place of a programme and describes the performance that will be streamed live from the Metropolitan Opera House in New York. She smiles at him and he grins back at her.

'Not quite as good as the real thing,' he says, unable to shake off this slight sense of inferiority – which is rather foreign to him – but hoping that she'll really enjoy it.

'It's great,' she says. 'It's so intimate. Rather like being in someone's private cinema. And wonderful to be able to see first-class productions.'

They begin to talk about other operas that will be coming during this autumn season and Jack is aware of an invading sense of pleasure; of the prospect of a new beginning. The lights dim and they sit back in their seats, alert with happy anticipation.

As they come out into the darkness, Cara pauses for a moment under the stone archway to look at the great medieval hall set in its courtyard of buildings. Lights shine from the mullioned windows; shadows slant across the lawn. It's like a Cambridge college.

'Magical,' she says. 'I must come and see it in daylight.'

'You must,' agrees Jack, as they walk together to the car park. 'The gardens are at their best in the spring but it's always worth a visit.'

He takes his phone from his pocket and switches it on.

'I'll just tell Amy we're on our way,' he says, but immediately a message pings in and he pauses to read it. 'Oh, right. Amy's decided to stay the night with Charley. Probably tomorrow as well. She'll bring her home on Saturday.'

He taps out a message and then puts his phone back in his pocket.

'That's rather nice,' Cara says. 'I like impromptu things, don't you? They often work so much better than pre-arranged events. There's no time to get expectation all worked up so there's less chance of failure.'

Jack laughs as he unlocks the car and they climb in. 'And there was I just about to suggest that you and Sam come over for coffee or a drink on Saturday. You could meet Amy properly, and Charley, too, if she stays around that long.'

'Well, that's a bit different,' says Cara, putting on her seat belt. 'I was really talking about big events like Christmas or special birthdays. Drinks on Saturday has a nice casual sound.'

They join the line of cars leaving the car park and heading down the long drive to the main road. She's surprised at how much she's enjoyed her evening: going down the stairs in the interval, into the Roundhouse with its huge beam and white-washed walls, to find their glasses of wine waiting for them, set out on a table with their names printed on a piece of paper. They sat together on one of the sofas and discussed the merits of Papagena and the Queen of the Night and agreed that it was impossible not to clap just like the live audience at special moments. Yet even as she laughed and talked with him, there was the ever-present knowledge that she mustn't allow herself to be drawn too closely to him. Too many secrets and lies, too much to hide. She knows that Jack could get under her skin: he's so easy, so amusing, so confident. With Philip alive she was able to live and love and laugh with him, skating above the darkness – the suppressed chaos that might overwhelm her – always in denial. Now, she can't imagine trusting anybody else

enough to tell them the truth about her life, though occasionally she imagines the luxury of confession.

'So that's a plan, is it?' Jack is asking, as they turn on to
the main road, heading into Totnes. 'Saturday? Coffee and
lunch at the pub? Will Max be back?'

'Yes,' she says, glad to be distracted from her thoughts. 'He's
coming home tomorrow. I'll have to check with him and Sam.
Either sounds great.'

Another thought crosses her mind. 'Have you met
Cosmo yet?'

'No.' She hears him chuckle in the darkness. 'Amy's not letting on about Cosmo.'

Cara remembers the little sense of shock in the Coffee
Shop when she first saw Cosmo, the way he reminded her of
Giovanni, and she has a sudden need to reach out to Jack, to
put her hand on his arm or his thigh so as to tether herself
to someone who might protect her from her demons.
Deliberately she crosses her arms, tucking her hands into
her armpits.

'Like I was saying earlier, Sam is making a great guide,' she
says lightly, deliberately changing the subject, 'and I'm having
a wonderful time, but I'm still totally confused about where I
ought to be. I think everyone's right about advising me to rent
but the million-dollar question is where.'

'Salcombe,' he answers at once. 'Why not? You've got
family there and you're making friends. Why go out on a limb?
Especially when . . .'

He pauses and she smiles into the darkness.

'It's odd, isn't it,' she asks, 'how difficult it is to speak the
language of grief?'

She hears him sigh and the silence stretches between them.

'I used to dread going out after Sally died,' he says at last. 'There were people who'd cross the road because they simply didn't know what to say to me, and others who would immediately put on sad faces and talk in special hushed voices and tell me how terrible I must be feeling.'

'Yes,' she agrees. 'It's hard for everybody, I know, and it's impossible to get it right, but I prefer those people who give me a hug and say, "God, isn't life shit? Let's go and have a drink."'

'Yeah, that's it,' Jack says. 'You need people to be drawing you out of it, not commiserating until you want to scream or leave you feeling utterly depressed. I was lucky to have Amy. She kept me going.'

'Well, I have dear old Max,' Cara says lightly. 'Or at least I do until Judith comes back. Judith doesn't totally approve of me. I was always the tiresome little sister and I always will be. There were only the two of us, you see, and our parents were rather dysfunctional, so Max tended to watch out for me. Poor Judith. It must be very irritating for her. And now here I am again, being needy and inadequate.'

'Is that why you're reluctant to get a place in Salcombe? You always seem to back off a bit when anyone mentions it.'

Cara is touched by his perspicacity. 'Probably. I don't mean to irritate her but it just happens. Having me living in the town must be her worst nightmare.'

'OK, then you need to make your own group of friends so that she doesn't feel threatened.'

'How easy you make it sound,' marvels Cara. 'Well, so far I have you, Amy, Sam . . . and I'm beginning to get to know Cosmo.'

'Cosmo?' He's clearly startled. 'You've met Cosmo?'

'Yes, I have. And a very nice-looking fellow he is too. I met him in the Coffee Shop.'

'And you liked him?'

'He was very easy to talk to. He had a dog with him. Reggie, I think he said his name is. Yes, he was amusing, friendly. You know what it's like round here. Everybody talks to complete strangers. He's only here for a short while, dog-and-house-sitting. He's on a sabbatical and he'll have to get back to his job.'

She feels her own sense of relief as she says these words. Soon Cosmo will be gone and maybe she will be able to regain that self-defence, that quietness of mind, that she's created so carefully over the years. Cara glances sideways at Jack's profile. She suspects that he's trying to think of a way around her staying in Salcombe without causing problems with her sister-in-law and once again she's touched by his compassion. She tries to lift the atmosphere to a lighter level.

'So perhaps you should invite lots of lovely people to your lunch party,' she suggests, 'so that I can make all these new friends.'

She sees him smile. 'I'll think about it,' he says.

As he sits at his laptop, Sam turns as he hears the front door open and glances at his watch. It's rather early for Cara to be back from the opera and he switches his laptop off, gets to his feet and goes to the top of the stairs. Oscar is already there, tail wagging expectantly.

'Only me,' calls Max. 'Thought you might have gone to the pub.'

'We weren't expecting you till tomorrow,' says Sam, stepping back as Max climbs up towards him.

'Yes, sorry about that. I texted Cara, forgetting that she was going to the opera, and I was nearly here when I remembered so there didn't seem much point in ringing. Paul is back from his conference at Harvard and it's a bit of a squeeze so we decided that I was surplus to requirements now he's back.' He strokes Oscar. 'Hello, old chap. Have you been a good boy?'

'Tea?' offers Sam. 'Coffee?'

'Actually,' says Max, 'I think something stronger might be in order. It was a long drive home.'

Sam grins. 'You sound like Hal. Let me guess. Gin and tonic?'

'Now you're talking,' says Max, subsiding at the table. 'I am feeling very, very old. Gin's over there. Tonic and lemon in the fridge.'

Sam makes the gin and tonic to Hal's strict specifications – plenty of gin, not too much tonic – and hands the glass to Max, who takes it gratefully and sips.

'Aaah. I approve of someone who knows how to make a decent G and T. You've clearly had training from Hal. Good man. So what's new?'

'Nothing much.' Sam sits opposite and tries to think of anything that's happened since Max left for Oxford.

'Oh, come on,' says Max encouragingly, stretching his legs comfortably beneath the table, one hand on Oscar's head. 'So I left you at The Keep . . .'

He looks expectantly at Sam, who nods. 'OK. So we all had coffee with Fliss and Hal. They really hit it off with Cara and she's coming over for lunch next week. Well, you too, of course, if you want to come. And then I drove Cara to Dartmouth and along the coast.' He wonders whether to mention the breakfast at Blackpool Sands but for some reason decides against it.

'Really, I've just been letting her get a feel of the area. It's been great fun.' He pauses. 'So when's Judith coming home?'

Max sips some more gin and tonic. 'Don't quite know. It's easier now Paul's home and Freya's ankle is on the mend, but it's still a tough call with Poppy, who's very demanding, and the baby due any minute. I have a feeling Judith will hang on a bit if they want her.' He smiles at Sam. 'Families, eh? So how are you doing?'

Sam looks at his godfather, longing to confide in him but he resists it.

'I'm having a great time, actually,' he answers. 'I hadn't realized how good it is to show places I really love to somebody who's never seen them. It's made me think . . .'

He hesitates. It's not in his nature to bare his soul but one of the reasons he's come to Salcombe is that he's hoping to bring his confusion into the open: the thought that somehow, by simply joining the navy, he's inviting into his life the same kind of disaster that happened to his grandfather and father.

'To be honest,' he says, 'it sounds a bit weird but since I passed the AIB it's like all my past has suddenly resurfaced. You know? Mole being blown up and my grandparents being killed out in Kenya? It's like I'm hearing it for the first time and having to deal with it. And at the same time I never knew any of them so I've nothing to work with. It's always been a part of my life – I've grown up with it – but suddenly I'm having this problem with it.'

Max turns his glass round and round, his eyes fixed on it while he thinks about what Sam has said.

'I suppose,' he says at last, 'we all come to that moment when we cross the divide between childhood and adulthood. Suddenly, you're assuming responsibility for yourself, making up your own mind about things, taking your own decisions. Who we are plays a big part in that. It seems to me that two major things have happened to you. Lizzie, who has been your continuum, has married and moved on, and you've passed the AIB. Right so far?'

Sam nods. He feels uncomfortable, already wishing he hadn't spoken out, but he's got to run with it now.

'Up until now,' says Max, 'you've been part of a big noisy clan of people and you've been swept about in all the activities and excitements that go with being a small part of a large family. But now, suddenly, it's time to step forward and stand alone. Oh, they'll always be there – they've got your back – but it's time to be independent.'

There's a silence. Sam knows that there's a great deal of truth in what Max has said and he feels a strong affection for his godfather. He doesn't know quite what to say but Max helps him through.

'And all that pomposity,' he says reflectively, 'on one gin and tonic.'

'But they were navy rations,' says Sam, smiling. 'Have another?'

'I think I might just do that.'

The door opens below them and they can hear Cara calling goodbye to Jack. The atmosphere changes as Cara comes up the stairs, exclaiming at seeing Max. Now the story of his Oxford trip must be told again and Sam is able to relax. He knows what Max has said is good sense: at this moment in his life the opening of the door to his past is a necessity but it's still going to be difficult to come to terms with his family's tragic history. As Cara and Max talk, Sam wonders again why he's never told Max about Ying-Yue. Was it because he thought

Max wouldn't understand; wouldn't be able to accept the intensity of his loss? And what about teaching? How can he explain to Max – his naval role model, his father's friend – of his doubts about joining the navy, and his pull towards a different vocation, especially when his memories of teaching in Shanghai, the pleasure he took in it, are so inextricably linked with his love for Ying-Yue? Some deep instinct warns him against talking with anyone about his confusion. This is something he must deal with alone. After all, who else would understand his dilemma?

Cara is telling them about the opera, about Jack inviting them to a lunch party, and Sam sinks back in his chair and prepares to join in the conversation.

CHAPTER TEN

By the time Alistair has dropped Cosmo off at the station in Totnes, driven back to Salcombe and given Reggie a walk, it's nearly lunchtime. Cosmo has stocked up with a few necessities such as milk and bread, and there are some frozen meals in the freezer, but Al isn't particularly impressed with the selection. He remembers his parents taking him to a pub in the town on one of his weekend visits so he settles Reggie, checks his water dish, and then walks off round the creek towards the town.

It's been a damp grey morning and the wide bowl of the estuary reflects the clouds, brimming over with silver light. The boatyard is busy – people are putting their boats to bed for the winter – and it feels strange to Al to see the car park full of boats instead of cars. The town is quiet, no tourists, just a few locals shopping in Cranch's and The Bake House, and he walks on past Whitestrand, looking for the flight of steps that leads down to the pub. And here they are. He hurries down, goes into the bar, and looks around: low beams, a fire alight in the wood-burning stove. It's not very busy yet so he buys a pint, takes a menu and goes to sit by one of the big windows.

Al stares out, distracted by the view even on such a gloomy day: golden beaches, rocky inlets, a few boats still on their moorings, sails furled loosely on their yards. He takes a pull at his pint and studies the menu. A group of people comes in, talking, laughing, greeting the bar staff; clearly locals. Briefly, Al envies them. It must be good, he thinks, to belong to a small town like this, where you are part of its life, involved with its survival, but on reflection he wonders if perhaps the anonymity of a big city is preferable to the suffocation of a small community. He wonders how his parents will enjoy it here, how long it will take for them to be accepted, although they have already joined the Sailing Club. Certainly Cosmo seems to be falling in love with it all, and not just with Salcombe and its magical surroundings. He was in a very odd mood – jokey, brittle – turning the subject away from Becks or this girl Amy. Instead he talked about his photography, asked Al how things were back in town, at the bank. Oddly, this was more disturbing than if Cosmo had been prepared to discuss how he was feeling and the real reason for preventing Becks from coming here to visit him. After all, it's no secret that he's still not absolutely committed to Becks; that he has reservations about taking that last step and giving up his small flat finally to move in with her. Even so, Al feels uncomfortable with this new situation. He doesn't much like Becks but he admires her intelligence and commitment to her work, and he's hoping that when Cosmo sees her again this romantic dream will fade in the face of reality.

Al glances again at the group at the bar. He tries to categorize them all but can't quite make them fit. Their ages range from young to old but none of them quite belongs together. There is no possessive or familiar behaviour that suggests that any of the three men or the three women are an item, nor do any of them look alike. He wonders what the relationship between them is – perhaps they all belong to a club – and then his thoughts drift on to the girl Amy, and whether she has fallen in love with Cosmo. Clearly she knows nothing about Becks and, just for a moment, Al feels angry with Cosmo. He wonders if Amy is like Becks: late twenties, sophisticated, smart, cool, focused. Perhaps she is younger, pretty, casual, rather like the girl in the group at the bar, with long curly brown hair and an animated face, who is talking to the young dark-haired fellow.

The group is moving away, sitting down at a table, and Al gets up and goes to the bar to order his lunch.

Across the bar, Amy has been watching the man sitting alone at the window table and wondering if it could be Cosmo's friend. She's never seen him before around the town and it's unusual to see a young man sitting alone in the bar, especially out of season. As they all talk, order drinks, choose their lunches, she wishes she had the courage to stroll over and ask him if he's Al.

She turns back to talk to Sam, to ask him about the navy, but he deflects the conversation, describing a flat Cara has seen in Dartmouth.

'It's tough,' he says, 'trying to choose where to live when you don't really know the area and you're all on your own.'

Amy smiles at him, liking his concern. In different circumstances she could have rather gone for Sam.

'I've just got a job decorating a flat that will be coming up for rent soon,' she says. 'Come and have a look and see what you think. Seems silly for Cara to be in Dartmouth when her family is here.'

Charley joins in, asking Sam how long he's staying with Max, and the conversation turns to her part-time job in a primary school, and then he's telling them about his year at university in Shanghai and those weeks he spent teaching English to Chinese children. Charley is really impressed, asks lots of questions, and Amy can see that Sam loved the experience.

'Sounds to me as if you've got a vocation,' Charley says. 'Have you thought of teaching?'

Sam looks embarrassed and Amy says: 'He told you just now. He's going into the navy.'

Charley simply raises her eyebrows, as though the question still stands, and Sam shrugs.

'No,' he answers, but slowly, as if it's not totally true, and Amy, knowing Charley's persistence and how she loves her own teaching job, suggests that they should order their food. Sam glances at her gratefully, gives her a little smile as if to thank her.

'Come and see the flat,' she says to him impulsively. 'Bring Cara with you. I'm starting work there on Monday. It might be just the thing for her.'

'Thanks,' he says.

He looks surprised, slightly shy, and she thinks how nice he is. Max is asking her what she wants to eat and then they're all moving to a table by one of the big windows. She glances across at the man sitting alone, studying the menu, and thinks how surprised he would be if she approached him and asked him if he knew Cosmo. He'd probably think she was crazy. Tomorrow, maybe, she'll stroll out to Batson Creek, up to Snapes Point, and see if she can see Reggie having a walk. The idea amuses her and she sits down and begins to talk to Cara.

Sam is relieved to be sitting next to Jack. He's slightly surprised himself by suddenly opening up to Charley about his time in

China but, after all, it's not a secret, though it's getting harder to dissemble about passing the AIB, to admit that the prospect of teaching foreign children to speak English *is* beginning to feel like a vocation. He knows it's foolish to be so secretive about this – after all, no one is forcing him to go into the navy – yet it's been accepted for such a long time that he feels unable to make a change; to follow this newer dream. But suppose he should be mistaken about it and miss the tremendous opportunity of a career in the navy? It's strange how Charley got under his defences so easily when he's managed to keep this idea so closely concealed. He hardly knows why he's unwilling to discuss it. Does he fear being talked out of it? Or is he actually afraid of being taken seriously; encouraged into it when he's still so uncertain about his true feelings?

Sam moves back a little as the lunch arrives and plates are passed around the table. He realizes that the decision to follow in Mole's footsteps is a way of connecting with this father he never knew, making the relationship more of a reality. Way back, when he first arrived at The Keep, he was given Mole's bedroom, which still held the reminders of his father's childhood – including a whole shelf of Tintin books – and showed his father's passion for the navy and especially for submarines. As a small boy, Sam was fascinated by the books and the photographs, and especially by the iconic, big, black-and-white photograph of his father on the bridge of a nuclear submarine as it sailed into Faslane, which was framed and mounted and hung in the hall. Neither Fliss nor Hal has particularly encouraged Sam to join the service – none of their own children has – yet it slowly morphed into an accepted way of thinking and, after all, nothing else particularly fired Sam up whilst he was at school. He was good at languages, good at sport and sufficiently adequate academically to get into Durham University to read languages . . .

He is aware that Jack is watching him.

'I know you're only a half-wit,' he says pleasantly, 'but which part of "Pass the salt" don't you understand?'

Sam laughs, apologizes, picks up his knife and fork and concentrates on the people around him.

Jack thinks about Sam as he eats his pie of the day – steak and ale – and he wonders what the boy has on his mind. He can see that there's something that's preoccupying him. Of course, it might be a girl, but some instinct tells him that it isn't that. Sam's too detached, too contained; too ready to come to stay with Max and offer his services indefinitely as chauffeur to Cara. Jack notices that Sam doesn't consult his phone, checking for messages or sending texts, nor does he talk about his friends. This preoccupation of his is at a different level and it's clear that Sam intends to keep it to himself. The only clue is how he deftly bats away any conversation about the navy except at the most superficial level. He clearly doesn't want to engage in a discussion about his future.

Jack sits back and sips his pint. It's odd that a young man about to embark on a new and exciting career shouldn't want to talk about it.

Jack glances around the bar. To begin with, when he first saw the man sitting at the table by the window, he'd wondered if it might be Cosmo. He's a stranger but he doesn't look like a holiday-maker and no one has joined him. It was clear, however, that Amy doesn't know him and he doesn't know her; there wasn't even a flicker of recognition. Jack is disappointed: he really wants to meet Cosmo, to size him up, but Amy remains vague about bringing him home or their having a drink all together at the pub. He catches Charley's eye and smiles at her. Perhaps Amy has told her about Cosmo. Jack wonders how he might lead the conversation round to it if he can get Charley alone, though he wouldn't expect her to tell tales out of school, of course. It's just that he feels uneasy about Cosmo, just as he feels slightly anxious about Sam.

Old fool, he tells himself, and raises his glass to Charley across the table.

Charley lifts her glass in response.

'For God's sake,' Amy said last night, when they'd had supper and were finishing the wine, 'don't mention any of this to Dad. He knows I see Cosmo around but he doesn't know how I really feel. I mean, it's crazy, isn't it? I hardly know him.'

Charley didn't say much. She listened, nodded, made the occasional response when it was required but she just let Amy talk. She was at that stage when she simply needed to talk about the beloved; to mention his name, things he said, the silly jokes. Charley had never seen her like this before and she was touched and amused.

'He sounds great,' she said, when Amy paused for breath. 'So what's the problem? He's not married, is he?'

'No, of course not,' Amy answered quickly. 'It's just that he works in London and he'll be going back any time soon.'

'So?' asked Charley. 'It has been known that two people can have a relationship whilst living apart. Or you could move to London. Or maybe he could relocate?'

'He's mentioned that,' Amy said. 'He's really keen on photography and he'd love to make a career out of it, but it's a huge step.'

'So what's the big deal?' asked Charley. 'Why all the secrecy and silence? Why don't you want Jack to meet him?'

Amy shrugged, made a face. 'You know Dad. He's being silly and saying Cosmo is a posh name. I'm afraid he'll do that yokel thing and embarrass me.'

Charley laughed. 'Of course he won't. And even if he does it shouldn't bother Cosmo. He's big enough and old enough to take care of himself, isn't he? Do you want me to meet him first? Would that help?'

Amy considered, biting her lips, and Charley wondered what was at the back of all this reticence. Perhaps Cosmo wasn't ready to be quite so involved; perhaps he wasn't prepared yet to meet Amy's father or her friends.

'Well, see how it goes,' Charley said easily. 'I'm here if you need me. But I have to say, whatever this is you're looking great on it.'

This made Amy smile and relax and they finished the bottle, said goodnight and went to bed.

Now, as Charley finishes her goat's cheese tart and puts down her fork, Max turns to her and she smiles at him.

'Amy tells me that you're about to have another grandchild,' she says. 'I think she said your family live in Oxford. I was at St Catz . . .'

Max listens whilst Charley tells him about her student life in Oxford, and afterwards going from one course to another, the perpetual student. Max is fascinated by her casual approach to life, though he knows Judith wouldn't approve. The thought irritates him. He wonders if other couples are like this: judging new acquaintances through the eyes of their spouses and being influenced by that judgement. Judith always makes her feelings very clear, though she adds the rider that he must make up his own mind. This is not as easy as it sounds. If she does dislike or disapprove of anybody it is almost impossible not to be aware of it, and by some subtle method she indicates that by having a different opinion he is being disloyal. He's finding Charley amusing and intelligent, he's enjoying their conversation, but he knows it wouldn't be a good idea to invite her for coffee when Judith gets back. He's seen that Cara has been getting on well with her, however, and when Charley mentions Cara's quest for a place to live an idea suggests itself.

'Amy says you live in Totnes,' he says casually. 'You must let us know if you see anything that looks good coming on the market.'

'I'll do that thing,' she answers, smiling at Cara, who is now enjoined in the conversation. 'You do know, don't you, that Totnes is twinned with Narnia? It's true! Just saying!'

They laugh, and Max sighs with pleasure, trying not to feel so happy at this sense of freedom, knowing that guilt will follow.

Cara watches him with sympathy and affection. She likes to see Max having fun and she's suffered too much at Judith's hands to feel particularly loyal to her.

'She's a passive-aggressive,' Philip used to say. 'She never comes right out with anything so that you can challenge her. It's just hints and observations with an accompanying look of contempt if you should feel differently. That drawn-in chin and tight-lipped mouth signifying disapproval. She needs to be in control and she's perfected a way of doing it. But she's been a good wife to Max, she's supported him, and coped with naval life, so who are we to criticize?'

Who indeed? thinks Cara, but she's anxious about how it will all play out when Judith comes home.

Cara wonders in which, out of all the places she's seen so far, she could imagine settling down. She knows that it's sensible to rent to begin with but even that seems a huge step to take at the moment. She wonders what Philip might have advised, knowing that he would have stayed in London. Here, she loves the friendliness of the shopkeepers and hospitality staff; the way a few locals are beginning to recognize her, especially if they see her with Oscar.

'Just don't agree to join anything or run anything,' Max advised her jokily, 'and you'll be fine.'

'No fear of that,' she said, laughing. 'I can't even decide where to live so I wouldn't be much use to anyone at the moment. Even poor Sam is beginning to despair of me.'

She looks across the table where he and Jack are in deep conversation and feels an odd and surprisingly strong affection for both of them. They share a strong sense of self-containment, of inner strength, yet they can both be very amusing. She feels lucky to have found a momentary berth here in this magical place where she can try to adjust to her grief and fear. The panic attacks have receded just a little but that is due in part to the fact that, because of all these people around this table, she is rarely on her own. She glances across the bar and notices that the man at the window table is still alone. To begin with, seeing him sitting by himself, she was reminded of Cosmo sitting in the Coffee Shop; of how he'd made her think of Joe and the secret she's kept for so long. Even as she watches him, the man prepares to leave. She wonders if he, too, is on his own in the world, and what he is doing here today. Then Amy claims her attention and she forgets him.

Al stands up, walks out of the bar into the gentle mizzling rain, and heads back to the creek. It's odd that he felt more alone in that friendly bar, with its log fire and amazing views, than he's ever felt amongst strangers on the Tube or in the streets or in the cafés of the capital. Is it because he isn't a local, that the bar staff didn't have a friendly quip for him or know which ale he prefers? Was it because all the other people in the bar seemed to be having such fun? Al feels out of place and he wonders what it is that Cosmo has seen here, what he's experienced in these last few weeks that has given him such a passion for the place. Al liked Salcombe better when it was teeming with summer visitors, the estuary crammed with water traffic, the shops busy to bursting point, yet he was still able to maintain his anonymity as he walked amongst it all. Of it but not in it.

He wonders how Cosmo is getting on and, on an impulse, steps to one side to send a text. He knows he must keep it simple in case Becks is there. Just at this moment, Al feels an affinity with Becks, with her straightforwardness, eye always on the goal, her refusal to be deflected. He wonders if she's believed Cosmo's story about wanting his camera equipment and his need for a fix of the bright lights. After all, she's a lawyer: she must be able to tell when someone is lying. He texts:

Reggie is missing you. Love to Becks.

As Al presses Send he's surprised that he added those last three words. He's always been careful to play it cool with Becks. But now there's been a change, as if they're all playing by a new set of rules, and he's slightly irritated at being called in to be the stooge for this weekend. He puts his phone in his pocket and strides on, shrugging his collar up to keep out the more persistent rain. He feels depressed. The rest of the weekend stretches emptily ahead and once again he wonders what on earth Cosmo finds to do all day. Al begins to feel slightly guilty that he persuaded Cosmo to come down here to dog-and-house-sit, even though he'd already decided he wouldn't stay in London for his sabbatical but might go travelling. Al wonders what kind of girl could present a challenge to Becks. Perhaps this evening he should check out the pubs to see if he can spot Amy. But how would he recognize her?

The rain is blowing soft curtains of mist across the estuary, obscuring the far shore, settling in cushions of fog on the hills. Al climbs the steps up to the garden, lets himself into the house. He drags off his jacket, kicks off his shoes and calls to Reggie, who comes to greet him, happy to have him home again.

The rest of the weekend passes slowly, and there is no answering text from Cosmo except the one on Sunday afternoon, which confirms that he is on the train, travelling west and he'll see Al at Totnes Station. Al sighs with relief and begins to get his belongings together. He tidies up, checks around and then puts his bag and Reggie into the car. Rather than take the lanes he drives up to the main road, and heads towards Kingsbridge. He is surprised at the lightness of spirit he is experiencing, as if he has been appointed an unpleasant task of which he is now being relieved. It is only as he approaches Totnes that he realizes he is actually feeling very angry at having been made complicit in this deceiving of Becks – and of Amy. He resents it. Cosmo might be one of his oldest friends but Al feels he has been used and he wishes he'd never agreed to it.

He finds it even more irritating when Cosmo comes swinging off the train looking so pleased with himself. He gives Al a hearty one-arm hug and lets out a great gasp of pleasure.

'Hey,' he says. 'It's great to be back. Thanks, mate. I'll do the same for you one day.'

'I hope you'll never have to,' Al retorts. 'Did you get my text?'

Cosmo opens the car door, calls a greeting to Reggie and hefts his camera case and bag inside. He begins to laugh.

'I did,' he says. 'And I conveyed your message to Becks. She was touched and surprised. But not as much as I was. What was all that about?'

'Perhaps I was just trying to make it up to her for all the shit you're giving her,' Al answers sharply.

Cosmo raises his eyebrows. 'Ooh,' he says, grinning. 'Get you.'

'Oh, for God's sake,' says Al. He takes a deep breath. He knows he's wasting his time. 'Look, I'll go back over the foot-bridge and wait for my train. It's not that long to go. You can give Reggie a walk before it gets dark if you hurry.'

Cosmo hesitates and then nods. 'OK. If you're sure. Thanks, mate. Really. Thanks. Are you sure you're OK?'

'I'm fine,' answers Al. 'But what will you do next time she wants to come down?'

He watches while Cosmo makes a face, mimes despair, horror, then he shakes his head, turns and walks away. As he crosses the footbridge he glances back to the car, which is pulling out into the road, sees Cosmo's hand waving from the window as he drives over the bridge. Al lifts his own hand in response and descends the steps to the platform to wait for the up-train to London.

CHAPTER ELEVEN

As he drives, Cosmo can hardly contain his delight; his happiness to be back here driving in these narrow lanes; catching glimpses of the estuary, of two small dinghies crammed together under a low stone bridge as the tide rises. He's finding it difficult to understand these emotions that have him in their grip. After all, he's had a good weekend in London. Becks was pleased to see him. In fact, he was flattered by her response and joked that perhaps he should go away more often. Despite that, despite the fun of going to a film and having supper at the new Italian restaurant, despite a slow, sexy start to Sunday morning, he could hardly wait to be back on the train and travelling west. He could tell that Al was baffled by his behaviour, and unusually judgemental, but Cosmo simply can't contain his high spirits.

The clouds are packing away to the east. The sun shines on fields and hedgerows, painting them gold and scarlet, and on an impulse Cosmo turns the car down the steep lane that leads past Lincombe Boatyard towards the coastal path around Snapes Point. He parks in the little car park and gets out to release Reggie. The air is warm, soft, and he laughs quietly with sheer pleasure. He decides to walk down the path at the edge of the field, just a short walk so he can reconnect and so that Reggie can stretch his legs. As they come out from the shelter of the hedge he gazes around him, away to Kingsbridge at the head of the estuary, across to the entrance to Frogmore Creek opposite and then around to Salcombe in the west. He can't wait to see Amy again. She is a part of all this, rather like a princess in a fairy tale, belonging to this landscape, which seems set apart from the real world. He is obsessed, possessed, by her and all of this and he can't give any of it up; not yet.

Even as he thinks of her a figure appears, walking round from the coastal path, a black Lab running ahead. It's not Amy, it's the woman he met in the Coffee Shop: Cara. The dogs meet, tails wagging as if they are old friends, and Cosmo raises his hand to her, calling a greeting. She waves as she climbs the field towards him and he smiles at her and gesticulates around him with an expansive gesture.

'Isn't it amazing?' he asks. 'Do you ever get used to it?'

She shakes her head. 'I wouldn't know,' she answers. 'I've only been here a few weeks. But I should think it's very unlikely. It's never quite the same.'

He remembers that she's staying with her brother, looking for somewhere to live, and he envies her that freedom: to be able to choose without any restriction of work or relationship.

'Is this your brother's dog?' he asks.

'This is Oscar,' she answers. 'They seem to know each other, he and Reggie. I think you said that's his name, didn't you, when I met him in the Coffee Shop? Or perhaps they're just naturally gregarious.'

'Like me,' he says, laughing down at her.

As she looks at him he is aware that this is more than just a friendly encounter. She seems to be studying him, observing him closely, as if she is trying to remember something, looking through the surface niceties to a deeper knowledge of him. He feels slightly discomfited, guilty. It's almost as if she might have guessed that he has just returned from a weekend with his girlfriend and is already planning a meeting with another girl, with Amy.

'I'm just having a quick leg stretch,' he says randomly, looking away from her. 'I've been on the train for a couple of hours and I wanted to breathe this wonderful air again.'

'The train?' she asks. 'You've been away?'

He stares across the estuary, cursing himself for his stupidity. Nobody, except Amy, would know he's been away and he doesn't want to explain himself, his life, to this unusual woman who acts as if she might already have guessed his secrets.

'A quick dash back to London,' he says lightly, 'to pick up some of my camera equipment. I had no idea it was going to be so photogenic here.'

He's turning, as he speaks, heading back towards the car, and she walks with him, the dogs following behind.

'Did you take Reggie with you?' she asks.

'No,' he answers. He feels cross with himself and with her. Now he is going to have to explain about Al. 'The owners' son came for the night,' he says.

After all, this is quite true. No need to tell her that Al is an old friend, that they work together. It's none of her business and he wants to keep the distance between Salcombe and London: between romance and reality.

In the car park they encourage the dogs into their cars, then they smile at each other and Cosmo climbs into the driver's seat and switches on the engine. He checks to see if Cara is ready to leave but she's still standing with the door open so he reverses and drives away. He waves as he goes, heaving a sigh of relief, and wondering why he feels unnerved. His earlier sense of exultation has been quenched and he is determined to regain it. As soon as he gets home he'll text Amy: make a plan.

After he's gone, Cara sits for a moment, gazing over the steering wheel, wondering about Cosmo. It's clear that he's in the grip of some great emotion. The landscape might be spectacular, his enthusiasm for photography might be exciting, but that doesn't quite explain the sheer joy that sparkles in his eyes and lights up his face.

So what does it matter if he's in lust with Amy – why should she feel anxious? And why does she feel the stirrings of her own past, the remembrance of that same look on Joe's face when he drove her from Fiumicino Airport to his flat in the city? Her hands tighten a little on the steering wheel. She recognizes the expression now. It's the expression of a man in the grip of a strong visceral emotion who believes that he is getting away with it; that he can have it both ways. Cosmo was uncomfortable when she mentioned London. He didn't want to talk about his quick dash away. She could tell by his body language that he was concealing something. But why? It's no business of hers so why should he be wary?

Cara sits back, putting on her seat belt, starting the engine. She's seen Cosmo with Amy and she can tell by the way that Amy looks at him that she's falling in love, but Cara knows it's crazy to make this connection with her and Joe.

That was then and this is now, she tells herself. But the memories begin to crowd in and with them comes the old familiar panic churning her gut.

Quickly she starts the engine, drives out into the lane. She won't think about it – she must keep it sealed away – but she longs for Philip: for his presence standing between her and the darkness. From nowhere comes the memory of him holding her calmly as she sobbed, her head buried in his chest. He wasn't surprised to see her: Max had phoned him to say she would be in Rome. She clung to this man she'd known all her life, Max's closest friend, knowing he would help her.

'For God's sake,' Max said, when she told him of her plan to visit Joe in Rome, 'it sounds a bit crazy. How well do you know this man? Are you staying with his people? What does Father say? Does Hermione know you're just blinding off into the blue?'

'She thinks it's a great adventure,' Cara replied, laughing. 'She's all for it. Don't be so stuffy, Max.'

'She would be,' he answered grimly. 'Look, be sure to take Philip's address. You know he's at the Embassy in Rome? He's First Secretary now. Promise to take his address, Cara. I'll phone him and tell him you're going out. I'll be at sea by then. Look, I wish you'd reconsider this . . .'

How excited she was to have Joe's call inviting her to visit him in Rome; how relieved. She'd begun to think that she'd imagined his love for her but the minute she heard his voice, laughing, expostulating, insisting that she should come, all her doubts vanished like smoke. He loved her. He would propose to her and they would be together for ever. She can't recall the flight, but she can remember how he bundled her into the little Fiat, how they'd driven through the city in the early summer evening. She was expecting to go to his parents' town house – or even to their villa – but instead he took her to a flat on the top floor of an old house. It was clearly his own pad. They couldn't wait to make love – she wanted it as much as he did – and only when it was over and she began to talk about the future did she realize that Joe had no thoughts of marriage. In fact he admitted – expecting her to understand – he was already engaged to an Italian girl whose family were wine exporters like his own. Cara was to be his mistress.

Her mind blanks out the scene that followed. She fled to Philip. He listened calmly, asked several questions, and then he went away to telephone the airport and make some other calls. All the while she simply remained in shock, trembling, bursting into tears, until he came back into the room, gave her some brandy and explained he'd arranged a few days' leave and that they would both be on the next flight home . . .

A Land Rover pulls out of a gateway ahead of her and Cara stamps on the brakes, realizing that she's driving too fast. She lets it go ahead of her and follows more slowly. The sudden shock has broken the train of thought and with a huge effort she thrusts the memories away, wondering instead if Max and Sam will be back. They've been sailing Max's boat up from the Bag to bring it ashore for the winter and she hopes they'll be finished and back at the house. She needs company, distraction.

The minute that she and Oscar come through the front door she sees that she's going to get it. There is an air of bustle, of emergency. Max's bag stands ready packed and she can hear him talking on the telephone. As she climbs the stairs to the kitchen Sam turns to look at her. He makes a face, a kind of amused grimace and she raises her eyebrows questioningly.

'There's a bit of a panic,' he says. 'Freya's gone into labour and her mum has arrived from Denmark. It seems that there might not be room for everyone so Max is going up to bring

Judith back as soon as the baby's born. They'll stay in a hotel or something. It all seems a bit of a pig's breakfast. Judith's in a state.'

'She and Freya's mum don't get on awfully well,' Cara tells him. 'But I expect Freya will be glad to have her mum with her.'

'I think,' he says rather awkwardly, 'that I might make myself scarce if Judith's coming home again. It'll be a bit of a squash.'

She smiles at him, glad of his presence. 'You mean you're ratting on me?'

He laughs. 'No, I'm not. But you see what I mean? It won't be quite the same, will it?'

She laughs too. 'It certainly won't. You and Max sitting up late, getting rat-arsed while he yarns about his navy days . . . suppers down at the pub.'

'I had a thought,' he says, rather shyly. 'I was wondering if you might like to come and stay at The Keep for a few days? I know Fliss and Hal would love it. Did I tell you that they've decided to rehome a Labrador? You must meet her.'

'That's very sweet of you,' she says, touched. 'But I'll need to stay here and look after Oscar if Max is going to Oxford.'

'No, I get that. I meant once they're back again. We could do some more exploring.'

It's odd how his thoughtfulness touches her. These days, since Philip died, small acts of unconsidered kindness almost move her to tears.

'I'd really like that,' she says. 'Thanks, Sam.'

Max appears, looking irritated, anxious. 'Freya's gone into labour,' he says to Cara. 'Judith wants me to go straight away, if you don't mind staying with Oscar. Freya's mum has arrived and it's easier if Judith and I check into a hotel. We'll be home as soon as the baby is born. I'm really sorry about this, Cara.'

'Don't be silly,' she says quickly. She pats Oscar, who is sitting watching anxiously, sensing trouble. 'It's nobody's fault. I'm quite happy here with Oscar. Are you going now?'

'I told Judith I would. Everyone's in a bit of a panic, apparently.' He looks at Sam. 'Your visit hasn't quite worked out the way we planned, has it?'

'Honestly. It's not a problem. Babies come first. I'll stay with Cara and we'll carry on house-hunting until you come home again. We've got lunch at The Keep to look forward to as well.'

Max looks relieved. 'That's great. Take care of each other. I'll let you know how things go on.'

'Text when you're safely there,' says Cara, kissing him. 'Give my love to everyone.'

In the silence that follows Max's departure Sam and Cara look at each other.

'Have we got any plans for supper?' she asks him.

He grins at her. 'Yes,' he says. 'Let's go to the pub.'

Jack's in the bar, having a pint with his mates. He looks pleased to see them and gestures for them to join him.

'Amy's abandoned me again,' he says. 'She's got a last-minute date. Where's Max?'

Cara explains. 'We can't be bothered to cook so we're going to have supper here,' she adds. 'Want to join us, since you've been stood up as well?'

'Sounds like a plan,' he says. 'What are you drinking?'

Later, when they come out into the quiet town, a huge moon is rising beyond the headland.

'It's so bright,' says Cara, awed by the sight of it.

'It's the hunter's moon,' Jack tells her.

'What does that mean?' she asks.

'It happens every autumn, usually in October. It's called the hunter's moon because its light is so brilliant that even the smallest animal can't hide from its predator.'

Cara shivers. 'That's rather scary.'

Jack looks at her. 'Only if you're an animal,' he says. 'Come back for a nightcap. Neither of you has seen our little house yet. Amy might be back by now,' and they all head off to Courtenay Street.

Cosmo is unable to sleep. Cold, bright moonlight pours into his bedroom and he gets up and goes to the window as if he is being drawn by invisible tides. He stares out at the mono-chrome landscape and suddenly, on some impulse, he begins to drag on his clothes. He needs to be out in this strange night-time world, in this uncanny light.

Reggie raises his head as Cosmo comes into the kitchen but he makes no attempt to rise. Cosmo pulls on his jacket and lets himself out into the night, walking up towards the coastal path, gazing around him in awe. There's a chill little breeze that rif-fles the waters of the estuary so that the moon's reflection is shivered into a thousand jagged silver pieces that resemble a shattered glass bauble. He walks with his hands driven deep into his pockets, noting the definition of each twig and stone, listening to the high-pitched scream of a small stricken animal and the eerie screech of an owl. There is something exhilarating about this light, which ruthlessly searches out each hiding place and exposes every secret. It seems to probe deep into his own heart, showing him his weaknesses; his faithlessness.

Cosmo pauses, clenching his hands into fists, examining his conscience.

After all, he excuses himself, nobody is being hurt.

He can't understand this passion that makes it absolutely necessary to surrender himself to this moment in time, which is offering him an extraordinary alternative universe, including this magical place – and Amy. He needs to take it, to explore it, to experience it, whilst, at the same time, keeping London and his work and Becks in a separate time capsule. This evening with Amy has been so good. How warm she was, how pleased to see him, and he remembers how she'd breathed the words 'I think I love you' when he'd held her tightly in his arms.

Cosmo stands drenched in the moon's brilliance, seeing himself clearly in its merciless light yet unable to accept its truth. He knows that he is cheating, lying, yet he cannot give up this excitement; this sensation of feeling so vitally alive. There is a noise in the hedge behind him, a scuffling of dried grass, the snapping of a twig. He turns quickly in time to see a shadow racing along the ditch, disappearing into a burrow. Cosmo glances around him, hearing again the owl's cry near at hand. One creature at least is safe from those talons and the cruel curved beak, and Cosmo smiles to himself. He sees it as a sign, a portent. Success is to the swift: to those who see their opportunities and seize them. Somehow things will work out, he knows they will. He turns up his collar and heads for home.

Back in Buckley Street, Sam says goodnight and disappears away to bed but Cara is not sleepy. The moon's light shining into the house is like an ineluctable tide, towing her towards it, dragging her up the stairs into the kitchen. She stands still for a moment, gazing out, and then very reluctantly she opens the doors that lead on to the balcony. Gripping the door jamb, she watches the reflections that gleam on the rooftops and on the water. She doesn't dare to look down, yet she feels compelled to take a step, to leave the safety of the kitchen and walk out on to the slatted floor of the balcony. Beneath her all is blackness, and she experiences that all-too-familiar longing to cast herself into it. Letting go of the door jamb, she steps forward. All is darkness and light; brilliance and shadow.

Cara gives a tiny sob, and stretches out a hand, as if someone might be there to take hold of her. She feels dizzy, losing all sense of where she is, and suddenly she almost falls. Her legs have encountered something unyielding and warm. She slides down, knees giving way, and encounters the solid body of Oscar, who stands across her, blocking her way. Cara crouches, putting her arms around his neck, seeing the glint of moonlight reflected in his kind, anxious eyes. Gently he edges her back towards the kitchen, and she goes gratefully, clutching his collar, closing the doors behind them. She collapses into an old wicker chair whilst Oscar stands beside her, watching her reproachfully. Cara strokes his ears, lays her cheek briefly against his warm, hard head, then she gets up and they go downstairs together.

Amy lies, wakeful and alert, watching the moonlight wheeling slowly across her bedroom ceiling. Its light reveals each well-known object, dazzles on the small mirror, picks out the books in the tall, narrow bookcase her dad made for her when she was little. Even from this distance she knows each book from its spine: *The Wind in the Willows*, *Winnie-the-Pooh*, *The Hobbit*. She remembers how Mum would read to her and, idly, Amy wonders what her mum would think of Cosmo.

Nobody could help liking Cosmo, she tells herself almost defensively, as if there's some question about it. He's such fun, so full of life and energy.

She feels slightly embarrassed as she remembers how pleased she was to see him earlier, after she'd got his text inviting her round for a drink and supper. It was the first time she'd spent any time there. Usually they went off walking, or to Dartmouth or Kingsbridge, but she decided to accept the invitation. It was as if this moved the relationship on a little bit. She's invited him back to hers but somehow he always slithers away from accepting. Never with a definite refusal but simply by turning the conversation a little so that she feels awkward repeating the invitation.

Amy rolls on to her side, gazing out of her window into the blaze of white light. Earlier, walking out to the creek, she wondered if she'd feel a bit shy, but somehow just the sight of him, flinging open the door, beaming at her, Reggie at his heels, dissolved her anxiety. She beamed back at him and then she was in his arms and kissing him, and it just felt like heaven. He'd poured her a glass of wine, taken something from the freezer to put in the oven, and they'd just fallen back into the pattern of all their previous encounters. When he kissed her she knew he wanted more than that – and so did she – but something held her back. He was so sweet, not pressing or trying to force the pace, that she'd held him tightly and muttered that she loved him, and then her shyness and uncertainty returned and she said that she must get back or Dad would start worrying. It was a bit feeble but he let her go, walking her back into the town but leaving her at the bottom of Buckley Street. He hadn't said he loved her in return and now she feels even more anxious.

Restlessly, Amy turns back on to her other side and pulls the duvet over her head. She longs to feel more secure with him but he never talks about the future and she doesn't know how to frame the question: how does he see their future together?

The moon sinks away into the west and between one thought and another she falls asleep.

PART TWO

CHAPTER TWELVE

When Fliss wakes, Hal is already up and gone, the sheet beside her cold to the touch. She lies for a moment, her eyes still closed, caught between sleep and wakefulness, her thoughts straying between the present and the past. Memories flit like moving pictures behind her closed eyes, all muddled up with other later experiences, and she shakes her head like a swimmer surfacing, opening her eyes to the present.

Suddenly she remembers why Hal has risen and gone quietly away and she sits up, pushing back the duvet and swinging her legs out of bed. She pushes her feet into slippers, then, pulling on her dressing gown, she goes out, along the passage and down the stairs. In the kitchen, Hal is sitting at the table, turned sideways, talking to Honey, whose tail is beating against the table leg.

Fliss smiles to see them and Honey immediately scouts around for the ancient battered teddy, which is her constant companion, and hurries to bring it to Fliss.

'Good girl,' says Fliss, stroking the smooth, warm head. 'Good girl. Is that for me?'

'You know it isn't,' says Hal, getting up and refilling the kettle. 'She's just showing it to you.'

Fliss pretends to take the toy, to shake it free, but Honey grips on, tail wagging, enjoying the game.

'Another good night?' asks Fliss. 'No problems?'

'Good as gold,' replies Hal. 'We've struck lucky. She doesn't chew things she shouldn't and there are no accidents. I've let her out for a pee and she seems very happy.'

'She's been used to walks in the park, they told me,' Fliss says, 'but not much more. With her owner being elderly she's been fairly restricted. It will be good to show her some freedom. We'll take her up on the moor. She needs to become a country dog.'

Hal passes her some coffee and Honey goes to her basket to check out her other toys.

'Do you remember Mrs Pooter?' asks Fliss suddenly. 'And Mugwump?'

Hal laughs. 'I never did know why we let my crazy sister name the dogs.'

'She loved them so much. And she was always spot on. She's going to love Honey.'

'Thank God she's got a name already,' says Hal. 'Kit's a nutter.'

'But such a nice nutter,' says Fliss. 'So do you think Honey's ready for Dartmoor? Nobody knows what she'll be like with stock. It'll be interesting to see how she behaves when she sees her first sheep or a pony.'

'She's been very well trained,' says Hal, 'but she's a city dog and I'm not taking any chances. We'll keep her on a lead until we're totally sure. By the way, I had a text from Sam last night. I've just seen it. He's asking if he and Cara can come for lunch today. Apparently Freya has gone into labour and Max has rushed off to Oxford again.'

'Oh, good grief! Poor Max. It's all go, isn't it? I hope Freya's OK. Yes, of course they can come. That would be great. Perhaps we can all take Honey out afterwards.'

She sits at the table, sipping coffee, wondering what to give them for lunch, whilst Hal scrolls through his messages, making comments about various members of the family: what they're doing, the latest news. As she watches him, Fliss wonders if she and Hal are so happy because they came together so late; each with the failures and disappointments and lessons learned from their first marriages. They know how to give each other space, to respect the other's feelings, and to have such delight in the love that they were both denied for so long. Perhaps it helps that they've known each other all their lives, lived within this extended family, shared so much.

Fliss wonders what their grandmother would think of them now.

'You're a long way off,' says Hal, watching her, pushing his iPad to one side. 'Penny for them?'

'Oh, they're worth much more than that,' she protests. 'Shall we keep lunch simple or make it a feast?'

'Simple,' he answers at once. 'Especially if we're going to walk Honey afterwards. Sam will be driving so he can't drink, and nor can I if we're going up on the moor.'

'Suits me,' she says. 'I've got some soup in the freezer but I might dash over to Riverford and get some really nice cheese.'

'I'll take Honey out on the hill for a walk,' he says. 'Sam says "late morning" in his text so I'll be around if they're a bit early.'

'Fine,' she says. 'So breakfast, then shower, or the other way around?'

'Breakfast first.' He gets up. 'Admiral's Special, I think.'

Fliss laughs. It's Hal's son, Jolyon, who has named his father's legendary fry-ups by this name. Hal is raiding the fridge: bacon, eggs, mushrooms, tomatoes.

'Bring it on and then I'll go foraging for lunch,' she says.

The shadows of the past have receded: the day ahead is full of promise.

Out on the hill, Hal follows the well-worn paths, crisscrossed with sheep tracks, listening to the harsh shouting of a crow, whilst Honey trots obediently at heel, though she looks alert. At intervals he encourages her to run ahead, to explore, but she remains close beside him as if she is baffled, even nervous, at this expanse of open land. He pauses beside a slab of granite beneath a hawthorn tree and looks out across the valley to the moor, and down to the spinney of beech and oak below him at the bottom of the hill. When Mole was small, running round the spinney was a game. He and Susanna sprinted round the small belt of trees whilst Fox stood here, where Hal is standing now, watch in hand, and timed them. It became a test, an important part of the nursery routine. Times were checked, improved, written down. But the real test was that Mole should one day run round the spinney alone. With the terrors of the massacre of his family in Kenya still upon him, even those few minutes out of sight, unable to see Fox on the hill above him, or The Keep on the opposite slopes, filled Mole's heart with dread. The whole family knew and waited patiently for that great moment when Mole might feel secure enough to run round the spinney alone.

Now, Hal stands on the hill, arms folded across his chest, with Honey waiting patiently beside him, thinking about Mole's son. What a bloody tragedy that Mole didn't know that he was to have a son. What a damned waste of a lovely man; a first-class officer. Hal thinks of Sam, hoping that if Mole is watching somewhere he'll approve of the way Fliss and he have tried to make sure that Sam is secure, confident, loved. If only they could be absolutely certain that all is well with the boy, that this reserve is simply his natural genetic inheritance from his father and not something deeper.

Hal's aware of a movement and glances down. Honey is looking up at him hopefully, tail brushing to and fro across the short sheep-grazed turf.

'Sorry,' he says. 'Sorry, old girl. Come on. Let's get going or Sam and Cara will be here. Go on. Run. Rabbits! Go get 'em!'

But Honey remains at his heel. Clearly she is as nervous of leaving his side as Mole was at running round the spinney.

'But Mole did it,' he tells her, 'and so will you, in time. There's no rush but it will happen.'

Honey wags her tail obligingly and they return the way they've come, down the hill and home to The Keep.

Fliss arrives only minutes before Sam's Mini passes under the archway and into the courtyard.

'Hope you don't mind us being early,' he says, getting out. 'We'll have to get back after lunch because of Oscar.'

'Oh gosh, I forgot all about Oscar,' cries Fliss, coming to kiss Cara. 'You could have brought him with you.'

'I wasn't sure how it might go with Honey,' says Sam, taking Fliss's shopping from her car. 'It's early days for her and it's a pity to cause any unnecessary stress.'

'We thought we'd all take Honey for her first walk on the moor,' says Fliss, as they go into the kitchen. 'What a shame. It would have been such fun.'

'Well, that might be a bit much for poor Oscar,' says Cara. 'He's already had a good walk and he's an old boy now.'

'So am I,' says Hal, getting up from the rocking chair by the Aga, 'but nobody seems to care much about *me*.'

Sam grins, filled with affection for him, gives him a friendly buffet on the shoulder and bends to greet Honey.

'Here she is,' he says to Cara. 'Isn't she a Honey?' and laughs at his foolish joke.

Whilst Fliss unpacks her shopping, Hal makes coffee and then suggests that he shows Cara some of the garden. Taking their coffee with them, Honey at their heels, they wander out, and Sam looks at Fliss to check that she's OK about the sudden lunch invitation.

'Max went off rather unexpectedly,' he tells her, 'and I thought it would be good to bring Cara over. Anything I can do?'

'It's fine,' she assures him. 'Of course it is. No, sit and drink your coffee. How are things in Oxford?'

He shrugs, sits at the table, picks up his mug. 'I think everything is going to plan. Judith will be back soon so I shall come home then, anyway.'

'You don't think it's a bit rude to leave so quickly?'

'I don't think so. After all, with Cara staying there it's a bit of a crush and Judith'll probably be tired after these last few weeks.'

Fliss hesitates as she sets food out on the table, takes a quick sip at her coffee, and glances at him.

'You've told Cara she can come here if she'd like to, haven't you? There's loads of space. She needn't feel like she's in the way.'

He nods. 'I've told her and I think she's considering it. That's one of the reasons I brought her over today, so as to get her used to the idea of it. I'm not sure she and Judith get on terribly well.'

'Nobody gets on really well with Judith,' says Fliss shortly. 'Sorry. Shouldn't have said that. Judith's got lots of good qualities but empathy isn't one of them. Well, I'll leave it to you. Cara might like some space to decide what she's going to do and there's plenty of that here. It's very early days for her after her husband's death and it's all very well to put on a brave face and be all gung ho, but you're not thinking straight when you've just lost somebody very special.'

Sam looks down at his coffee. He thinks: well, you certainly know all about that.

He feels the same kind of tenderness and love for Fliss that he felt towards Hal earlier. He owes them both so much. Suddenly he has one of those rare longings to open up, tell her his dilemma, but he can hear Cara and Hal coming back along the passage and he suppresses it.

As they drive along familiar lanes, past Buckfast Abbey, through Hembury Woods up towards Holne Moor, Fliss is thinking of times past and how Hal and she drove this way twenty years before. Back then, it was a spring day: a chiff-chaff swinging on a branch of budding crab apple, a clump of early purple orchids on a grassy bank, two painted ladies fluttering above a patch of violets growing in a crevice of a dry-stone wall. They parked by Venford Reservoir and walked out to Bench Tor, looking down into White Wood; seeing the gleam of water far below, between the branches of the trees that clung to the coombe's steep sides. They heard the cuckoo, and suddenly they spotted him, watching his dipping flight as he dropped down towards Meltor Wood. Then Hal had taken her in his arms and kissed her and the next afternoon, when the family was gathered for tea in the hall, just before he went back to join his ship, he'd announced to them all that he and Fliss were going to get married.

As the car bumps over the cattle grid and up on to the open moor, Fliss stretches out a hand and lays it on Hal's thigh. He gives her a quick sideways glance.

'Do I deserve this token of affection?' he asks.

She smiles. 'It's good to be bringing a dog up on the moor for the first time again,' she says. 'There have been so many. Mrs Pooter, Mugwump, Rex, Rufus. And now Honey.'

'I think we were right to resist a puppy,' Hal says. 'I think a seven-year-old is a good age for us.'

Fliss looks out at the autumn face of the moor, a patchwork of rusting bracken, bleached grasslands and tall stands of golden gorse. Venford Reservoir reveals itself: a shining jewel of blue, reflecting the clear sky, set within its banks of rhododendrons and trees.

She's surprised at how quickly she and Cara have bonded. Fliss guesses that it's because of their shared experience of grief: that each recognizes in the other the extent of suffering and respects it. But it's more than that. She senses in Cara the inability to confide easily, the in-built barrier that prevents the luxury of speaking of things close to the heart. Whether this is an imposed barrier or one that is natural to her, Fliss can't quite decide, but this act of connecting lowered Fliss's own defences. It's clear that Cara has grown very fond of Sam and, after lunch, whilst Hal and Sam cleared up, Fliss found herself talking about Mole, about her grief and horror at his death. They sat together on a bench in the courtyard, Honey leaning against their legs, and it was as if the presence of the dog were a conduit through which their thoughts could be shared. As they stroked Honey, it became easier to talk about loss and grief and loneliness. For the first time in many years Fliss talked about her beloved older brother, Jamie, and how he died out in Kenya with their parents; how she tried to be a little mother to small Mole and Susanna whilst feeling quite incapable of the responsibility, and her relief when they arrived home, to The Keep and to their grandmother. She relived the horror of Mole being utterly silent during the weeks following the massacre.

'It would be called PTSD now,' she said to Cara. 'But back then nobody knew about that and we were all so worried. I was terrified that Mole would never speak again.'

Remembering that awful time, she bent to smooth Honey's head, feeling the fear fresh again in her heart, tears filling her eyes.

'What happened?' asked Cara gently, after a moment. 'Was it gradual or was it some kind of shock that restored Mole's voice?'

Fliss stared across the courtyard, blinking away tears, reliving the scene in her mind. 'Fox had gone to Staverton Station to pick up Hal and Kit and Aunt Prue from the train,' she said. 'Hal was the same age as Jamie, and they were very alike. Mole was asleep in the hall when they drove into the courtyard. I shouted out something like, "They're here" and Mole woke up. Hal got out of the car first, and stood looking up at the house, and then Prue started to get out and Mole suddenly screamed out: "It's Mummy. It's Mummy and Jamie!" He ran out and flung his arms round Hal . . . and then he realized.' Even sixty years on Fliss can remember her guilt. 'I'd told him they were coming, you see, but when he woke I think he forgot just for a moment. Perhaps he thought it had all been a dreadful dream and nobody had died. It was terrible. Awful. But his voice had come back.'

There were tears in Cara's eyes, too, as she listened. Briefly she touched Fliss's hand in sympathy, and then Sam appeared and said that he and Cara should be getting back to Oscar.

Now, as she gazes out across the moor, Fliss longs to share the glory of it all with her.

'I hope Cara will come and stay,' she says to Hal. 'It would be so good to show her Dartmoor.'

'Well, even if she doesn't,' Hal says, 'I'm sure Sam will bring her up here at some point. He loves it all, too. But I agree. It would be fun if she were to decide to spend some time with us.' He hesitates. 'I felt that the boy was looking a tad less introspective, did you? More like his old self. He positively sparkled at lunch.'

Fliss nods, smiling. 'I think he's coming to it. To telling us what's troubling him. Mole was like that, wasn't he? Always anxious that he shouldn't worry you with some confidence. As if it were some kind of weakness not to be able to cope.'

Hal nods. 'Dear old boy,' he says rather sadly. 'And Sam looks just like him. It takes me aback all standing sometimes.'

He pulls into the car park opposite the reservoir, switches off the engine and looks in the rear-view mirror. Honey is sitting up, staring out rather anxiously at the great expanse of open moorland, and at the several ponies which loiter nearby. Hal turns round and reaches for her lead.

'I'm not sure we'll need this – she won't leave my side as a rule – but I don't want to take any chances. The ponies might suddenly kick up their heels and dash off and that might spook her. I'd hate to have to chase her halfway over Dartmoor.'

Fliss opens her door and gets out. The air is clear and fresh and she breathes deeply. There is a sense of infinity here: a brief glimpse of the eternal. Hal is out of the car, releasing Honey, clipping on her lead.

'Rule one,' he is telling her. 'We do not chase persons who have four legs. That'll do to begin with.'

Fliss goes to join them. She slips her hand in Hal's and they set off together towards Bench Tor.

CHAPTER THIRTEEN

Cara puts into a folder all the sheets of paper containing house details that Sam has printed off for her, gives Oscar a pat and takes the folder down to her bedroom. All the while she is listening for the sound of the front door opening and Judith's return from Oxford. Sam has already driven away to The Keep and now Cara is alone again.

She is no nearer finding a place to live than when she first arrived, although she is becoming familiar with the countryside. The anxiety makes her heart beat fast. With Sam gone, and Max back in his role of attentive husband, who will hold up the mirror for her? How will she be sure of her existence? She remembers the mirror in the loft of her childhood home, and remembers the joy and relief with which she greeted her reflection. She was real, she existed, and she was no longer alone in the big quiet house with her indifferent, unpredictable mother. She laughed and danced and talked, leaning forward to kiss the cold lips of the little girl who lived in the mirror and convinced Cara that she had a friend. How old was she when her mother discovered her? She was shocked by what she called Cara's 'showing off', angry at her vanity, and the mirror was covered up. It was not long after that she'd been sent away to school.

Cara turns away from the chest of drawers and sits on the edge of the bed. Can any other child have been so happy to go away to boarding school? The children – even the bullies – convinced her of her reality. None of the hardships, the deprivations, could quench the happiness of being with friends who loved her, teachers who encouraged her. During the holidays Max was down from university and then, when he joined the navy and their mother died, Hermione came into her life.

How relieved their father was, how delighted, that Cara embraced his mistress so wholeheartedly. Later, she wondered whether her father's relationship with Hermione was the result of her mother's cold, withdrawn detachment, the drinking bouts and crying jags, or whether she was the reason for it. Either way, she, Cara, blossomed into a happy teenager under Hermione's warmth and guidance. Max, now engaged to Judith, was relieved, though not entirely comfortable with Hermione. It was becoming clear that Judith was irritated by his sense of responsibility towards his little sister and she was keen to plan their wedding and move to a married quarter in Gosport. With a distinct lack of enthusiasm she agreed that Cara should be a bridesmaid.

'Judith's just like her mother,' Cara said privately to Hermione after the wedding. 'Rather bossy and not much fun.'

'Hmm,' said Hermione. 'Max can't say he hasn't been warned then. Like mother, like daughter.'

Hermione took Cara to boutiques, to the theatre, to exhibitions. She visited her at school – 'She's a kind of cousin,' Cara told her friends – and when Hermione met Philip she welcomed him into the warm circle of friendship.

Cara clenches her hands between her knees. Philip: loyal, kind, faithful. How can she manage without him? They were a great team and their parties were legendary amongst their colleagues in the FCO. He collapsed with an aortic aneurysm and died instantly. Gone between one moment and the next. Each morning when she wakes, there is a split second before reality strikes, a split second in which she thinks, something terrible has happened. What is it?

When she told him that she was pregnant with Joe's child, he put his arms around her and held her close.

'What shall I do?' she asked him, unable to stop weeping with the shock and fear of it all.

'Marry me,' he said, his face hidden in her hair. 'Marry me and we'll bring the baby up together. It will be my child.'

She clung to him, dear, familiar Philip, always there in a crisis. She'd always loved him; why shouldn't she marry him? It seemed impossible that she would ever marry anyone else. He was still holding her tightly, and saying she must consider his offer carefully, and then he was explaining that he was gay, that he wanted to be in a stable relationship so as to pursue his career. She'd never suspected that he was gay. He'd had several girlfriends, though never a serious, long-term relationship, and he was very popular with women. But after that first moment of shock her instinct was to hold him even more tightly. They would protect each other, keep each other's secrets. Later, as she saw their friends being unfaithful to their partners, getting divorced, or living in a kind of permanent unspoken truce of indifference, she knew that she and Philip were happier than most.

The front door opens, she hears voices, Oscar barks, and instinctively she gets to her feet. She stands for a moment, listening, wondering when she should emerge. Then she hears Max call her name and she opens the bedroom door and goes out to greet Judith.

Despite her good intentions, Judith is filled with the usual faint irritation at the sight of her sister-in-law. It has always been thus. From the beginning, Max's devotion to his younger sister has always seemed over the top: his concern and anxiety for her unnecessary and rather embarrassing. Judith smiles and embraces Cara but her critical eye notices that in those jeans and her oversize sweater Cara hardly looks like a grieving widow. But then, thinks Judith resentfully, she's always looked and behaved like a teenager. Philip and Max encouraged her and, of course, the boys adored her. They loved it on those rare occasions when she came to stay – she seemed to prefer to be with the children than with the adults – and later, when he was away at school and at university, their younger son Christopher always insisted on spending some part of his summer holidays with her and Philip wherever they were posted. He came back full of the jaunts they'd been on, the crazy things they'd done, the fun he'd had. Cara could do no wrong.

'How long is she planning to stay?' she asked Max in the car on the way home, once they'd finished talking about the baby and how sweet Poppy was with her new little sister.

'Oh, come on,' he said wearily, as though she were being unreasonable. 'I haven't asked her. She needs time to think about where she'd like to be.'

'I can't think why she sold the house in Fulham,' Judith answered, irritated as usual by this instant display of partisanship. 'It was the obvious place for her to be. Shops. Theatres. She could see all their old FO friends when they were on leave.'

'I'm not sure she thinks of London as home,' he answered.

'I don't think she sees anywhere as home, but you have to admit that it was crazy to sell before she had anywhere else to live.'

He was silent and she felt she'd scored a point. Only Cara would sell her home without having the least idea where she might want to go – except to big brother Max, of course. Judith silently enjoys her minor victory but, at the same time, she wants to think through an idea not yet mooted to Max. She needs to pick her moment before she suggests it to him.

Now, as they all climb the stairs to the kitchen, Cara is asking about the new baby, the little family in Oxford, but Judith answers rather briefly. If she's honest, she is always annoyed at being stepped down for Freya's mother, having to give way, and, of course, Paul never sticks up for his own parents. He's too afraid of Freya's sharp tongue, thinks Judith crossly.

She looks around the kitchen. Everything looks clean, tidy; nothing out of place. Max takes the bags into their bedroom and Cara fills the kettle and gathers mugs together.

'Tea?' she asks.

This is another irritation, being offered tea in her own home, but Judith can see that it would be churlish to refuse. She makes an effort to pull herself together, to remember that Cara has lost her husband, though in her view it was an odd relationship. Despite Philip's responsibilities they *both* behaved rather like a couple of teenagers. Perhaps that was because they had no children. Judith had never quite had the courage to ask outright why not, although she'd dropped a few hints. Apparently a miscarriage early on in their marriage had left Cara unable to have more children, although no details were ever given.

'It's none of our business,' Max said, whenever she mentioned it, but at least, thinks Judith rather bitterly, if Cara had children then she'd have somewhere else to go now.

'How's the house-hunting going?' she asks, making her voice bright and interested. 'Seen anywhere nice?'

Whilst Cara describes some of the places she's seen, Judith hopes she won't buy in Salcombe, although if her own plan works out it won't matter much. The thought of this raises her spirits and makes her feel more generous towards her sister-in-law. She takes her mug of tea and brings her phone out of her bag so she can show Cara photos of the new baby. Cara makes all the right noises and for the moment there is harmony.

Max, coming into the kitchen, is relieved to see it. He's never quite understood the antagonism that exists between his wife and his sister. Judith, studying to be a teacher when he first met her, has always disapproved of the fact that Cara has no formal training in anything, but it's much deeper than that. It seems that Judith resents Cara just as some women resent their mothers-in-law. From the beginning she was irritated by the closeness between Max and his sister, by the bond formed by those early, lonely days. Although he's tried to explain his anxiety for the small Cara, left alone with their unreliable and occasionally violent mother, Judith could never truly understand. She lives within her own reality; she can't connect with feelings and actions that don't chime with her own, and dismisses them as unworthy or weak.

As Max drinks his tea and watches the two women he wonders if it was her capacity to take responsibility, to be reliable, that first attracted him to Judith. After his indifferent, disinterested mother, Judith's strength and capability was a novelty. Her need to be in control has been an asset to her as a naval wife and the mother of two boys, but now he is retired Max is beginning to find it an exhausting quality to live with on a daily basis. He's enjoyed this brief respite with Sam and Cara, the jokes and laughter, the impromptu visits to the pub. He really misses Christopher, now that he's moved to Dubai. Chris is more volatile, more ready to take risks than Paul, but he's also great fun. He comes home each summer for what he calls 'some R and R' and they go sailing, walking, checking out old haunts together. His visit is the high point of Max's year.

Max has had the third degree in the car about how long Cara would be staying and where she might live but there seems to be another matter on Judith's mind. Something is distracting her and he can't quite decide what it might be. Perhaps it's simply the arrival of their second granddaughter that's pre-occupying her thoughts, and the usual annoyance of being sidelined by Freya's mother, although it's natural that Freya should want her mother with her at a time like this.

Max finishes his tea, rinses his mug under the tap and stands it on the draining board. He feels disquieted. He knows that Judith won't want Cara with them for too long yet how can he possibly ask her to leave?

'I'm going to take Oscar out for a walk,' he says. 'Shan't be long,' and he and Oscar clatter down the stairs and out into the late afternoon sunshine.

He walks down Buckley Street, letting his hand brush over the feverfew that is still flowering on the stone wall opposite, glancing between the houses to the harbour beyond. The evenings are drawing in and the sun is already slipping behind the hill. He decides to walk round to the head of the creek and back again. He still feels edgy, knowing that he didn't find out the real reason for Sam's visit, and still worrying about Cara. As he comes out of Island Street he sees Amy walking ahead of him. He is about to shout to her when a young man with a dog steps out from between two boats parked in the boatyard into her path. It's clear from the affectionate greeting that this is an assignation. Amy bends to stroke the dog, and then they all walk on together.

Max slows his steps, not knowing who the young man is but fairly certain that he's not a local. He knows that he's seen him around, in the Coffee Shop, in Cranch's, and he wonders if Jack knows him. Max follows them along the edge of the creek, unable to decide if he should turn back or whether he should catch them up and seek an introduction. But, after all, it's none of his business. Yet he continues to follow slowly until they round the head of the creek, climb some steps and disappear into the garden of a converted barn.

Still puzzled, Max calls to Oscar and turns for home.

Jack lets himself in, checks that Amy's not at home and then sits down at the kitchen table to study the programme for the Barn Theatre. He's hoping that Cara will accept another invitation to go with him to the opera, and wonders if she's decided where to live. He can't understand why she simply doesn't take a let in the town for the winter and postpone the final decision, but she is unwilling to commit.

'You're dithering,' he told her. 'No good comes of that. Make a decision and go for it.'

She laughed at him. 'You make it sound so simple.'

'It is. What can go wrong with taking a six-month let while you continue to look around? You said you won't want to be with Max once Judith comes back.'

'Only because I shall feel like a spare part hanging around,' she said quickly. 'You know what I mean.'

He grinned at her, raising his eyebrows, indicating that he knew just how tricky it might be to live with Judith, and she tried not to smile back. He knew she didn't want to be disloyal and he changed the subject.

'*Der Rosenkavalier* is on next week,' he said casually. 'Fancy another night at the opera?'

'Yes, please,' she answered at once, and he was gratified at her swift response. He's surprised at how important she is becoming to him; at how the prospect of her company brightens his day.

'I'll check it out and let you know,' he said.

Now, he picks up his phone and texts her with the date, glances at the mail Amy has left on the table and wonders what he might eat for supper and whether she will be in tonight. Just lately Amy's been in an odd kind of mood but she's always been difficult to pin down. Nevertheless he worries about her.

'Still seeing Cosmo?' he asked her casually, a few days ago.

She shrugged. 'On and off,' she answered. 'Why?'

It was his turn to shrug. 'Just thought it might be nice to meet him. Why not bring him round? Or we could meet up in the pub for a pint.'

She hesitated, looked uncomfortable, and he felt uneasy.

'Where did you say he was staying?' he asked. 'Didn't you say he was dog-sitting?'

She nodded. 'Round the head of Batson Creek.'

His anxiety increased. He hoped that his girl wasn't falling in love with this young man who would probably disappear back to London when his dog-sitting stint was over. He didn't want her hurt but was powerless to prevent it.

'Bring him to quiz night,' he suggested lightly.

'I'll ask him,' she said, and that was the end of the conversation.

A text pings in and Jack looks at his phone. It's from Cara.

Sounds good. Could I come round for a drink? Now?

Jack laughs softly to himself and taps out a message.

Bad as that, is it? Of course.

He sends it and stands up. The place is fairly tidy but he does a quick check round and then looks to see what he's got to offer her to drink. In a few minutes there's a tap at the door. He hurries to open it, letting her go past him into the kitchen, then shutting the door behind her.

'Running away?' he asks. 'That didn't take long.'

She grimaces guiltily. 'I told them we'd made a plan before I realized Judith would be back. I have to say she was rather surprised. I don't know what came over me.'

'Judith's a very formidable lady,' says Jack, holding up a bottle of Shiraz. 'Although I should have thought you were used to that after all these years.'

'The thing is,' says Cara, 'what with us abroad most of the time and Max away at sea, we've actually spent very little time together. Yes, please, I'd love a glass. It's very kind of you. I had a kind of panic attack.'

'I'm afraid it goes with the territory.' He pours them both a drink. 'Nothing is the same and you feel in uncharted waters. It's hard, sometimes,' he adds, 'being with married couples. You feel so terribly alone.'

'Yes,' she says, looking at him. 'That's exactly what it's like.'

He sees her eyes fill with tears and curses his tactlessness.

'It's so good,' she says, 'to be with someone who really understands. Thanks, Jack.'

He raises his glass to her, seeking for a distraction. 'So tell me,' he says. 'Do you know anything about this young fellow Cosmo?'

Cara sips her wine, not wanting to talk about Cosmo. 'Well, I met him in the Coffee Shop, as you know. And I met him walking the dog – that's all. Why?'

Jack says that he wonders if Amy and Cosmo have something going between them and that he's hoping she'll invite Cosmo to quiz night.

'I'll come along, too. We'll give him the third degree,' Cara says, trying for a lighter note. 'So what day is *Der Rosenkavalier*?'

Jack is distracted, reaching for the programme, talking about dates, and she takes another sip of wine and relaxes.

CHAPTER FOURTEEN

S am puts the car park ticket on the dashboard, slams the car door and locks it and then glances round as someone calls his name. He sees a woman waving at him, smiling, and he recognizes her as Amy's friend Charley. She locks her own car door and then comes towards him.

'Hi,' she says. 'So we meet again. What are you doing in Totnes?'

'I live near Staverton,' he answers. 'I was only staying in Salcombe.'

'Oh, yes. I remember now. With Max. Your godfather?'

'That's it,' he says, smiling at her. There's something attractive in her slightly boho appearance: a long swirling skirt with boots, and a shaggy, woolly kind of jacket. 'His wife's back from Oxford so I'm at home again. I've been detailed off to do some shopping.'

'Time for coffee first?' she suggests. 'I've come in for work a bit early and they do a very tasty brunch in the Terrace Coffee Shop.'

'Sounds good to me,' Sam answers, slightly surprised but very happy to go along with it. 'I thought you said you were a teacher. An art teacher.'

'Part time,' she says, as they cross the car park together. 'I also work in the Potting Shed.'

She gestures to it as they walk past, between racks with pots and plants for sale. Sam tries to remember what else he'd learned about her as he follows her up the steps and says 'Good morning' to Rob and Andy. Fliss often comes in here for coffee when she's been shopping so he knows them well. He likes this café, built on the ruins of the old priory, with its massive stone fireplace, and set high above the pavement. They settle at a table by the window and order breakfast for Charley and coffee for them both.

'So,' says Charley, shrugging off her jacket, 'have you come to any decision yet?'

He stares at her in surprise. 'Decision?'

She smiles at him. 'I had the feeling, back there in Salcombe, that you weren't one hundred per cent sold on this navy lark. You seemed much more fired up about your experience teaching Chinese kids to speak English. Or have I got that wrong?'

Sam is so taken aback that he can't answer. Nobody else has questioned his decision to go to Dartmouth, not even Fliss and Hal. Yet here is this woman, whom he met for such a short time, getting under his guard and guessing his secrets. He looks away from her, out of the window, but she doesn't back off or change the subject.

'The thing is,' she says, thoughtfully, 'I felt, when you talked about it that lunchtime, that here was someone with a vocation. Like the ministry, or medicine. Teaching is so crucial, isn't it? And you've either got it or you haven't.'

He looks at her again. She stares back at him with her clear brown eyes.

'But how do I know?' he asks at last. 'How can I really tell that it's what I should be doing? I mean, I was there just for a year. It was different. Exciting. Those kids were so keen to be learning, growing. How can I be certain that it wasn't just a one-off thing? Is it enough to take a risk on and give up the prospect of a career in the navy?'

Charley sits back in her chair as Andy brings the coffee. Sam thanks him, glad of the interruption. In a way it's a relief that it should be brought out into the open. Once or twice with Cara he's nearly talked about it but because she's Max's sister he's felt it a bit unfair. He has a feeling that Max, with his naval past, would be disappointed if his godson were to pass up this opportunity. It's good to be able to discuss it with this unusual woman who has no axe to grind and hardly knows him.

'I've thought about it,' he admits, stirring sugar into his coffee. 'But I just can't make up my mind.'

'When do you start your naval training?' she asks.

As she sips her coffee, holding the cup in both hands, her elbows propped on the table, Sam is aware of her personality. Her brown eyes seem to look into him, challenging him, willing him to take the chance, yet there is something else that makes him hesitate to accept that challenge.

'In January,' he answers. 'A couple of months yet. It's a tricky one, though, isn't it? To be able to tell the substance from the shadow?'

Just for a moment her expression changes. She looks startled, as if he has wrong-footed her: as if the boot is on the other foot and he is challenging her, questioning her own life choices.

'How do you mean?' she asks almost defensively.

He shrugs. 'I just think that it might be easy to be distracted by what could be something that's almost like an ego trip,' he says. 'It was a terrific experience but it was in an unusual set-ting, in unusual conditions. Would it be sustainable for me? It's terribly tempting but I need to know which is reality, for me. How is it possible to be sure of that?'

He finishes speaking, watching her, trying to remember what she'd told him about herself. He remembered about the teaching, that she met Amy at Falmouth Uni on some kind of course, but what else? He senses that by turning the challenge, he has in some way hit a nerve and she looks relieved to be dis-tracted by the arrival of her breakfast. His own sense of being on dangerous ground, of identifying a quality in her that might lead him into sharing confidences he might regret, seems to be warning him to quit whilst he's ahead. He finishes his coffee quickly and smiles at her.

'That was good but I need to dash. I've promised to get some things for Fliss and she's waiting for them. See you again sometime.'

'Yes,' she says, almost absently. 'Fine. Yes. See you around.'

He stops at the counter, wonders if he should pay for her breakfast and compromises by paying for her coffee. Then he goes out into the High Street, still feeling that he's been on the verge of talking about his confusion and fear despite the fact that he barely knows Charley and he's not given to baring his soul readily. His private feelings, especially those for Ying-Yue, are not to be shared lightly over a cup of coffee with a woman he's only just met, even if she is very attractive and amusing. He's glad to be beyond her disturbing influence.

Charley sits eating her breakfast but not really aware of it. Sam has surprised her. She really thought that she'd touched a nerve during that lunchtime in the pub in Salcombe. He was really fired up when he talked about his experience in China and she could tell that he was unwilling to discuss any aspect of a career in the navy, despite all the others encouraging him; telling her how wonderful it was for him.

To be honest, she rather likes to encourage mutiny, rule-bending. It's always made her popular with her young pupils but has never endeared her to her superiors, which is probably why she's never held down a long-term teaching job. She was confident that she could fill Sam with a kind of rebellion against that solid military background; encourage him to break the mould. It always gives her an odd sense of secret pleasure when she encourages others to push the boundaries, take chances.

'You're a free spirit,' people say to her admiringly.

But being a free spirit has led her to having lovers who won't commit, and several jobs. Perhaps inspiring others to rebel makes her feel less lonely. She thinks about Amy and Cosmo. Personally, she can't see what all the fuss is about. Just because he lives and works in London doesn't mean that he's off-limits. Seize the day and let the future take care of itself, is her motto. Now that Simon has got this temporary job upcountry, she's feeling restless. She needs a new challenge: a new man.

The café radio is playing 'Holding out for a Hero'. Charley smiles at the irony, finishes her breakfast, has a chat with Andy and Rob, and then heads off to the Potting Shed.

As he strides up the High Street towards the ironmonger's, Sam is trying to make sense of his confusion; that continual pull back to Shanghai, Ying-Yue, the children he taught. He knows that he's being entirely irrational. Charley has put his feelings into words. She saw this unlikely vision of his future in a positive and exciting light, and yet his reaction was negative. He's spent weeks hiding the possibility of exploring this new career from the people around him lest they should rubbish it and yet, when someone finds it praiseworthy, he immediately backs off.

'What is the matter with you?' he mutters to himself. 'For God's sake, get a grip.'

He knows that he should talk to Fliss and Hal about it but there never seems to be the right moment to introduce the subject. And, anyway, the trouble is, the only advice anyone ever really wants is the sort that confirms them in their own decisions. And, since he hasn't made a decision, that's not going to happen. He hoped that he might be able to broach the subject with Max but he can see that, even if Cara hadn't been there, he wouldn't have known how to start.

He finishes his shopping and heads back towards the car park. As he passes the Potting Shed, Charley is outside, tidying the racks of garden equipment and potted plants. She straightens up and smiles at him and he is once again aware of her attraction; her magnetism.

'Shopping done?' she asks.

She looks amused, as if she is aware that he was escaping from her earlier, avoiding answering her awkward questions. He feels uncomfortable but he nods.

'Yes, thanks. All done.'

'And thanks for my coffee,' she says, as he makes to go. 'You must let me return the favour.'

'That would be good,' he says, embarrassed. 'See you around then.'

And he hurries away before she can suggest a date. He suspects that she is watching him go, laughing at him, and it's a relief to get into the car and drive away towards Staverton.

Charley watches him go, smiling a little to herself. He's very attractive and she wonders if there was a girl out there in China. Her phone vibrates and she takes it out of her pocket. It's a text from Amy.

`Coming over to see a client. Meet up afterwards?`
`I've got Cosmo with me!`

Several emojis – laughter, fear, a bottle of wine – follow this and Charley laughs out loud. She types a message.

`Finishing at two o'clock. Is that any good?`

The reply comes straight back.

`See you in the tapas bar. Act surprised.`

Charley puts her phone away, and arches her eyebrows. She *is* surprised – and pleased – that Amy should feel ready to introduce her to Cosmo, even if he has no idea that it's going to happen. Charley chuckles inwardly. The prospect delights her. This is just up her street. What doesn't surprise her, though, is that Amy wants to make this introduction on neutral territory. This will be the first test. Amy wants to see how Cosmo makes out in these circumstances before she moves closer to home. It's interesting that she hasn't warned Cosmo, that she wants to take him by surprise. This is clearly not a straightforward relationship. From what Amy has told her there may be reservations on Cosmo's side: he seems to be a bit slippery, difficult to pin down. This is where she can be useful. What would be more natural than for Amy's old friend to ask casual questions? Maybe she can be a little more cunning than Amy – after all, she has nothing to lose – and she suspects that this is part of the reason behind Amy's plan. She wants reassurance, approval, courage to move forward. Charley takes a deep breath. She simply can't wait.

As soon as Charley walks into Ben's Wine and Tapas, Cosmo knows he's been set up. He's not in the least deceived by the cries of amazement from the two girls or their reasons for being there without telling the other. All the way from Salcombe he was aware of a little buzz of excitement just below Amy's natural cool. She talked about her client, just a very quick visit to discuss sourcing some garden tubs and pots, and how Reggie would enjoy a walk along the river out to Longmarsh, but all the while he was aware that she was distracted. It hadn't occurred to him what it might be: the old uni friend called in to make her assessment.

He's partly annoyed and partly amused. This woman, Charley, is in her thirties, quite a bit older than Amy, and dresses like a seventies flower-power child. She doesn't constitute a threat, in his opinion. In fact he can tell pretty quickly that she's ready to approve, to encourage her friend in this little adventure. He guesses that she'll give him the third degree and so by the time they're all sitting at a table together he's ready for her.

He goes along with it, putting himself out to make an impression without making it too obvious, determined to give nothing away.

'That sounds pretty cool,' Charley says, when he tells her what he does, though he suspects that she has no idea what his work entails. He talks instead about how he's blown away by this part of the world, how he's taking lots of photographs, working up his blog. It's easy to make her laugh, to pretend that he finds her witty and attractive without overstepping the mark, but all the while his brain is darting to and fro, seeking ways of holding her out of his private life. He guesses that she's definitely on Amy's side in that she wants to encourage their relationship, rather than being in any way protective about her. She's the kind of woman who thinks it's cool to live on the wild side and this, oddly, has the opposite effect on him. Unexpectedly he wants to turn to Amy and tell her the truth: that he's living in two worlds, both of them are equally real to him, and he doesn't know what to do about it.

He doesn't do it, of course – he's not quite that crazy – but it occurs to him that this Charley might be rather dangerous. She's rather like the witch in the fairy story who promises the prince that he can have it all. Despite being able to see this, he's still attracted to her. He wants to believe that she's right, that his wish *can* come true and that he *can* have it all.

By the time they part they are all good friends, and if it weren't for poor old Reggie stuck in the car they'd be making an evening of it.

Thank God for Reggie, thinks Cosmo, as they all say goodbye. He wonders what Amy will say as they walk back to the car but to his surprise she says nothing. She talks instead of the party she's planning for her father's birthday but she doesn't invite Cosmo, which slightly surprises him. After the meeting with her friend he suspected that Amy would be ready to try to move things along but he's relieved all the same. He doesn't know how he would behave towards her father.

He drives through the now familiar lanes, slightly thrown by the afternoon, hoping Amy will come in when they get back. They could have a drink and he'll make some supper and perhaps, this time, she'll stay longer than she did last time. Making love can solve so many problems.

Amy sits beside him, seething with various emotions. She is really angry with herself for arranging the meeting the way she did. It was clear almost from the get-go that Cosmo knew he'd been set up, and she feels embarrassed and at a disadvantage. He behaved perfectly, fielding Charley's remarks with grace and charm, telling everything and nothing, and now Amy feels like a complete fool. If she was hoping that this would move the relationship forward she couldn't have been more wrong. Knowing that he saw through her plan is humiliating but she tries to see a way out of this; to turn it into something more positive. She decides that honesty is the best policy.

'Well, that didn't work, did it?' she observes cheerfully.

She sees Cosmo stiffen slightly. His hands on the wheel take a firmer grip. She loves his hands with their long elegant fingers. He slips a look sideways at her.

'Sorry?' he says cautiously.

'I thought you might freak out if I told you Charley was coming, so I decided to set you up. You knew right off, didn't you?'

She can see that she's taken him by surprise and that he's first shocked and then amused. He begins to laugh.

'It did just cross my mind,' he admits coolly. 'I hope I passed the test.'

She sees her advantage, that he actually admires her for being upfront about it, and decides to push it further.

'I'm tired of you fobbing me off every time I suggest you meet my dad or my friends so I decided to take it into my own hands,' she tells him. 'You didn't do badly, but you'll have to be better than that with my dad.'

Her audacity has paid off. Cosmo glances at her, his eyes alight with amusement.

'I still think it was underhand,' he says, determined to take advantage of his own position and not let her off completely.

'So do I,' she admits. 'But you were asking for it. Admit it.'

'OK.' He raises one hand from the wheel as if signifying defeat. 'But you can't blame me. It's always scary, meeting the rellies.'

'Had a lot of experience, have you?' she asks swiftly.

He groans, but he doesn't answer, and she sits back in her seat, more relaxed now. Nevertheless, she needs to consolidate her position, hold the advantage she's won.

'I just might invite you to Dad's party,' she says, 'but I'm still thinking about it.'

'And I just might need some persuading,' he answers.

She grins. 'What have you got in mind?'

'A drink when we get back?' he suggests swiftly. 'Supper?'

She laughs, feeling a huge relief that everything has sorted itself out, and that it looks like he's reconciled to coming to the party. Relief makes her generous.

'Sounds good to me,' she agrees lightly. 'I've got nothing else planned.'

Her anger and embarrassment have passed and she is glad, now, that she took the chance. She'll text Charley later and let her know that all is well. She longs to know what her old friend thinks about Cosmo and decides to ask her to Dad's party, too. She glances sideways at Cosmo and is filled with all sorts of sensations: happiness, excitement, lust. He senses her glance and stretches a hand to her, his eyes on the lane ahead. She holds his hand tightly, rerunning the scene in the tapas bar.

'How did you guess I'd set it up?' she asks.

Cosmo laughs, gives her hand a squeeze and releases it.

'Male intuition,' he says.

Charley smiles when Amy's text comes in: she's been expecting it. It's rather sweet that Amy's seeking approval, reassurance. Perhaps it's because she doesn't have a mum that she looks to the older woman for confirmation of her feelings. Now that she's met Cosmo, Charley can understand Amy's anxieties. Despite his friendly, confident, extrovert approach, he's very clever at diverting questions he doesn't want to answer, at protecting his privacy. She was frustrated by his slickness. At the end of their afternoon together she still didn't know a great deal more about him than the things that Amy has already told her and it was impossible to pin down his intentions as to what he might have in mind when his house-sitting commitment is over.

Charley has an unwilling respect for Cosmo's deft handling of the situation but she can't see that Amy should be too worried. He's clearly fallen head over heels in love with the South Hams, with Amy, with the converted barn he's living in – even with Reggie. He's utterly sold on the whole experience and Charley feels certain that Amy should be able to take full advantage of it. Although she can't imagine Amy ever moving to London, it's not impossible that Cosmo should relocate to Bristol or Exeter.

As she rereads Amy's text – So what did you think of him? – Charley wonders if Cosmo has a girlfriend in London. It seems unlikely to imagine that he hasn't – he's a very attractive, amusing man – but, if he has, it's odd that he should take a three-month sabbatical alone, and when he talks about his flat, making fun of its lack of space, it's clear that nobody else is sharing it with him.

Charley shrugs away the problem of the mythical girlfriend. All's fair in love and war, and Amy should take her advantage and run with it. Seize the day and let the future take care of itself. Even as she repeats her mantra to herself she is aware of its treacherous repercussions. Nevertheless she refuses to acknowledge them. To do so would mean that she might have to acknowledge the flaws and failures in her own life. She mustn't allow herself to think about Simon, who finds it difficult to commit to a settled life, or her own inability to hold down a serious job for any length of time. She must continue to play the part of the fun, independent, up-together woman. She must never let anyone see behind the smoke and mirrors, not even herself: especially not herself. Instead she taps out a reply to Amy:

Gorgeous. Go for it xx

When another text comes in – Cosmo's making supper. Would you like to come to Dad's birthday party next weekend? – Charley is filled with pleasure, not only at the idea of Amy and Cosmo enjoying an intimate supper together, but also at the prospect of a party. Smiling to herself, Charley sends a quick acceptance, hums a bar or two from 'Holding out for a Hero' and goes to pour herself a glass of wine.

CHAPTER FIFTEEN

J udith comes out of Cranch's and pauses on the pavement to
check her shopping list. Max has suggested that they should
meet up in the Coffee Shop when she's finished but for the life
of her she can't imagine why they would do that when they can
have coffee at home five minutes away. When she said so to
Max she saw a fleeting expression on Cara's face: a blend of
puzzlement, amusement and pity.

Annoyance at this almost patronizing look was very difficult to control but Judith simply replied that she'd never had
time for café society – if that was what it was called – and it was
probably too late to start now. As far as she can tell, in the few
days she's been away, Max and Cara have spent most of their
time in the Coffee Shop or in the pub.

'Good morning, Judith.'

Jack Hannaford is smiling at her. Time was he would have
called her Mrs Watson but now he considers himself to be almost
a friend of the family. In fact, they've been invited to his birthday
party. It's very difficult in such a small community to maintain
the required distance between neighbours and the people who
work for you, but it's necessary to try to hold on to your privacy.

She nods at Jack, tries to think of something that will sound pleasant whilst keeping him in his place, but doesn't succeed. And now here is that girl of his, standing beside him, dressed in paint-splashed overalls and smiling at Judith as if they are old friends.

'Hi,' she says cheerfully. 'How are you doing?'

'I'm well, thank you,' Judith answers coolly, but remembering to smile. 'How are you?'

'I'm good,' answers Amy, and Judith is seized with another pang of irritation. She wants to point out that she is enquiring after Amy's health, not her moral well-being – why do the young talk in this irritating way? – but she contains herself and nods again.

'And congratulations on the new grandchild,' adds Amy. 'That's really great.'

Judith feels herself thawing a little, warming to this generous remark.

'Thank you,' she answers. 'It's all very exciting.'

'We were just going to grab a quick cup of coffee,' Jack says. 'Would you like to join us?'

'No, no,' says Judith quickly – rather too quickly. She smiles again to cover any rudeness. 'Max will be wondering where I am. But thank you.'

'See you later, then,' Amy says. 'Glad you can come to Dad's party.'

Jack Hannaford grins, as if he can guess exactly what Judith is thinking, and she simply nods again, and turns away. She's already told Max what she thinks about the party but Max is standing firm. He's always liked Jack; all those silly quiz nights, and sailing together. Judith's view is that surely Max has plenty of other friends at the sailing club he can go sailing with.

Judith climbs the steps beside the Fortescue, thinking about the party. The trouble is that Jack always makes her feel uneasy. She suspects that deep down he is laughing at her, that he lacks respect. This is all part of the problem with living in a small community, of course: people are so friendly – too friendly. Max enjoys it – and so does Cara – but personally she prefers the anonymity of the city. Not too big, of course. Somewhere like Oxford. Outside their house Judith pauses for a moment, staring up at it. The idea in her head has expanded and taken shape. And now another thought occurs, blinding in its clarity, and she stands, gazing at nothing, thinking it through, trying it out.

Max comes out on to the balcony above her and looks down at her.

'Got a problem?' he calls. 'Want me to let down a rope and haul you up?'

He bursts out laughing, as though he has said something funny, and calls to Cara behind him in the kitchen. It occurs to Judith that Cara never goes out on to the balcony but the thought doesn't distract Judith from her new and exciting idea. She nods at Max, acknowledging his witticism, and goes in through the gate to the front door.

'What's her problem?' asks Amy as she leads the way into the Coffee Shop and waves to Lydia at the counter. 'She always looks like she's swallowed a glass of vinegar.'

'She has difficulty in forgetting that I'm the handyman,' Jack answers. 'She finds it hard to treat me as an equal.'

'Seriously?' Amy stares at him. 'What is she? Royalty or something?'

'You have to remember that Max retired as a four-ring captain,' Jack tells her. 'That's very senior. It's uncomfortable for Judith to be like the rest of us after living for all those years at the top end of a hierarchy.'

'Max doesn't seem to have a problem with it,' retorts Amy.

Jack smiles. 'Max doesn't have anything to prove. An Americano for me, if you're getting them. Cold milk on the side. Thanks.'

He sits down, waves a greeting to a couple of cronies, and wonders if it was wise to invite Max and Judith to his party. It's become complicated, now that Cara has become a friend, to maintain the delicate balance he's managed so far with Max and Judith. Max understands the situation and is flexible, but now everything has changed. Jack wonders how Judith will react when Cara tells her that she's been to the opera a couple of times with him. It's not really Judith's fault. She put her own career to one side to follow Max to his postings around the country and abroad, and she believes that her status is directly related to his. She's been a naval wife and she's used to a hierarchy that everyone within that special close-knit group understands and respects. But that was then and this is now – and it's cold outside the services.

Jack feels a sympathy for Judith, which he knows would outrage her. He turns round as a dog jostles behind him, nudging his sleeve, and glances up at the dog's owner. The young man is tall, dark-haired, and Jack knows with absolute certainty that this is Cosmo. This certainty is confirmed by the way the man is staring at Amy, who is chatting to Lydia and hasn't seen him come in. His look is intense, expectant, and Jack draws a deep breath.

'Hi,' he says casually, putting out a hand to the dog, smiling up at the dark man. 'We haven't met yet but something tells me that you're Cosmo.'

*

When Amy turns away from the counter and sees Cosmo pulling out a chair and sitting down opposite her father, she feels a thrill of apprehension. It's happened at last, unplanned, unpremeditated, and suddenly relief sweeps away her fear. She's been slightly dreading the party, and she didn't want to repeat the mistake she made with Charley of setting up a meeting, so this is the best way. Everyone on the back foot, everyone equal. Both men look cool, friendly, both acknowledging that this is not quite a casual meeting of two strangers.

Taking courage from their relaxed body language, the amusement on her father's face as he strokes Reggie, she goes to join them.

'Hi,' she says, hoping she sounds as casual as she feels. 'So you seem to have introduced yourselves.'

'Your father recognized me,' Cosmo says, half getting to his feet, grinning at her, 'not because of your glowing reports, I hasten to say, but because I'm the only stranger in here.'

His eyes sparkle. He seems to be enjoying himself, equal to the situation. As she sits down beside her father she can tell that he's not totally taken in by Cosmo's apparent equanimity and she hopes that they really will hit it off. Unexpectedly, she thinks of how she and Cosmo made love last night, how exciting it was, and, as she catches his eye and he sends her a tiny wink, her face is suffused with bright colour and she wants to burst out laughing – and at the same time simply to run away.

Cosmo is talking enthusiastically to her father about the town, the creek, the magic of it all, distracting attention from her confusion, and by the time Lydia arrives with the coffee

Amy is able to behave with some semblance of normality. Cosmo gets up to go to order his own coffee and Amy waits for her father to make a comment.

'Well,' he says, pouring milk into his Americano, 'I can now see why he's called Cosmo. It's so absolutely the right name for him. Cosmopolitan, smooth, and not easily fazed.'

There's a little silence whilst Amy tries to work out if this is a compliment.

'Does that mean you like him?' she asks uncertainly.

Her father smiles at her, purses his lips and shrugs. 'You know me. I never make snap decisions. But he's welcome to come to my party.'

Amy bends to stroke Reggie so as to cover her relief. From her father, this is quite a positive statement.

'That's good,' she says casually. 'It would be embarrassing to have to cancel our invite.'

Suddenly her father moves, twisting round in his chair, and she sits up to see what has attracted his attention. Cara has come in and is putting her belongings on a table by the door. As she goes to order her coffee it's clear that she's alone and her father pushes back his chair. He grins at Amy.

'Two's company, three's a crowd,' he says. 'See you later.'

And, picking up his coffee, he goes to join Cara.

Cara has just come from the bookshop, collecting some books she ordered from Jessica, the owner, and enjoying a chat with her. She's delighted to see Jack.

'May I join you?' he asks. 'I'm tired of playing gooseberry so I'm counting on you to save me.'

Puzzled, she glances across the café, waves to Amy and then sees Cosmo coming back from the counter.

'You've met Cosmo at last?' she asks. 'What do you think of him?'

'He's very smooth,' says Jack, sitting down. 'He didn't turn a hair.'

'You mean this wasn't arranged? You just met him by chance?'

'That's right. Amy and I were already here when he arrived with his dog. Took it all in his stride.' He glances across at Cosmo, who is making Amy laugh. 'Good-looking devil, isn't he?'

Cara watches the two young people. There's a new ease to their behaviour, a new intimacy.

'I wish I knew a bit more about him,' Jack is saying, 'but I suppose there comes a point when you just have to let go. You've met him a couple of times, you said. What do *you* make of him?'

She is not going to tell him that because of Cosmo's resemblance to a man she knew nearly forty years ago she wouldn't trust him for a second. It would sound so crazy. Instead she casts around for a light-hearted response.

'The dog likes him,' she says, nodding towards Reggie, whose head rests on Cosmo's knee. 'That's supposed to be a good sign, isn't it?'

'Dogs like anyone who feeds them,' he answers cynically. 'You'll have to do better than that.'

'Amy likes him,' she offers. 'Does that count for anything?'

'Are you kidding? Look at him. Even I can see that he's an extremely attractive young man. He's older, sophisticated, London-type. All guaranteed to turn her head.'

Cara laughs. 'What a cynic you are. Well, he'll be gone soon, from what I gather, so we must hope he doesn't break her heart.'

She wonders how she can talk so lightly, but what else can she do?

'It's at times like this,' Jack is saying, 'that I really miss Sally. You know? A woman's instinct and all that? I know Amy talks to Charley but Charley's more like a sister. She doesn't have quite that same sense of responsibility as a parent. It's just that I don't want Amy to get hurt, which is a stupid thing to say because everyone gets hurt one way or another, don't they? You can't protect the people you love from life.'

For a moment he looks so serious, so vulnerable, that she wants to reach across and take his hands, which are lightly clenched on the table as if they are holding on to Amy, keeping her safe. She wonders how to cheer him, but at this moment Lydia brings her coffee, the tension is broken and Jack sits back again. He turns to look at Amy and Cosmo whilst Cara sips her coffee. Amy is getting up. She comes across to them, smiles at Cara and taps her father on the shoulder.

'If you want that lift to Kingsbridge we need to get going,' she tells him.

He nods, stands up and looks down at Cara.

'We'll be seeing you at the party,' he says.

He and Amy go out together and Cara drinks her coffee, deliberately not looking at Cosmo. As she gazes at her cup, held between both her hands, she sees that there's a little blue sail painted on it. She's never noticed it before. Out of the corner of her eye she sees that Cosmo is standing up, grabbing Reggie's lead. They pause beside her table and she looks up at him. His smile is infectious; his vitality is almost tangible. She smiles back at him, longing to be wrong; willing him to be trustworthy, loyal, and in love with Amy. Yet even as he smiles she recognizes the gleam behind its friendliness, a kind of exaltation, as if he has got away with something, brought off something risky. It's the look of a gambler; of someone who risks all on the roll of the dice.

'I've been invited to a party,' he says. 'Shall I see you there?'

She nods. Cosmo laughs, tips his head towards the words on the beam above her head, *Dolce far Niente*, and goes out into the sunshine with Reggie.

As Cosmo strides away from the Coffee Shop, out of the town, he's still feeling on a high. It was a shock, meeting Amy's dad like that but, after all, it's always been on the cards. It was bound to happen sooner or later, and better in that natural crowded environment than formally at the party amongst their friends and family. Amy was a tad tense to begin with, which wasn't surprising after their previous evening together, but she was able to get over it.

Gradually, though, as the high subsides, Cosmo feels slightly less euphoric about his ability to hold all this together. The whole adventure is too good to let go. Amy is a darling and he is definitely in love with her, as he is in love with this whole place. And it's clear that she is in love with him. But that doesn't mean that it's necessarily a long-term thing. The trouble is, he can no longer see where reality lies. Is it here with Amy or in London with Becks? His work and his flat are in London, and it would be a very big step to change all of that but, at the same time, it will be a huge wrench to leave this place: to leave Amy. Some part of him tries to believe that somehow, magically, it will all resolve itself and, just for now, for his remaining few weeks, he can go with the flow.

Even as he tries to convince himself that this is the truth, a message pings in and he pulls his phone from his pocket. He's expecting Amy, making some comment on the meeting with her father, but it's a text from Al.

Hi. Thought I'd pop down again this weekend. Something the parents want me to check. Sorry it's such short notice. Arriving Saturday. Same place.

Cosmo stands still to reread the text. His euphoria is vanishing and a real anxiety is taking its place. Reggie tugs at his lead and Cosmo walks on more slowly, trying to decide how to reply. After all, the house belongs to Al's parents; Cosmo can't refuse him access. And Al won't be fazed by the news that his friend is going to a party on Saturday evening. Knowing Al, he'll ask if he can come along. Now all the excitement, the euphoria, is gone, leaving a very chilly reality. The thought of Al meeting Amy, Jack, even Cara, makes Cosmo very nervous indeed. He tries to imagine Amy's face if Al were to slip up and mention Becks, and his gut churns. As he walks, his mind darts to and fro trying to find a way through and he can think of only one solution. All he can do is to say that if Al is coming down then he, Cosmo, will take advantage of his visit to dash to London to see Becks. Al can look after Reggie again. It means missing Jack's party but that's definitely the lesser of two evils. Quickly Cosmo texts Becks, telling her of this opportunity of coming to see her. Even if she refuses, he'll go anyway and stay at the flat. But why should she? Unless, of course, Al has dropped him in it with her. Once again Cosmo's gut churns but, to his intense relief, Becks texts back almost immediately.

Great. Text me times. Off to a meeting xx

Cosmo feels weak with relief. He swallows several times, takes a great gasp of air and then taps a text to Al.

```
That means you can look after Reggie while I
dash up to see Becks. Great stuff! See you at
the station.
```

He's almost home before he receives Al's text. It's rather laconic.

```
Not quite what I had in mind but OK.
```

As he climbs the steps, lets Reggie off the lead, a new problem occurs to Cosmo. What on earth will he say to Amy? Even as he thinks about it another text pings in. It's from Amy.

```
That was amazing. You've passed the first test.
Let's see how you do at the party! xxx
```

This is followed by several emojis depicting happiness and fun. Cosmo stares at it and groans aloud. He goes into the house with Reggie at his heels, his mind busy with what kind of crisis he can dream up as his excuse. The family party he invented was one thing; this will need to be something else altogether. Perhaps it will be best to wait until almost the last minute, until he's on the train to London, so that there's no chance of an actual confrontation.

Cosmo makes several attempts at a reply to the text but in the end simply types:

```
It was great to meet him.
```

It's lame but just for now it's the best he can do. Cosmo stands at the kitchen window and stares out, but for once he is unaware of the view. He's visualizing his two universes spinning towards each other, on a collision course.

CHAPTER SIXTEEN

S am is on his way back to Salcombe but this time he's
driving. This late in the year he should be able to find a
parking place somewhere and it's good to have his own wheels.
He's pleased that Amy has invited him to Jack's party. Max
passed the message on to Sam, phoning him to check that he
was free.

'It's going to be much the same as last time,' Max said. 'It
seems that it might be a bit of a squash at Jack's so we're going
to the pub again. Same group as last time, plus Judith,
of course.'

Sam wonders how Judith will fit into the group. He can't see
her bonding with Charley, somehow. The thought makes him
smile just a little bit. Judith: correct, smart even when she's
casual, not very relaxed out of her comfort zone. Charley: so
laid-back as to be horizontal, very peace 'n' love. However, if
they're all at the pub it should go smoothly, everyone on neutral
territory, no judgements to be made.

He thinks of that last lunch at the pub and the way Charley
had drawn him out and he determines that this will not happen
again. She's put a bit of a spell on him, clouding his vision

rather than making it clearer. Each time he decided he would talk to Fliss and Hal about it, during the last few days, the words seemed to stick in his throat. He couldn't quite find a way to start the conversation and he slightly dreads their expressions of surprise, disappointment. Part of him wonders if it's simply the commitment that the navy demands that's beginning to worry him and that the idea of having a vocation is just a way of backing out whilst looking as if he's doing something rather noble. Certainly Charley was impressed but he's not certain that Hal and Fliss would see it all in that light.

Driving through the quiet roads in the autumnal landscape, he finds the tension sinking away from him. The bare bones of the countryside are beginning to show through: crisp yellow and brown leaves drifting from the tall, stark trees; the last of the scarlet berries trailing in bare twiggy hedges. Glimpses of the distant moors, barely more than a charcoal scribble against a golden western sky, and, nearer at hand, small dun-coloured fields and round green hills, dotted with sheep that look like small granite boulders.

He drives on, feeling calmer, though he has yet to take a decision. Instead he thinks about the coming weekend: Jack's party, seeing his friends again. He wonders if Cara has any clearer ideas about her future or if she feels as indecisive as he does.

When he arrives at the house in Buckley Street, Judith is talking on her phone, Max is sitting at the kitchen table staring at the screen of his laptop whilst Cara sits opposite writing in a birthday card. They look round as he ascends the stairs. Max raises a hand, Cara beams at him, Judith glances at him, gives a little nod and moves away, along the passage towards her bedroom, still talking. Oscar's tail wags as he gets up to greet him.

'Bit of a crisis in Oxford,' Max tells him, as if to apologize for Judith's offhand welcome. 'Good to see you, Sam. How's everything? How are Fliss and Hal?'

'Everything's fine,' he answers. 'People staying, family at the weekend. Usual stuff.'

'It must be rather wonderful,' says Cara, 'to have lived in the same place for all of your life, and your ancestors before you. Such a sense of continuity. Of belonging.'

She sounds wistful and Sam sees Max glance at her.

'You wouldn't have wanted to stay in Sussex,' he says, almost bracingly. 'It's not always as idyllic as it sounds.'

'No,' she says quickly. 'No, I wouldn't. But The Keep seems rather different somehow. Wonderful vibes.'

Judith comes into the kitchen, greets Sam, and begins to talk to Max about some drama with the family in Oxford. Max stands up and they move back towards the bedroom. Cara smiles at Sam.

'Families, eh?' she says. 'Fancy a stroll? Oscar hasn't been out for a proper walk yet.'

'I'd like that,' he answers at once.

He feels slightly *de trop* with the discussion going on in the passage and he's aware of a different atmosphere now that Judith's home. The easy, laid-back feeling has evaporated and there's a faint tension.

'Good,' says Cara. 'I've got to post this card and then we'll take him round the creek and up to the Point. We don't want to bother with cars, do we?'

She calls to Max and Judith, telling them her intentions, and she and Sam go downstairs, followed by Oscar. Sam's wondering whether to invite Cara to The Keep but can't decide if it looks like he's assuming that she feels as he does. On previous occasions when he visits, Max usually takes him sailing and to the pub. He doesn't really know Judith very well and it might be wrong to assume that Cara doesn't get on well with her sister-in-law, although she's hinted once or twice that it's not an easy relationship. Better wait to see how the weekend goes. He follows her out, clips on Oscar's lead, and they set off together.

Judith hears the door close behind them and she moves back into the kitchen. This is the perfect moment to tell Max her new plan. A new series of problems in Oxford, Freya's mother needing to get back to her work and her own responsibilities: the timing is right.

'There always seems to be so much drama going on,' Max is saying, impatiently. 'I can't see why Paul being on a lecture tour is such a big deal. I used to go away to sea and leave you coping with babies and moving house.'

'I wasn't working,' Judith reminds him. 'We moved around too much for me to keep a job. But I've been thinking, Max. It would be good to be more involved with the children. I'm not just talking about childcare, I'm talking about spending time with the whole family. I'm thinking we should sell up here and move to Oxford.'

He is staring at her in amazement. She can see dismay behind the shock and she stiffens herself as if she is preparing for battle.

'Are you serious?' he asks. 'I thought you were happy here.'

'We have been,' she assures him quickly. 'But things move on. I want to see my grandchildren growing up. Staying with them is going to be even more difficult now, space-wise, and Oscar is always a problem. I know it's lovely when they come here but that doesn't happen very often, does it?'

Max still seems knocked sideways by her suggestion. She can see him calculating all that he would miss, here in Salcombe, and she cunningly makes her next move.

'I had another idea, too. Cara seems to be settling in so well here, making friends, and she clearly loves the area. Why shouldn't she buy this house? Then she'd be in a lovely community and you could come down and stay with her and go sailing and see all your friends.'

Quite deliberately she doesn't say 'we'. She knows perfectly well that Max and Cara enjoy each other's company and she's trying to make it more attractive to him.

'We can all come down,' she adds quickly. 'It would still be a family house. And Cara can afford it. I checked on Zoopla. She got a small fortune for the house in Fulham.'

Max begins to laugh, but not in an amused way.

'You never cease to amaze me, Judith,' he says. 'So how long have you been planning this for us all?'

'I told you. The idea came to me when I got back, although I was thinking about it a bit when I was in Oxford. I love it there. You know I do. It's so central for everything and it would cut out all this awful travelling when we want to see the children. That won't get easier as we get older, you know. I think it solves a lot of problems in one go. Why are you frowning?'

He shakes his head. 'I think it's the casual way that you decide Cara's future for her. We don't actually know that she wants to be in Salcombe. She came here to be with us.'

'To be with *you*,' Judith corrects him sharply. 'Be honest. She has to stand on her own two feet, Max, to build a whole new life, and this could be perfect for her. She loves it here. It means you could keep the boat, go sailing with your friends, and spend time with Cara, and the children could come to stay with her. Try to see it clearly.'

'How ruthless you are,' he marvels, but his eyes are cold.

'No, I'm just realistic,' she answers. 'You like Oxford, you love to spend time with the children, it seems a very good solution to several problems.'

Max sits down at the table. She knows that he is trying to marshal all kinds of arguments against her plan but is unable to think of anything really plausible, apart from the fact that he wants to remain in Salcombe. She also knows that it's in his nature to weigh up both sides and see things rationally. She's counting on this and on his loyalty. Once Cara and Sam come back it will be difficult for him to be as outspoken as he might be if they were alone. She's factored this in and hopes it will count on her side.

'If you're totally committed to spending the rest of your life here,' she says lightly, 'then that's that, I suppose we'll stay. But do at least consider it. We'll ask Cara what she thinks when she comes back.'

He looks up at her, almost alarmed. 'You're going to tell her?'

She stares back at him as if puzzled by his question. 'Of course. Why not? Cara's part of the equation. We could sell the house, anyway, but I think we'd be doing her a favour as well as saving money on fees and things. Want a cup of tea?'

He nods and she turns away to fill the kettle. Some instinct tells her that the first round is to her.

Max listens to the sound of the tea-making, his thoughts fluttering in his head like moths around a lamp. His first reaction is dismay. Ever since they bought the house back in the eighties, when the submarine was running out of Devonport, he's loved being in Salcombe. They never spent very long here – Judith preferred to move with him, letting out the house when they went to Washington and Naples – but it was here to return to, waiting for the time when they could retire and live here permanently.

If he's honest, he knows that Judith hasn't been quite so happy in Salcombe as he has since he retired, but then Judith has very specific requirements and he's not certain that he knows where the perfect home for her might be. Nevertheless, it's a very big step to take and he's not sure that he's ready for it. And as for suggesting that Cara should buy the house! Max gives a little snort of disbelief at Judith's presumption. Why should Cara, after just a few weeks here, suddenly agree to make it her home, whilst he and Judith disappear away to Oxford? He had a twinge of temptation at the thought of trips down to see her, to be able to keep his boat and go sailing, to go to the pub and the Island Cruising Club, which would definitely be a plus, but the whole prospect dismays him. To pull up their roots and move to a place where they know very few people fills him with a kind of panic. Slowly he tries to see this panic clearly. He loves his family, loves to spend time with them, but he realizes that he needs his friends, too. The camaraderie of the navy has meant a great deal to him. He misses it. He finds it hard that he no longer has a specific role, a job that defines him. This sense of belonging, of being viable, has been replaced in part with his cronies at the sailing club and people like Jack Hannaford and a few others: mates down at the pub. He tries to imagine a life where there is no relief from Judith's company and feels another shiver of panic, and an even stronger sense of guilt. Judith has been a loyal, capable wife and she's devoted to Chris and Paul, but he worries that she is beginning to rely too much on her grandchildren as the focus of her life; to want too much influence in their lives. He tries, sometimes, tactfully to remind her how she resented her own mother's interference when their boys were small but she can't see the connection.

Judith puts the mug of tea down in front of him and he glances up at her, smiling his thanks. His smile isn't particularly convincing and she pats his shoulder as if he is a recalcitrant child.

'If you can just give yourself a chance to think about it clearly,' she says, 'you'll see that it could be the best of both worlds.'

She puts her mug next to his and sits down beside him, pulling his laptop towards her, opening it. He watches her, puzzled, as she taps away.

'This is just so as to give you some idea of what we could afford,' she tells him, 'assuming we decide to go for it. Now then . . .'

He looks at her, wondering if he's ever truly known her, feeling the indomitable strength of her will.

'One thing, though,' he says, hitching his chair so that he can see the screen. 'I'd rather you don't mention this to Cara until after the party tomorrow night. I don't want everyone talking about this before we've had enough time to discuss it properly.'

He can see Judith considering this, seeing the wisdom of it whilst believing that she's won a point because he hasn't rejected it out of hand. She nods, starts to show him properties. Max picks up his mug and begins to drink his tea, wondering how Cara and Sam will react to this suggestion, trying to prepare himself for the battle ahead.

CHAPTER SEVENTEEN

Alistair and Cosmo make the changeover at Totnes Station again but this time it's in reverse. Cosmo is taking his bag from the car as Al comes off the platform and he can see that Cosmo is not in that ebullient mood of their last meeting. He is slightly uncomfortable, brittle.

'Hi,' Al says, swinging his own bag into the back of the car, giving Cosmo their usual one-arm hug. 'I'm sorry you're dashing off. I thought you were going to show me the sights. By now, you must know Salcombe much better than I do.'

'I know.' Several expressions pass over Cosmo's face: embarrassment, apology, confusion. 'It just seemed too good an opportunity to pass up.'

Al watches him, remembering Cosmo's pleas for help when Becks announced her impromptu visit and the reasons that he didn't want her there. It's clear that the weekend Cosmo spent in London with her must have alleviated any fears she might have had, but still Al doesn't quite trust him.

'So how's Amy?' he asks casually, as Cosmo shuts the car door and hands him the keys.

Cosmo hesitates, shakes his head. 'If you want the truth, I'm in a mess.'

For a moment he looks so confused, so desperate, that all the instincts of an old familiar friendship reassert themselves and Al feels a stab of sympathy for him.

'What's the problem?' he asks, almost impatiently. 'Are you in love with her or something? If so, why are you rushing away to Becks? Why don't you just tell Amy the truth?'

'Because I don't know what the truth is,' Cosmo almost shouts. He glances quickly round to see if anyone is watching him. 'Sorry, mate. I know I'm behaving like a complete arse-hole but I simply don't know what to do.'

'You mean you can't choose between them?'

'It's not that simple.' Frustrated, Cosmo thrusts his fingers through his hair. 'It's like I'm living in parallel universes. London and Becks. Salcombe and Amy.'

'And you want the best of both worlds?'

Cosmo stares at him. 'I suppose I do.'

'And you don't think this is unfair on Becks and Amy?'

'Of course I see that but . . .' Cosmo hesitates.

'You're not going to say, "But it's OK as long as nobody is being hurt," are you?'

'OK. OK. But after all, if neither of them knows, then neither of them is being hurt,' says Cosmo.

'What about you?' asks Al.

'What about me?' Cosmo looks puzzled.

'You don't think that lying and cheating is hurting you? Making you a lesser person? Cheapening yourself?'

Cosmo stares at him, amused and slightly affronted. 'Not being a bit holier than thou, are we, mate?'

Al shrugs. 'Probably. Just putting it out there. You'd better go and catch your train. See you tomorrow.'

He gets into the car, reverses out and drives away, leaving Cosmo staring after him. As he heads off up the hill Al knows that he sounded priggish and he experiences a mix of emotions: frustration, irritation, regret that he and Cosmo parted so abruptly. They've been mates for so long and it would be crazy to fall out over something like this. Nevertheless, Al feels very strongly about cheating. He's seen the result of it with the break-up of two of his closest friends' marriage. In his view, nobody wins, and irreparable damage can be done, yet what can he do about it? It's as if some kind of spell has been cast over his old friend and Cosmo's caught up in the magic and the rapture of it.

As he drives, Al's mind darts to and fro, seeking for some way out of the situation. Of course, in a few weeks' time Cosmo must return to London, but will it end the affair with Amy? And how will she feel about it? Clearly Cosmo hasn't told her the truth so it won't be simple for him just to walk away without hurting her. And for the life of him Al cannot imagine Cosmo settling happily in Salcombe, giving up his work, which he loves, giving up the clubs and restaurants and cinemas that are so integral to his life. Al knows that part of his own distress is that he feels responsible. If he hadn't persuaded Cosmo to come down to Salcombe it wouldn't have happened.

As Al drives up the track and parks the car, an idea occurs to him. Perhaps he could invent some kind of crisis, plead the need for time off work and come down here to stay. Cosmo could stay on, or go, but either way his style would be cramped. Al considers this plan, wonders if it might work. He gets his bag and goes into the house to find Reggie.

*

Amy sits in the Coffee Shop watching out for Cosmo. She hasn't heard from him since yesterday afternoon and she's excited and nervous about the party. She wonders how he will cope in this rather large group of people; whether he will feel daunted or quite cool with it. He was certainly very self-possessed with her father, and he already knows Cara. Amy hopes that Charley won't make her feel shy about him and she is suddenly almost overwhelmed by nerves. She needs to see him come walking in, to see his smile and the confidence and vitality he always carries with him. She glances up every time the door opens but he doesn't come and, as she sips her coffee, she feels her phone vibrate and pulls it out of her pocket.

A text from Cosmo. She opens it, reads it and then reads it again.

I'm so sorry about this. A real crisis in London. Had to dash back. I'm on the train. Be in touch xx

Amy stares at it, trying to make sense of it. A crisis – and it sounds as if he is already on the train so he must have known for a couple of hours at the very least. Why wait until now to text? Disappointment washes over her and she sits staring out into Fore Street, trying to come to terms with this sense of desolation; of being let down with a bang.

What kind of crisis could call him back so suddenly? He doesn't mention family or work? And why such short notice? She wonders what's happened to Reggie. Worse than all of these, she wonders how she'll explain to everyone why Cosmo won't be at the party. Even as she sits there, miserable, hurt, and cross, the door opens and Sam Chadwick walks in. He glances round, sees her and raises his hand in greeting. He hesitates, clearly wondering if it's OK to join her, and with a huge effort she smiles back at him and makes a welcome gesture. As he orders his coffee, she's rehearsing what she might say should he mention Cosmo. She remembers how well Sam got on with Charley at their last meeting, that he's going into the navy, and hopes that she can deflect him from any awkward questions by talking about it. Nevertheless she needs to prepare what she's going to tell everyone so it's no good shirking it. Amy drops her shoulders, takes a breath.

'Hi,' she says brightly. 'How're you doing? Getting ready to party?'

Sam sits down, laughs at the question.

'I certainly am. It was great fun last time. Thanks for inviting me over.'

She's such a pretty girl; so vivid and confident. Yet as he looks at her, he notices something rather febrile about her, a slight lack of poise that shows a vulnerability. He wonders if she's anxious that the evening at the pub might not go so well as that last lunch did; that it's important her father enjoys his party.

'I think it's such a good idea to go to the pub,' he says rather randomly. 'Not so much pressure. It's a kind of shared responsibility, isn't it?'

He can tell by her faintly puzzled expression that this is not what is worrying her, and he feels a bit of a fool, but he doesn't let himself get fazed.

'Cara was telling me earlier that her big horror is organizing parties. They always had staff to do it for them at the embassies, of course, but even so, there's quite a lot to oversee. I was just wondering if you might be having last-minute cold feet.'

She smiles then, gratefully, as if she thinks it's nice of him to be concerned.

'I think the whole thing will run itself,' she says. 'Especially as we've done it before and we all know each other . . .'

She trails off, biting her lip, as if she's said something she regrets but he can't think what it might be. Everyone knows each other, even if only slightly – and then he remembers that Cara told him that this guy Amy is seeing, Cosmo, is coming to the party. He wonders if this is making her feel a bit shy at the thought of them all sizing him up, but before he can speak his coffee arrives. The girl who brings it pauses to chat to Amy and Sam leans back, wondering how to proceed.

After the girl goes back to the counter, Amy sits forward and picks up her cup. She's frowning, as if she's coming to a decision, and then suddenly she speaks out.

'To be really honest with you, Sam, I'm feeling a bit upset. I don't know if anyone's told you that I invited this guy I've met to Dad's party? His name's Cosmo and he's house-and-dog-sitting for friends for a couple of months or so in Batson Creek. We've got to know each other and . . . Well, Dad wanted to meet him so I invited him and everything was great. And now I've just had a text saying he's had to rush back to London. Just that. No explanation. I mean, it's so embarrassing. Everyone is kind of sitting round waiting to meet him, teasing me about him, and what will I say?'

Sam is taken aback by this unexpected confession and he can see that she is both angry and hurt, and very embarrassed. He casts about for some comforting answer that is in no way patronizing or diminishes her reaction.

'That's tough,' he agrees. 'I suppose it must have been a pretty big disaster to make him go rushing off. But surely everyone will get that, won't they? I mean it's not your fault, is it?'

'No,' she agrees, rather reluctantly, 'but it's embarrassing that he doesn't say what it is so I have no real explanation. It's just weird that one minute it's all on and the next he's on the train to London without any warning.'

Sam can see that it's costing her to tell him all this, to take him into her confidence and expose her embarrassment to him. He longs to help her.

'Look,' he says, 'let's not make a big deal out of this. OK, so Cosmo hasn't given you an explanation. Maybe it's just too complicated to do it by text. If it's some kind of emergency he might not be thinking straight. Meanwhile nobody is going to be that shocked, are they? If you like, I can tell Cara. And Max and Judith, too. Just in a casual kind of way. You can tell your father. Who else is there?'

'Charley,' says Amy.

She says the name rather sulkily, as if her old friend is the person she is worrying about most. Sam can understand this. Charley is the kind of woman who might very well tease and joke about it. He wonders if Amy has talked to Charley about Cosmo, opened up to her, and now it will be embarrassing to tell her that he's gone off to London with no explanation.

'You'll have to tough it out,' he says firmly. 'Tell your dad as soon as you can and then Charley will be the only one you need to worry about and there will be too many of us around for her to be much of a problem.'

She stares at him in surprise and with a certain amount of admiration.

'Thanks,' she says at last. 'I guess that's the way to do it. If you'll tell the others and I tell Dad it won't be a kind of public announcement. Everyone will know beforehand.'

'You'll be fine,' he assures her. 'And I'll keep an eye on Charley.'

Amy begins to laugh. 'I can see why everyone says you've been chosen to be a leader of men. Your talents would be wasted elsewhere. I shall count on you to have my back.'

He's taken aback by her words. Is that really how people see him? He raises his coffee cup to her.

'It'll be fine,' he tells her. 'You're in control. Remember that.'

She clinks her cup against his and smiles at him.

'Thanks, Sam,' she says.

He smiles back at her, thinking that Cosmo is a lucky man, and hoping for his sake that he's got a really good reason for standing her up.

Jack comes in and pauses beside them.

'Thought you'd be here,' he says to Amy, 'but I thought that Cosmo would be with you, not this young warrior.'

'He's had to go back to London,' Amy says casually. 'Some kind of emergency.' She shrugs, almost indifferently. 'Says he's really sorry.'

'Yeah?' says Jack, disbelievingly. 'Just couldn't face being outnumbered. Ah, well. We'll manage without him.'

He grins at Amy and goes to order his coffee. Sam and Amy stare at each other. Sam gives a kind of 'told you so' shrug.

'You see? It won't be a big deal if you don't want it to be,' he tells her. 'You were really casual the way you told him. He took his lead from you. It'll be fine.'

She shakes her head, as if in surprise. 'I guess you're right.' She grins at him. 'Just be sure you sit next to me for supper.'

He is filled with delight at the prospect. 'You're on,' he says.

*

Jack waits in the queue. He feels relieved that Cosmo won't be joining them at the pub this evening. Though he likes the lad it might have been less relaxed, more formal, with a stranger in their midst. He glances back at Sam and Amy, who seem to be toasting each other with their coffee cups, and he smiles to himself. He'd much rather see her with Sam than with Cosmo. Somehow, though he couldn't have explained why, Sam seems to fit in better with them all. Cosmo is almost overconfident, smooth, showy. Sam is quietly strong; at ease in his skin, self-reliant. Jack would rather his girl was attracted to that kind of man than to Cosmo's extrovert liveliness. But then again, who could tell what might attract a woman to a man or, for that matter, a man to a woman? He could never quite see what chemistry worked between Max and Judith, for instance. She's so buttoned up, so proper, as if she needs to protect herself from ordinary people. Whilst old Max is such a hail-fellow-well-met kind of guy. Jack slightly wishes that Judith wasn't coming to the party either – fears that she might put a blight on it – but he hopes that there will be too many of them for it to have any real effect. He intends to enjoy himself. He's glad that Amy doesn't seem too worried by Cosmo's sudden departure, wonders what's happened to make him back out, and rather hopes that it keeps him away for a while.

He orders his Americano and turns back to join Amy and Sam. He has every intention of enjoying his birthday. They've already pulled up a chair for him and, as he sits down, the door opens and Cara and Max come in. Everyone begins to laugh.

'You've started early,' says Max. 'Happy birthday, Jack. May we join you?'

'Why wait till this evening?' asks Jack, pulling two tables together so that they can all fit round. 'Let's do the show right here.'

Amy is laughing. She looks relaxed and cheerful. Sam is watching her with an odd, almost protective look, and Jack feels another surge of affection for him.

'Get the order in, Sam,' Jack says. 'I bet you know what everyone wants by now. And I'll have a piece of that tiffin. It's my birthday, after all.'

'Aye aye, sir.'

Grinning, Sam gives him a mock salute and gets to his feet. He checks with Max and Cara, raises his eyebrows towards Amy's empty cup. She shakes her head and then just as suddenly changes her mind.

'Why not?'

Another little look passes between the two of them and Jack is intrigued, but Max is explaining why Judith isn't with them, and Cara pauses before she sits down to give him a birthday hug, and he forgets about it.

Pleased though he is to see his friends, Max is slightly irritated not to be able to have a quiet word with Cara about Judith's new plan to move to Oxford. He didn't want open discussion – not yet – but he wondered if he might just moot the idea to Cara in the privacy of the Coffee Shop so as to give her a warning shot across the bows. He hadn't expected to see Jack and Amy with Sam already here, and now the opportunity is gone. His anxiety is that Cara might somehow imagine that she ought to take up Judith's proposition so as to help them; to enable the move. He can imagine how Judith will cleverly emphasize the benefits of his being able to keep his boat, of the fun they'll have together when he comes down to see Cara and all his friends. Cara knows how he loves his boat, how much he would miss his life here in Salcombe, and she might feel pressured to help him. He wants to assure her that this is not necessary.

Now, as he watches her talking and laughing, he can see that it might be the right thing for her to stay here, amongst this friendly group of people, but not in a large, expensive house that would not necessarily be her choice. Max wonders how she will react to the news that he might be going to Oxford. He knows that it will be a shock – that she believes he and Judith are settled here – and he feels cross and sad that he doesn't know what is best for his sister. It would be crazy to suggest that she should come to Oxford with them, and Judith certainly wouldn't be pleased. He can't see a way through it and feels frustrated and angry.

Sam sits down beside him and Max turns to him, glad to be distracted.

'We looked for you earlier,' he tells him. 'Just to say we were going to do some shopping and then pop in here, but you were nowhere to be found.'

'I went out for a walk,' says Sam. 'Just getting my bearings. So many little streets and passages. The thing is, I just want to check with you if it's OK if I whisk Cara off to The Keep for a few days? Seems a bit rude, pinching your guest, but Hal and Fliss asked me to invite her over so she can meet Jolyon and Henrietta and the kids. I think I mentioned they're down for the weekend.'

'I think it's a great idea,' answers Max, 'and I'm sure she'd love to. I think that she'll be around for a while yet so there's no need to worry about poaching.'

'Great,' says Sam. 'And we can do a bit more exploring. I'd like to take her up on to the moor. Though I can't quite see her wanting to live up there.'

Max wonders what Sam would say if he were to tell him that Judith is planning a move to Oxford and that she thinks Cara should buy the house in Buckley Street. Suddenly he is filled with an odd sense of desolation. He loves both his boys but Paul is an academic, wrapped up in his research work, and they have very little in common. Chris, on the other hand, loves to come here to Salcombe, to sail with his father and have a drink with his friends. These visits are so precious to Max. Sam is watching him: he looks concerned.

'Are you OK?' he asks.

Max pulls himself together. 'Of course I am.'

He suddenly realizes that Sam seems to have lost the air of pre-occupation, his introspective look. He's relaxed, happy, and Max wonders what has happened to bring about the change. Instinct-ively he glances at Amy, who is talking animatedly to Cara.

'So I hear we are to be meeting Cosmo this evening,' he says. 'How serious is it? Do you know?'

'Oh, Cosmo can't come,' answers Sam casually. 'Some crisis has called him back to London. We'll have to do without him, I'm afraid.'

'Well, Amy doesn't look too bothered,' observes Max.

He watches Sam look across at her, notes the expression on his face and wonders if he's found the answer to his earlier question.

'No she doesn't, does she?' answers Sam. He grins at his godfather. 'We'll just have to make sure she doesn't miss him.'

Max bursts out laughing.

'I think you might find that Jack will be glad to encourage you in that endeavour,' he says.

More coffee arrives, the tiffin is shared around, and Max prepares to put his problems to one side and celebrate his old friend's birthday.

*

Cara raises her cup to Jack and smiles at Amy, wondering how Cosmo will fit in with this group of friends.

As if she is reading her thoughts, Amy says casually: 'Oh, by the way, Cosmo can't come tonight. Some emergency has come up and he's had to go back to London.'

Amy looks quite calm, unfazed, but Cara feels a little tug of anxiety. Something makes her want to say: 'That's convenient timing, isn't it?' but she has no reason to believe that Cosmo wants to avoid an evening with Amy's family and friends. Yet instinct tells her that all is not well. She likes Amy: she's so straightforward, so easy to be with, and she's such a pretty girl. Cara remembers how she met Cosmo out at Snapes Point on his last return from London.

'What's he done with the dog?' she asks casually.

Amy shrugs. 'Don't know. Maybe his friend's down again. Al, his name is. His parents own the house. And Reggie.'

'Is Cosmo coming back?'

Just for a moment, Amy looks slightly disconcerted. She frowns, then shrugs again.

'He didn't say in his text,' she answers. 'I should think so.'

It seems rather odd that Amy isn't very well informed but Cara is pleased to see a measure of indifference. Even if Amy is hurt or worried she isn't going to allow it to show. Cara remembers how they looked together, so much in love, so absorbed in each other, and she can't quite dismiss her fear.

Jack is offering her some tiffin, coffee is put in front of her. She smiles at him and she glances up again at the beam, remembering how she felt when she first saw Cosmo, how he pointed out the words '*Dolce far Niente*' and how he reminded her of Joe.

As she picks up the piece of tiffin, Sam slides into the chair opposite and smiles at her.

'You've got permission for a run ashore,' he tells her. 'How about we go to The Keep tomorrow to be in time for lunch? Shall I phone Fliss and ask her?'

'Yes,' she says. 'Yes, please.'

As Amy asks Sam about his family, Cara thinks that it will be good to go back to The Keep, to be with Fliss and Hal and Honey in that wonderful old house. She remembers how she and Fliss sat in the courtyard with Honey between them, and how Fliss talked about Mole and their older brother, Jamie, and how their deaths had affected her. These confidences were unexpected – Cara guesses that Fliss is not a woman who readily bares her soul – yet it seemed so right, as if The Keep's high walls were sheltering them both in this special moment of intimacy. It made her feel privileged and less alone.

Everyone is raising their coffee cups to Jack, toasting him, and Cara finishes her tiffin and joins in.

PART THREE

CHAPTER EIGHTEEN

Al, sitting at his table in the corner of the bar, sees the group come in. It's a few moments before he realizes that it's the same group that was here the last time and he's amused at the coincidence. Obviously this is their local and they enjoy a get-together. As he watches them at the bar he sees that there is a new addition: an older woman, rather formally attired. Whereas before he could see no obvious connection between any of the group, this time he guesses that she and one of the men are definitely a couple. The body language suggests that they are married. There is that familiarity of touch and exchange of glances that indicate a long relationship. The other two women, one dressed like a hippie, are talking to the other man, laughing and toasting him, whilst the two younger people – a boy and a girl – watch, smiling but slightly apart. The girl glances round the bar, her eyes meet his. She does a double take, and it's as if she gives a little jump of surprise.

He looks back at her, wondering if she remembers him from his last visit, surprised at her reaction. She's turned away now and as he watches her she leans towards the dark young man beside her and murmurs something in his ear. Both of them have their backs to him and neither looks at him again, but Al is intrigued. He wonders if this is Amy. They are all moving to a big table now, sitting down, and his own food comes and he begins to eat. He's still pissed off with Cosmo for calling his bluff and dashing away to London. Al's original plan was that they'd spend this weekend together, have some fun – and, no doubt, bump into Amy somewhere so that he could assess the situation more clearly and make Cosmo realize the damage he might be doing. Instead, Cosmo has outwitted him, and here he is bored and alone.

He glances across at the other table. Champagne has been opened. Obviously a celebration is in progress. There's laughter, a short chorus of 'Happy Birthday to You' and a round of applause. Clearly the birthday boy is well known and popular because now several other people have joined in, crossing over to his table and crowding round. Under the cover of the hulla-baloo, the younger girl pushes back her chair and comes quickly across to him. Al watches her approach, sitting quite still, his fork loaded with food in his hand.

'This is going to sound utterly crazy,' she says, smiling at him, 'but I just have to ask the question. I saw you here a few weeks ago, didn't I? Could you by any chance be Al?'

He hardly knows how to answer but he lays down his fork and smiles back at her.

'Well, actually, yes, I am.'

He wonders if he should ask if she is Amy but she is hurrying on, embarrassed but friendly.

'It's just that I know Cosmo, you see, and he told me that he's had to dash off again but last time he said that his friend Al would be down to look after the house and Reggie. It's just such a coincidence that I couldn't resist asking the question.'

'You're absolutely right. It's my parents' house.'

He hesitates; doesn't quite know what to say next, how to move forward.

'So I hope it wasn't something awful?' she asks. 'The crisis, I mean. It was all rather sudden, wasn't it? Actually we'd invited him to my dad's birthday party tonight.'

She gestures towards the busy, noisy table, and now Al sees why Cosmo ran away. How difficult to explain to his old mate that he was well in with this girl and her family and friends. Maybe he would have had to ask if Al could join the party. How difficult then, not to talk about their London lives, work, Becks.

'It looks like you're having a lot of fun,' he says awkwardly, avoiding her question. 'He'll be sorry he missed it.'

She stares at him, eyebrows raised just a little, as if she's still waiting for an explanation for Cosmo's sudden departure, and then she gives a little nod, turns away and goes back to her friends.

Al sits staring at his plate. He guesses that somehow he's given the game away, dropped Cosmo in it, although he's said nothing. His sheer inability to explain the situation looks as if he is shielding Cosmo and he is angry to be put into this position. He has no doubt that the girl is Amy, and that she suspects that there's something going on, and Al wants nothing to do with it. On an impulse he takes out his phone and taps out a message to Cosmo.

Just met Amy in the pub. She says you were invited to her dad's birthday party. She asked me why you just dashed off without giving a reason. What's all that about?

Al stares at the message for a moment and then presses Send. He finishes his supper, although his appetite is gone, and without looking again towards Amy and her friends he gets up and goes out.

Under the cover of the general conversation, Sam leans slightly towards Amy, seated on his left.

'So is he Al?'

'Yes,' she answers shortly.

She's glad now that she followed her instinct and, encouraged by Sam, went across and asked the question, but she is angry and embarrassed. Al's reluctance to talk about Cosmo confirms that something is going on and she feels humiliated.

'But he didn't tell you what the emergency was?' mutters Sam.

Amy shakes her head, aware of Charley watching them across the table. Charley has been the most difficult person to cope with; the one who wants to know what has happened.

'So where is he?' she asked when she arrived earlier. 'Can't wait to meet him again.'

She was ready to tease Amy, to enter into the spirit of the thing, and when Amy said Cosmo wasn't coming Charley stared at her in surprise.

'Oh, no,' she said, disappointment and sympathy flowing like honey. 'Why ever not, hon?'

Amy shrugged, pretending indifference. 'Some emergency cropped up. He's had to dash back to London. Never mind. We'll manage without him. The important thing is that Dad has a great time.'

She could tell that Charley wasn't convinced by this casual show and Amy prayed that she'd let it drop. Luckily, Dad came in and the moment passed, but Charley has been on the alert, waiting to have another chat. True to his word, Sam made certain that he was sitting next to Amy but even that seems to have alerted Charley's attention and she's been watching them across the table, catching Amy's eye, giving her a little wink, as if she knows something Amy doesn't. She's seen Amy go to talk to Al and now she's looking even more inquisitive and Amy would like to scream.

She picks up her wine glass, looking about, pretending she's enjoying herself, but all the while her mind is busy trying to work out the logistics of Cosmo's dash to London. How he managed to organize Al to cover him, then to drive to Totnes to catch the train, without finding the time to send her a text to say he was going. He hasn't answered her later texts and she's wondering how he's going to explain that when he gets back. A tiny thought wriggles into her mind. Suppose he isn't coming back? After all, Al is here. She turns quickly in her chair, half wondering whether she should ask Al the question, but when she looks across the bar she sees that his table is empty. Al has gone.

Judith finishes her champagne and wishes that it was time to go home. The noise is too much for her, the silly banter irritates her, but she continues to keep a smile pinned to her lips and to nod and seem interested when required. To distract herself she thinks about her Oxford plan, about some of the houses she has seen, and how good it will be to live closer to the little family and to be a part of their lives. With Christopher divorced and in Dubai it seems unlikely that he will be contributing much companionship for a while.

She's promised Max that they won't confront Cara with this proposition until Sam has gone home. Max is clearly anxious about Cara's reaction and wants to pick his moment, but Judith thinks he's overreacting as usual and that Cara will be prevailed upon to see how well it could work for all of them. Judith looks across the table at Cara, who is deep in conversation with Jack. They certainly seem to be getting on very well, though Judith can't quite understand what Cara sees in him. At least it's another positive reason for her to stay here in Salcombe. She's also becoming very friendly with the Chadwicks so it's really not necessary for Max to be so concerned about his sister. Judith feels the long-familiar stab of irritation. Of course, he's always been ridiculously protective about Cara – and clearly this is a very difficult time for her – but life goes on and Cara must learn to go with it.

Judith sits back to allow the waiter to put her plate in front of her. Her thoughts stray back to Oxford, her spirits rise, and she begins to eat.

Charley picks at her food feeling slightly discontented. She was looking forward to a really fun evening, teasing Amy about Cosmo whilst getting to know him better, chatting up Jack and making him laugh, probing a little more into Sam's plans for his future. But nothing's worked out quite as she hoped. Cosmo has done a runner, Jack is absorbed with Cara, and Amy and Sam seem to be developing a rather interesting new depth to their friendship. She's conscious of Sam's awareness of Amy, almost a protectiveness, which slightly puzzles Charley. Amy is being brittle, difficult to approach. Of course, it's easy to imagine that she's a bit miffed at Cosmo disappearing away like that – and with no very good explanation, by the sounds of it – but she's surprised that Amy doesn't want to have a little girly chat about it. And why did she suddenly dash across the bar like that to speak to the man sitting on his own in the corner? Clearly he isn't a friend, or he'd have come over when everyone gathered round to toast Jack, so who can he be?

Charley is used to being the confidante, the best friend, but suddenly she doesn't have a role to play. She's finding Judith very hard-going – it's clear that she's not particularly enjoying herself despite her efforts to look pleasant – and Max seems slightly preoccupied. Charley turns to him, determined to make some kind of effort to be involved.

'I haven't managed to speak to Cara properly yet,' she tells him. 'How's the house-hunting going? Has she found a place to live?'

To her surprise her question seems to touch a nerve. Max frowns, glances quickly across her at Judith, and then looks down at his plate.

'No,' he says quickly. 'That is . . . Well, no. Several things in the pipeline . . .'

He waffles on for a bit, clearly uncomfortable, and Charley sighs and shakes her head. The whole thing is beyond her. The last time they all met up it was such fun, so easy, everyone having a great time. She's been looking forward to this evening but somehow the magic ingredient is missing, although Jack seems to be having a great time. She tries to catch his eye, to raise her glass to him across the table, but he's talking to Cara and doesn't see her.

Al walks home, out of the town and along the creek. He hadn't realized how dark it is in the country with only the lighted windows of the few cottages at the head of the creek to guide him. It's so quiet; only the sound of the rising tide lapping gently along the shore. He looks up at the stars blotted with mist and into the dense shadows of the trees. Nothing is familiar and he glances behind him, feeling ill at ease and longing for company. As he climbs the steps up to the garden and crosses the lawn he's glad to hear Reggie's bark. He lets him out into the garden for a quick scout round, then they both go in and Al locks the door behind them. He wanders into the kitchen, back into the sitting-room, wondering what to do for the rest of the evening. At intervals he glances at his phone. Last weekend he went to a school reunion for the first time and met up with his old friends. They've been texting each other since and it's rather fun being back in touch.

He's still annoyed with Cosmo. Perhaps he should have given him more warning of his plan to come down to Salcombe, but the whole point was to take Cosmo by surprise and see just exactly what was going on. Al gives a disgruntled sigh. Well, now he knows. He thinks of Amy's face, of how he sidestepped her question, and he feels angry all over again at being involved.

He reaches for the remote. Reggie comes to sit beside him, and he settles down to watch the news. It's some time later before he gets a reply from Cosmo.

Thanks for that, mate! Becks saw your text and I got the third degree and she's chucked me out. I'm back at mine but I'm not giving in. I'll go round tomorrow so I shan't be coming back just yet. Over to you.

Al stares at the text in consternation. He hadn't foreseen anything like this. His first thought is of himself. If Cosmo doesn't come back he's stuck. He can't simply leave Reggie and go back to London. He presses the call button and Cosmo answers almost at once.

'What happened?' asks Al without preamble. 'How the hell did she see the text?'

'We were sitting on the sofa together,' says Cosmo. 'We'd been texting a mutual friend and she was looking over my shoulder at the replies. Yours came in and we both just read it.'

'Christ!' exclaims Al. 'Look, I'm sorry, mate, but you really shouldn't be playing away. You asked for it. Did she see Amy's texts, too?'

'I'd blocked them. It never occurred to me that you might sabotage me.'

Al is silent for a minute, feeling guilty. Then he remembers his own predicament.

'What d'you mean you're not coming back tomorrow? What am I supposed to do? I can't just leave Reggie.'

'I've got my own problems.' Cosmo sounds sulky. 'You dropped me right in it and I'm going to have to talk my way out of it.'

'And what about Amy?' asks Al. 'Does that mean it's all over for her?'

There's a silence. Al can almost hear Cosmo weighing up the situation. If he can't win Becks around he's got Amy in reserve. Cosmo likes to have a plan B.

'Have you told her anything?' asks Cosmo.

Al gives a disgusted snort. 'If you mean have I told her you've got a girlfriend in London, then no, I haven't. You realize you're behaving like a complete shit? And what am I supposed to do if you don't get back here tomorrow afternoon?'

'That's your problem,' says Cosmo.

The line goes dead and Al waits for a moment and then throws the phone down on the sofa with an exclamation of frustration. He sits, trying to see a way forward, wondering what he will do if Cosmo really does decide not to come back. Al has a pretty strong suspicion now that this is going to happen and that he'll be left in the lurch. He feels slightly responsible for the whole business because he asked Cosmo to help his parents out, but his anger is partly for himself and partly for Amy. She doesn't deserve this.

A message pings in and he picks it up. It's one of his old school friends hoping they can all meet up together again soon. He agrees about another group session and to a suggestion to meet up for a drink next weekend. No question but he'll have to be back in London by then.

CHAPTER NINETEEN

As they drive to The Keep in Sam's Mini the following morning Cara is rather quiet. A westerly is driving tattered clouds before it, whirling the autumn leaves high into the sky, flinging handfuls of rain across the windscreen.

'Everything OK?' asks Sam, glancing sideways at her.

She doesn't answer straight away but sits slightly hunched, with her arms crossed, frowning, as if she is considering his question.

'I think so,' she says at last. 'To be absolutely honest I was rather surprised at Judith's reaction to us going. It was almost as if she didn't want me to go, which is a bit surprising. I don't mean to sound rude or anything but I thought she might be quite pleased to see the back of me for a few days. She seemed almost put out.'

Sam nods. 'I know what you mean. I noticed it but didn't give it much thought.'

'And Max seemed a bit twitchy too, as if he half expected Judith to go off on one. It was like he was edging her away from something. I suppose I might have upset her somehow without meaning to, and she's cross and he was trying to keep the peace. It wouldn't be the first time.'

'The good thing about a big family like ours,' says Sam, 'is that there's plenty of us to deflect rows and arguments so it never gets too intense. By the way, Fliss says she's putting you in Lizzie's old rooms so I hope you'll be comfortable. They're in the west wing so they're best in the late afternoon and evening, though especially lovely in the spring.'

'And you're happy with that?' Cara asks. 'I know Lizzie's very special to you.'

'It will be nice to know they're being used,' he answers. 'The thing with a house as old as The Keep is that the rooms have always belonged to someone else at some time, if you see what I mean. Did you enjoy the party?'

'Yes,' she says at once. 'Yes, it was fun. Especially when all Jack's friends came and joined in. I loved that. I was sorry that Cosmo couldn't make it, though. Amy didn't seem too upset but I wasn't sure if she might just be putting on a brave face. I hope not.'

There's a little silence.

He glances sideways at her. 'You don't trust him, do you?'

'No,' admits Cara. 'I suspect him, but I'm not sure of what, and I don't want Amy to be hurt. I've nothing to go on except . . . nothing. Just an instinct that he's not playing straight. Did you find out why he had to rush away so suddenly?'

He shakes his head, slightly taken aback at her honesty.

'No. Amy texted him but got no reply. I suppose it might depend on the nature of the emergency.'

Cara makes a little explosive sound of disbelief.

'And the young man Amy spoke to at the pub?'

Sam begins to laugh. 'Quick, aren't you? His name is Al and he stands in when Cosmo's not there. His parents own the house and the dog.'

She nods, as if she knows it already.

'Odd, though, isn't it,' she says, 'that Cosmo was called away in such a rush that he couldn't warn Amy, but he still had time to organize Al and do the handover?'

Sam makes a little face. He can't deny it. 'You're not very pleased with Cosmo, are you?'

She stares out of the window, biting her lip, almost as if she is going to tell him something, confide in him. Then she shakes her head as if deciding against it.

'It's none of my business,' she says. 'But I'm very fond of Amy and I don't want her to get hurt.'

'Neither do I,' he says.

It surprises him how strongly that came out, how important Amy is becoming to him. Cara looks sideways at him, and she smiles.

'Good,' she says. 'That's very good. So let's forget the wretched Cosmo and talk about your family. Explain who it is I'm going to meet and their exact relationship to you, and remember, I'm a complete stranger.'

When they arrive at The Keep it's clear that celebrations are taking place. A television series is going to be filmed locally and Jolyon, Hal's son, has suggested to the producer that The Keep might be the perfect location for some of the scenes. Cara is slightly alarmed by the whirl of family life but is caught up by the excitement of it all. Jolyon is very like his father, and Cara takes to him at once.

'So are you, by extension, Sam's godmother or his god-sister?' he asks her. 'I've been trying to work out the relationship.'

She shakes her head. 'I take no responsibility for him at all.'

Jolyon laughs and introduces her to his pretty wife, Henrietta, his small son, George, and the baby, Alfie. Fliss and Hal are preparing a big Sunday lunch. Honey patrols, on the watch for titbits, and Cara settles happily at the big kitchen table, listening whilst the discussion continues about the prospective TV series.

'It's the perfect time for The Keep,' Jolyon says. 'The eighteen hundreds, when dear old however-many-greats-grandfather Edward was restoring it from an old hill fort and then adding a couple of wings. It's not going to be the main location for the series but it should earn you some money and it'll be fun.'

'And do Fliss and I get to be extras and dress up as Victorians?' asks Hal, putting glasses on the table and picking up a bottle of wine.

'Definitely not,' says Jolyon at once. 'That would be just so embarrassing, Dad.'

Hal winks at Cara, shows her the bottle, and she nods.

'Yes, please,' she says. 'But maybe Honey will get a part, like the dog in *Downton*.'

At the sound of her name, Honey looks up to gaze across the room at Cara, and then small George puts his arms around the dog's neck, hugging her.

'So what d'you think of our latest addition?' Sam asks Jolyon.

'She's great,' he answers. 'It's good to see the dog basket occupied again.'

Hal nods. 'Absolutely. Nice to have someone else in the dog-house for a change.'

There's more laughter, more jokes, and Cara sips her wine, fascinated as always by the behaviour of a large family *en masse*.

It's outside her own experience and she envies them their shared past and the ease that goes with it.

'Come and see your room,' Fliss says. 'Lunch isn't quite ready.'

She picks up Cara's small bag and leads the way along passages, up the stairs and along the corridor to the west wing. The rooms look down into the orchard, across the kitchen gardens, away to the west.

'They're quite small,' says Fliss, almost apologetically, 'but at least Lizzie had a little sitting-room so she could have some privacy when she needed it. And there's a shower in this cubbyhole, with a loo, but if you want a bath you'll have to muck in down the corridor. It wasn't easy to drag The Keep into even the twentieth century so this is as good as it gets.'

Cara looks around at the simplicity of the two small rooms, the pretty French furniture, the watercolours on the walls.

'It's perfect,' she says. 'Thank you very much. It's so kind of you, Fliss.'

'Not a bit of it,' says Fliss. 'We love having people here. You're welcome to stay for as long as you need to. It must be incredibly difficult to try to decide where you want to be when you've never had a settled base. The navy was like that, but I always had The Keep to come to whenever I needed it.' She glances round as if to make sure everything is in order and then smiles at Cara. 'Come down when you're ready,' she says, and goes out.

Cara picks up her bag and puts it on an old pine trunk at the foot of the bed. Then she crosses to the window. She imagines the orchard foaming with blossom in the spring; the kitchen garden, surrounded by its rugged stone walls and crisscrossed by grassy paths, filled with produce. She tries to imagine what it must be like to live with such continuity, the changing of the seasons, a sense of belonging.

She turns back into the room, opens her bag and takes out a few things. A mirror with a mahogany frame hangs above the small chest of drawers. Cara brushes her hair without looking herself in the eye. She can't bear to do that, to see the other self, the disapproval looking back at her. She prefers others to be her mirror so that she can imagine herself as they see her, not as she really is. She remembers how she danced before the mirror at the house in Sussex, how she talked and laughed with her mirror-image, her friend. How long it's been since she could look at her reflection and not see the accuser looking back at her.

She turns away, wondering what Philip would have made of Hal and Fliss. She is certain that he and Hal would have got on very well. They would have exchanged yarns of life at sea and in embassies in foreign countries. Philip had a knack of putting people at ease, creating a convivial atmosphere; he would have felt at home here at The Keep. She wishes he could be here with her, sharing this as they'd shared so many things. They'd had so much in common. He was a lonely only child, with a father in the army, and he'd enjoyed the companionship he found at school, especially with Max.

She can remember when she first realized, had known for certain, who Philip's true love was. They were in Copenhagen when Max's ship came into harbour for a Show the Flag visit. He'd grabbed a taxi and come straight to their flat much earlier than expected. She let him in, hugged him, then Philip came out of his study and stopped in surprise. The expression on his face – joy, love – showed her everything, explained so many things. How odd that she hadn't minded: that it simply brought them all even closer. These two men had been the constants in her life and she loved them both.

After Philip died, when she was packing up in London, she'd found a photograph tucked between the pages of one of his books. On the flyleaf was a brief inscription: 'Philip. Congratulations. Max' and a date, July 1970: the summer before Philip went up to Cambridge to read History. The book was a copy of *1066 and All That*. In the photograph, the two young men stand together. Max, slightly taller, has propped his elbow casually on Philip's shoulder and is smiling nonchalantly at the camera. Philip is looking at Max with an oddly touching mix of affection and admiration. Somehow the photograph says it all.

Now, Cara picks up a bag that has a box of chocolates in it, a little present for Fliss, and makes her way downstairs and back to the kitchen.

After lunch, leaving Hal to fill the dishwasher and Henrietta to settle the baby down for his nap, the others take Honey and set off for a walk on the hill. Jolyon and Sam walk on ahead, with Honey close at heel as usual, despite their efforts to make her run freely. Fliss and Cara follow more slowly, battling into the strong westerly wind.

'So was it a good party last night?' Fliss asks. 'Sam seems to have enjoyed himself.'

Cara guesses that Fliss is trying to find out a little more about Sam's activities in Salcombe and wonders how much he's told her about Amy.

'It was a birthday party,' Cara tells her. 'Jack Hannaford. He's one of Max's friends. They go sailing together. He's interesting. Gave up a teaching career to go self-employed as a decorator. He brought me over to see *The Magic Flute* and *Der Rosenkavalier* at Dartington. His daughter's about Sam's age,

Amy. She works with him but she's spreading her wings a bit, from what I can gather. Starting to source things for clients, that sort of thing. Beginning to be a bit of an interior designer.'

Fliss smiles. 'Perhaps that's why Sam enjoyed himself so much. He's been a bit quiet lately, a bit introspective. Perhaps Amy is helping him out of it.'

'They seem to get along very well together,' Cara says. 'I think you'd like her a lot, but I wouldn't want to say that it's anything more than friendship.'

'Sounds good to me,' says Fliss.

They walk for a while in companionable silence, heads bent against the wind and the little splatters of rain. Ahead of them, Jolyon and Sam turn and start back towards them.

'It's going to start chucking it down in a minute,' Jolyon shouts, gesturing at the banks of clouds massing along the horizon. 'Time to go home.'

Cara is glad to turn her back to the wind and be almost carried down the hill. When they get back, the fire has been lit in the hall and Hal is sitting on one of the long sofas, reading newspapers, with George at his feet surrounded by toys. Cara guesses that these are family heirlooms: a wind-up jack-in-the-box, some rather battered Dinky cars, an old teddy, his fur rubbed thin with much hugging. Henrietta is sitting on the sofa opposite, the baby asleep beside her. Hal looks up.

'It must have been chilly out there. I can hear the wind rising,' he says. 'Come and get warm.'

They take off their coats and boots and go to sit by the fire. Fliss kneels down beside George, showing him how to wind up the jack-in-the-box. Hal clears a space beside him on the sofa and smiles at Cara.

'Just as well you're not going back.' he says. 'It's going to be a stormy old night. Though you might get a bit of a battering up there in the west wing.'

'There's something rather nice,' she says, 'about listening to really wild weather when you're tucked up safe and warm inside.'

She sees Sam take his phone from his pocket and glance at it. A smile touches his lips and instinctively she knows that the text is from Amy. He looks up, catches her eye and grins at her.

'All quiet on the Western Front,' he says, and she wonders if that means that Amy still hasn't heard from Cosmo.

She wonders what will happen when Cosmo returns to Salcombe, and gives an involuntary little shiver. Hal turns to look at her.

'Cold?' he asks. 'It wasn't the best afternoon for a walk. How about some tea?' He gets up, scattering newspapers. 'Come on, Sam. You can help me carry.'

Cara sits quietly listening to George and Fliss chattering together on the rug at her feet whilst Henrietta and Jolyon talk in quiet voices on the sofa on the other side of the long low table, and Honey stretches out before the fire. How peaceful it is. This is what a real homecoming must be like. Returning to the people you love best, in the home you've known for ever. Suddenly the baby wakes and begins to cry, and the dynamic changes as Henrietta picks him up. Fliss is asking if she needs anything; George takes some of the toys to show Jolyon. Tea arrives and is set out on the low table. Cara is absorbed by the life around her. She can't remember when she's been so happy.

The next few days are filled with companionship; walks on the moor, trips with Sam to do outside recces of two flats in

Dartmouth, and a visit to Dartington Hall, where she is introduced to Fliss's younger sister, Susanna, and her delightful husband, Gus, who live in the village. As Cara works in the kitchen garden with Hal and Fliss, she wonders why she should feel so relaxed with these people she's known for such a short time. They have a stability, a rootedness, that she's never known in her own life, and at this time of loneliness and adjustment it's very comforting.

'We just wanted to say,' Fliss says after lunch on Cara's last day, 'that you're always welcome to stay here. Don't let the pressure of finding somewhere to live get to you. We can imagine that it might get a bit cramped in Salcombe after a while, but we've got so much space here and we're used to having people around.'

A north-westerly is buffeting The Keep's strong walls, there's a sudden clatter of rain, and Hal comes into the kitchen with Honey, brushing the water from his jacket, kicking off his boots. Sam follows him, getting Honey's towel and rubbing her dry.

'We didn't quite make it,' he says. 'There's a real old gale blowing up. I think I'll light the fire in the hall.'

'Good idea,' says Fliss.

Hal and Fliss begin a conversation about one of their children and Cara slips out and goes upstairs to her room. It's colder today and she needs a warmer jersey. She's packed one of Philip's, a soft cashmere, warm and oversized, and she shrugs herself into the comfort of it and shuts her eyes just for a moment, acknowledging all that she has lost. She wraps her arms around herself, remembering his kindness, his sense of fun, their own ways of intimacy and love.

'I never guessed,' she said to him, after that visit in Copenhagen, 'that it was Max whom you loved.'

Philip was sitting reading the newspaper and she can remember his swift upward glance, the anxiety and guilt in his eyes. She went to him, kneeling beside him and putting her arms round him. Philip held her tightly, his face hidden.

'I love you, too,' he said, muffled. 'You know that.'

'It's OK,' she reassured him. 'I love him, too. If you have to love somebody I'm glad that it's Max.'

Cara stands up. Pausing at the bedroom window, she sees that the rain has stopped although the sun is almost obscured by the mist over the moor. To the south storm clouds are building, towering and toppling over the hills. She hears her name called and then a knock on the door. She calls a response, the door opens and Sam sticks his head around, eyes alight with amusement.

'Fancy an adventure?' he asks.

Cara laughs. 'That depends on what sort of adventure you have in mind,' she answers. But Sam has already gone.

'Bring a coat,' he calls.

Catching up her fleece jacket, she hurries to the door.

'Come on,' he calls impatiently from further down the corridor. 'We haven't much time!'

She goes after him along the passage to the big central landing and, as he turns left and climbs the stairs, Cara follows, keeping close to the wall. She hasn't been up to the third floor before. Something about the wooden stairs and banisters has seemed forbidding, unsafe, but Sam is climbing and she has to follow him. Here the building is less well decorated, less lived in. Even on this floor the ceilings are high, so much higher than in her cosy rooms in the west wing. There is a sense of space, of grandeur. The pictures on the walls here are fewer, and the paint on the walls is rougher, peeling in places. She is not surprised. After all, Hal and Fliss have no need for this extra space; its maintenance would not be a priority. On the top landing she looks around. There are several doors, which she assumes lead to bedrooms. Indeed, as Sam makes his way down the passage he gestures at an open doorway.

'That's my room,' he says, but clearly this is not his destination.

He is leading her towards an oddly narrow door at the end of the corridor. He has a large key in his hand, which he puts into the lock.

'Boxroom,' he says briefly, and pushes in.

She follows. The smell is enticing: warm and dusty and dry, scents of different kinds of wood, of old lavender. Around the room are piles of boxes, furniture, even paintings stacked against a wall. It is a treasure trove of the old and neglected, cast-offs of a long established family. In the wall opposite the door is a small window so covered in grime and cobwebs that it is difficult to see the countryside beyond. It doesn't cast much glow but Sam has flicked on a switch, and a bare bulb, hanging from a long cloth-bound cable, supplements the weak natural light.

As Cara takes it all in she is aware that Sam is busy. He has found a long, oddly shaped pole, which he carries into the corner on her left, which is clear of shelves and boxes. Here he reaches up with the pole to a latch in the ceiling.

'Keep back,' he warns, and with practised ease he flicks the catch to allow a long panel to swing downwards on sturdy hinges. There is a little shower of debris as the panel swings back and forth above their heads. Sam is still working; from the corner he collects a long, sturdy wooden ladder, which he lifts into place below the hatch. She can see that on the ends of the struts there are large brass hooks that match with eyes that are set in the wooden beam above their heads. Sam slots the ladder into place and turns to grin at her.

'Give me a moment,' he says.

He puts his hand in his pocket, rooting around for something, and draws out a small old-fashioned key. Holding it in his right hand, he puts a foot on the ladder and climbs quickly and smoothly to the top.

His head, shoulders and arms disappear from view and he stands still for a moment. Then he places one foot higher on the ladder and, with an audible grunt, he springs upwards. As the hatch opens high above, daylight floods into the room. Sam comes back a few steps so he can look down at her upturned and anxious face.

'I was fifteen before I could get that hatch open,' he says, grinning at her. 'Don't tell Fliss. Come on, Cara. You're going to love this.'

He springs back up the ladder, into the light, until he disappears from view.

Cara moves forward slowly, her heart speeding, her thoughts a jumble of tension, fear and determination. She does not want to climb that ladder. The wood seems solid but she doesn't trust in it. And yet neither can she bring herself to quit, to give up on Sam and let him down. He is so keen, so enthusiastic, and this is so obviously a gift he is offering her. How can she refuse him; how can she cope with admitting her fear to him? She is trapped, and so she touches the ladder gingerly, places a foot on the first rung. Clinging to the wood, she begins to climb.

It is a long way up. She stops twice, willing herself to go on, to put one hand above the next. Sam is calling, 'Come *on*, Cara, you'll miss it!' and for a moment she feels like the little girl she once was; that it is Max above her, transformed back into an eager youth, urging her to conquer her fears, and she climbs on, not daring to look down, until her head reaches the hatchway.

Above her, Sam stretches for her hand, grasps it, and half pulls her up, into the light and the wind. Cara steps up off the ladder, Sam's arm around her, steadying her. She looks out, across the gently sloping roof to the east, to the tiny towns, and to the distant sea, a sliver of blue, flashing and glinting in the setting sun. The wind whips at her clothes as she gasps in astonishment at the panorama all around her. And then Sam lets go and she is left unsteady, balanced precariously beside the hatch, as he saunters across the roof into the wind, towards the west and the setting sun. As she watches him he turns to face her, whooping in delight, revelling in the wind and the light. Laughing, he turns again and moves closer to the crenellations that surround the roof, facing into the brilliance of the sunset.

'Sam!' she shouts. 'Don't. Please don't, it's not safe.'

But he can't hear her because of the wind, which catches her voice and tosses it away. Around the base of the crenellations is a low terrace, a walkway from which a watcher might see whomever is approaching the house. Sam jumps on to it with practised ease. Now Cara is terrified for him.

'Sam!' she calls out urgently.

He turns to face her, his face bright with pleasure. Turning back to face the sun, he flings his arms up and wide and shouts at the top of his voice, 'Welcome to my kingdom, Cara!'

A huge blast of wind strikes the rooftop and, as Cara starts towards him, there is a tremendous echoing crash and she screams. She covers her face and screams again. In that brief moment the scene around her dislimns, past and present collide, and it is as if she stands once more on the landing of the old town house in Rome. Joe is facing her. He's laughing, protesting at her foolishness: 'Cara, *bellissima* Cara, where are you going, Cara?' His arms are stretched towards her, detaining her, and she raises her handbag as a shield between them. He pretends to be frightened of her anger, throws up his arms in mock defence, ducking back against the banister. There is a splintering, cracking sound, the banister disintegrates and he is falling back. His hand flails out, catches the railing, but it breaks off as he grasps it. Gracefully he topples backwards into the stairwell. She screams his name, rushes forwards, hears a sickening crack, and his shout abruptly cut off. Standing precariously by the broken banister, looking down from the top landing, she sees him three floors below. His neck is crooked at an impossible angle and a pool of blood is spreading from beneath his head. She leaps down the stairs, her bag still clutched in one hand, her case in the other, and crouches to look into his sightless, half-open eyes. A door opens at the end of a passage behind her, she hears voices, and then she is running; running away into the hot, noisy city.

CHAPTER TWENTY

S am hears Cara scream, sees her collapse down on the rooftop. By the time he reaches her she is curled up small, huddled against the wind, screaming a name over and over again. He drops to his knees, gathers her shaking body into his arms and sits holding her, utterly unnerved.

'Cara, what is it? Are you hurt?'

She shudders, wails quietly, and then her eyes roll up and she becomes limp in his arms.

'Cara,' he calls. 'Cara?'

There is no response. He forces himself to stay calm, to control his panic. The squall is on them now. The sun has set and in the noise of the wind and the rain he can't even tell for sure that she is breathing. Sam lays her flat, bends to her face and listens for breath. He feels it on his cheek and, sitting back, he places a finger on her neck; she has a pulse. He looks around the roof and sees that the crash had been caused by the hatch blowing shut in the wind. He is berating himself, cursing, even as he says out loud, 'We can't stay here.'

He leaps up, crosses to the hatch and, seizing the large metal ring in his hands, heaves it up from the roof, hoping that this time the wind will allow him time to act. Moving back to Cara, determined, he bends so that he can pull her up, gripping her under the arms. He lifts her till she is upright and then ducks down to allow her to fall across his shoulders. As he straightens, he is aware that she is light, very light, and it is not difficult to secure her in a fireman's lift, with her body secure around his neck and his arm locking her legs. Moving swiftly now, scared that the wind might once again catch the hatch door, he approaches the ladder and swings himself over on to the top rungs. The first few steps will be the most difficult. A moment to adjust his burden and then he is climbing down, hands on the rungs, relying on his balance to hold her in place. He is utterly relieved when his head drops below the entrance, out of the wind, but it is still not easy to make progress. Halfway down the ladder he has to pause, terrified that he might let her slip. But he adjusts her weight across his back and finishes the climb, gasping with the fear. He doesn't pause to savour his relief but rolls her off his shoulders and gathers her in his arms. Leaving the loft room to the elements, he carries her out on to the landing, shouting for Fliss and Hal at the top of his voice. As he begins the descent of the stairs he can hear the commotion below and shouts again. And here they are, hurrying up the stairs to meet him. They take charge, assisting him down to the ground floor, helping him to lay his burden on the sofa. Fliss is pulling Cara's shoes off and is removing the sodden fleece from her arms when Sam sees Cara stir, her eyes flickering open.

'Sam?' she asks. 'Where's Sam?'

'He's here,' says Fliss, 'he's fine,' although the look she gives Sam tells him that he is anything but fine; that he's in a lot of trouble. Far above them there is a boom that echoes down through the hall, and Sam knows that the wind has once again slammed the hatch closed. He flinches at the sound, unable to meet Hal's eyes.

Cara twists, dropping her feet to the floor, and pushes herself up into a sitting position, wedged in the corner of the sofa. She is attempting to summon her defences and barriers, trying to regain control. Fliss takes the rug that's draped along the back of the sofa and, sitting down beside her, wraps it around Cara's shoulders.

'How are you feeling, Cara?' she asks gently, 'Are you hurt?'

Cara shakes her head. Sam kneels beside her, taking her hand in his. His face is pale, shocked.

'Cara, I'm so, so sorry,' he says. 'I never thought . . . I didn't know it would scare you like that. Are you afraid of heights?'

She shakes her head again. 'It wasn't that. I wasn't scared for me.'

There is a moment's silence and then Sam says: 'Cara, who is Joe?'

Her eyes fill with tears, she doesn't want to speak, doesn't want them to know, but she sees in Sam's face the guilt, the horror at the pain he has caused her, and she is overwhelmed by the need to exonerate him. Fliss touches Cara's arm, smoothing her sleeve. This gentleness is Cara's undoing. She remembers how she and Fliss sat together in the courtyard, sharing; how Fliss opened her heart to her, talking about her brother Jamie, and about Mole, and it gives Cara courage. She knows that she cannot avoid this, that she owes it to Sam, and to Hal and Fliss. She has to tell them.

She begins to talk, randomly at first and then more coherently. She tells how she met Joe in London and fell in love.

How, when he went back to Italy, she feared it might be over but then, a few weeks later, he invited her to Rome. He sounded so keen, so passionate, that she believed that he was going to propose to her. Joe met her at Fiumicino Airport and drove her into the city.

She tells the whole story, exactly as she relived it just now up on the roof, leaving out none of the details. How she imagined that she might be going to meet his parents, to stay with them at their town house, but instead he took her to his flat on the top floor of a house in the old part of the city. It was early evening but he didn't want to go out. Joe wanted to make love. They both did.

Cara pauses. It's more difficult to explain how, afterwards, it became clear that there was going to be no proposal of marriage; to tell them how Joe explained to her that he was already engaged to be married and he was assuming that she'd be happy to be his mistress. She tells them how, ashamed, humiliated, shocked, she seized her case, which was still standing by the door, grabbed her bag, and ran out. Joe followed her, trying to prevent her, still behaving as though she was being totally irrational. Outside the front door of the flat he was laughing at her, calling to her. And when she shouted at him again, he leaned back against the banister rail and flung both arms up in mock fear, still laughing at her as the banister gave way. She can remember his scream as he fell, the thump as he hit the ground three floors below, and then the silence.

'I ran away,' Cara says.

She stares at her hands, now clasped together on her knees.

'When I got down to the hall I could see that he was dead – his neck was broken – and then I heard a door opening; voices. I panicked. I could only think that I knew no Italian, that I couldn't explain and that I might be thrown into prison. I ran out into the street and then I walked and walked. Eventually I remembered that Max had given me Philip's address. Philip was his oldest, closest friend and he was stationed at the British Embassy in Rome. I saw a taxi, showed the driver the piece of paper with the address on it, and he took me there.'

She takes a gasp of breath but she can't stop. It must all be told now. She doesn't look at Hal or Fliss, or at Sam, who kneels in silence watching her.

'Philip was amazing. He was calm, he let me cry, he looked after me. The next morning he took me to the airport and booked us on the next flight home. When we arrived in London he hired a car and then he drove me to Norfolk to stay with his mother. I loved his mother. She was the kindest woman I'd ever met. I don't know what he told her but she just treated me as if I was suffering from some terrible bereavement. She looked after me while he returned to Rome. He told me to speak to no one and that he would come back to see me in a few days.'

At last she raises her eyes and looks at them. They don't look disgusted, just horrified, shocked. Fliss reaches out and holds Cara's clasped hands tightly.

'What an utterly appalling thing to have happened.'

Cara stares at her, hardly able to believe what she hears: no condemnation or drawing back. She nods, wipes away some tears.

'I caused him to die, you see,' she says, just in case Fliss hasn't understood. 'He died and I abandoned him. I couldn't stop thinking about his parents.'

'But it wasn't your fault,' says Fliss. 'He should never have invited you out. He misled you. You were right to leave. But,

Cara, what happened was an appalling accident and it wasn't your fault.'

There is a short silence.

'And when did Philip come back to see you?' asks Hal.

'Philip came home a few days later, as he'd promised. He was in the Chancery section of the Foreign Office but he had contacts who were able to find out what had happened after I ran away. Apparently Joe often took women to the flat. It was thought that there might have been a lovers' quarrel but nothing was found or proved. Nobody had seen me, and certainly no one suspected a foreign national. Joe's family didn't want a scandal. Nobody thought that he'd been murdered, and since the banister was rotten with woodworm it was assumed to be an accident. It was all kept quiet, hushed up. Philip told me that nobody need ever know, but I told him that I would know and that I would never be able to forgive myself.'

She falls silent, wondering how to go on. This is always the problem with baring the soul: it's difficult for everyone to move on from it. It's Sam who breaks the silence.

'So when did you and Philip get married?' he asks, as if he is trying to carry her forward to a happier time.

She knows that only the truth will do and she braces herself to continue.

'A few weeks later I realized that I was pregnant,' she says. 'I was devastated but I couldn't lose the baby, I couldn't give it up. You see, it seemed like an atonement: it was Joe's, a part of his life. I phoned Philip and he came home on compassionate leave. He understood. He knew what keeping the child meant to me.' She pauses a moment before continuing. 'So he suggested that we should get married, that as far as everyone was concerned the child would be his.'

Fliss is still holding her hands.

'What was your reaction?' she asks gently.

'I'd known Philip since I was a little girl,' answers Cara. 'He was Max's best friend and I loved him, so it wasn't as bizarre as it sounds. And at that moment I needed him so much.' She pauses again. 'But then he said that if I would agree to marry him, he would not lie to me. So I knew his secrets just as he knew mine, and I kept them just as he kept mine.'

Cara falls silent. She takes a great breath and looks at them. They still look calm, totally sympathetic. She feels as if she is betraying Philip, that these are not her secrets to tell, yet she needs to be free at last of all the concealment.

'Philip was gay,' she says at last. 'Forty years ago that still meant a very great deal, and Philip was ambitious. As a married man nobody would suspect; no questions would be asked.'

Oddly, they look more horrified now than they did when she told them that she'd caused Joe's death.

'But how did you feel about that?' asks Fliss. 'Not about him being gay but his asking you to marry him? Was that fair of him? Surely he was taking advantage of the situation.'

'No, it wasn't like that,' Cara tells her quickly. 'It wasn't like a bribe or blackmail or anything. You see, I knew he loved me, very deeply, just not in that way. He was prepared for me to say "no" but he wanted to protect me. I was pregnant with Joe's child and he knew me well enough to know that I could never give it up. I had to deal with all of this, so why not with Philip?'

She pauses again. 'And then, not long after we were married, I lost the baby. I was devastated. I felt as if I'd killed Joe all over again. But Philip was there, he shared my grief, bound it up, carried it with me.' She stops, fresh tears on her cheeks. 'Philip was a good, kind man. I know he would have liked to have been a father, but I wasn't able to have another child.'

'It was the most terrible tragedy,' says Hal at last, 'but I wish you hadn't crucified yourself all these years because of it. Awful things happen – car accidents, all sorts of things. You weren't to blame.'

She looks up at him. 'I ran away,' she says. 'I left Joe lying there.'

'But you knew people would come. You knew they would deal with it. Your reaction was natural, Cara. How old were you? Nineteen? Twenty? Alone in a foreign country. For God's sake!'

He seems almost angry, but oddly his anger gives her courage, hope. They are on her side.

'And you've never told anyone?' asks Fliss gently. 'Not even Max?'

Cara shakes her head. 'Max knew about the pregnancy, but he never knew the child wasn't Philip's. It was best that nobody knew anything about Joe. Philip was implicated in a way. I mean, he could have reported Joe's death, couldn't he, but he didn't. It was best that we kept it all to ourselves. And we were happy. I miss him terribly.'

Suddenly she feels weak, exhausted, and embarrassed that they will not know what to say next. She makes a movement, shifting herself to the edge of the sofa as if to get up but Fliss gently presses her back down, not allowing her to leave. Hal stands up, throws some more logs on the fire. Cara sits quite still, Fliss beside her, and Honey comes slowly across to Cara and pushes her head into her lap. Her golden Labrador eyes look up unblinkingly. Cara meets her gaze and reaches out to stroke her soft head with a slight smile. She looks at them again.

'I'm so sorry. When I was on the roof with Sam . . .' She pauses for a moment, shakes her head. 'I don't know why; it brought it all back. I was so afraid he was going to fall too, and then it was like I was back there again, in Rome. I've never experienced anything like that.'

'It's called PTSD,' says Hal calmly. 'Your mind stores up the horror, feeds it, plays on it, and then something triggers a relapse and you find yourself reliving the trauma all over again. I'm glad you could tell us. Acknowledging it is almost the first requirement to finding a way through it. I think you've been through hell, Cara, but perhaps it's over now.'

His pragmatic response steadies her far more than any out-burst of sympathy could. Somehow it puts her confession into a new perspective: that maybe, somehow, it wasn't all her fault. That her reactions, her fears were natural, something that might happen to anybody faced with a deeply traumatic event.

'Thank you for telling us,' Fliss says. 'I know that it can't have been easy after such a long time.'

Sam is watching Cara anxiously and she smiles at him, needing to reassure him.

'I feel a complete fool,' she says honestly. 'But it was time. Thank you.'

Hal steps into the breach. 'I have an old friend called Claude who says that the sun is always over the yardarm somewhere in the world,' he says. 'Let's have a drink.'

Later, up in her room, Cara sits on the bed and tries to analyse her feelings. She can hardly believe that she has spoken out, told the secrets that she and Philip have kept for so many years.

Why now? she asks herself. Why now, and to three people I hardly know?

She knows the answer: that she had no choice, that she had to explain for Sam, to relieve his guilt. And yet the relief is overwhelming. Closing her eyes, arms clasped around herself, she tests herself: waits for the knot in the gut, the panic attack, the desolation. But all she feels is a slow unclenching, as if muscles she never knew she had are loosening, relaxing. Suddenly, as if to convince herself that this is not a dream, she stands up and goes to the mirror. She stares into her own eyes. It seems as if she is meeting herself again after a very long time. Her reflection is familiar, reassuring; it even smiles at her. She wants to burst into tears but is unexpectedly seized with an extraordinary weariness. Going back to the bed, she rolls on to it, kicking off her shoes. Turning on her side, drawing up her knees, she drops into sleep as if she has tumbled from a cliff.

CHAPTER TWENTY-ONE

Amy comes downstairs just as Jack is about to go to the pub.

'Sure you don't want to come?' he asks, pulling on his jacket.

She thinks about it and then shakes her head. She's been in an odd mood these last few days since his birthday and he can't quite decide if he should ask questions or leave it alone. Sometimes she needs a bit of encouragement to talk about her worries and he's not sure if this is one of them. There's been no sign of Cosmo and she hasn't mentioned him. At the same time she doesn't seem terribly cast down about it. Thoughtful, yes, almost as if she is working something out in her mind, trying to decipher a puzzle. But she's not grumpy or snappy or miserable. Despite his tendency to tease he feels an unwillingness, just at the moment, to make jokes about Cosmo, to ask why he never turned up to the party.

As if she guesses his thoughts she smiles at him.

'Well, get a move on then,' she says. 'Are you meeting anyone?'

'I said I'd have a pint with Max,' he tells her. 'I saw him in Cranch's this morning, looking a bit glum. Cara's gone off with young Sam again. Getting very thick, those two.'

Amy grins. 'Yes, you'll have to watch out, Dad. Liking opera might just not cut it. You'll have to try a bit harder.'

'You're not too old for a good smack,' he tells her.

'When you're big enough you'll be too old,' she retorts. 'For goodness' sake, go. Max'll be wondering where you are.'

He raises a hand in farewell and goes out into the street. Lights twinkle in the dusk, the water is smooth and grey so that the jetties and the little boats seem to be balancing on sheet metal. He goes down the steps and into the pub. Max is already standing at the bar, a pint of ale in front of him, and he turns as Jack comes in and nods a welcome.

'So,' says Jack when his pint has arrived, 'you were looking pretty damned miserable this morning and you don't look much better now. What's up?'

Max folds both his arms on the bar and stares into his pint. 'Judith wants us to move to Oxford,' he says.

Whatever Jack was expecting, it wasn't this. 'Oxford? But why? I mean I know you've got family there but . . . Is she really serious?'

'Very serious indeed. She wants to be nearer to the grandchildren.'

Jack takes a swallow of his ale, wondering what to say to this. Family comes first, of course, but this is a very big step.

'Is Paul suggesting this?' he asks cautiously. Just for a moment he's forgotten the name of Max's daughter-in-law. 'Do they need help with the new baby?'

Max shakes his head. 'It's totally Judith's idea. She thinks that as we get older the journey will become more difficult.' He shrugs. 'Well, I can't argue with that.'

Jack is silent. He knows how much Max loves Salcombe, his boat, sailing, all his friends. At the same time, he loves his family, too.

Max glances at him. 'Bit of a bummer, isn't it?'

Jack nods. 'I have to say it is.'

'There's more. She thinks Cara should buy our house, thereby enabling us to buy in Oxford without any delay or problems, and solving where Cara should live all in one stroke.'

'What?' Jack sets down his glass with a smack that nearly spills his ale. 'Are you serious?'

'Yep.' Max smiles wryly. 'She thinks that Cara has settled in so well here that it's the perfect answer, plus I would be able to keep the boat and we could come down for holidays.'

'And what does Cara say to these plans for her future? I thought she came here to be near you.'

'Cara doesn't know yet. Sam's taken her over to stay with Fliss and Hal for a few days. They're back tomorrow when Judith plans to break the happy news.'

'Sorry. Let me get this clear.' Jack shakes his head. 'So your family don't know you're coming and Cara doesn't know you're going?'

'I think that sums it up.' Max drains his pint. 'I don't know how Cara will react.'

Jack thinks about it. Part of Cara's happiness in Salcombe is due to being with her brother. Buying their house while he and Judith move to Oxford is something else.

'Does she need a house that big?' he asks.

He doesn't ask if she can afford it. Everyone knows that the prices of properties in Salcombe are off the wall, but it's none of his business.

'Of course not. But Judith thinks that all of us visiting will be an added attraction. I know that Cara's got to make a life for herself but it's still going to be a shock. I'm trying to think how I can warn her – how to break it to her gently rather than Judith just coming out with it – but I can't quite see how it's to be done. And I don't want her agreeing to it simply because she thinks it will help us out.'

They stand in silence together.

'If there's anything I can do,' Jack says at last, but Max shakes his head.

'Thanks, old man,' he says, 'but this is my problem and I'm going to have to try and sort it.'

Jack claps him on the back, tries to think of something encouraging and helpful and gives up.

'Let's have another,' he says.

Amy is listening to her music – Joss Stone, 'Pillow Talk' – and checking her phone. She's been FaceTiming with Charley, who's over the moon with joy because it seems that Simon might be coming home for Christmas.

There's still nothing from Cosmo. His phone has been switched off for the last twenty-four hours and she veers between a mixture of anger and hurt, and anxiety that something might have happened to him.

She wishes for the thousandth time that she hadn't told him that she was in love with him, that they hadn't made love. It all seems cheap now. What was special, magical, now is revealed as a chimera; something that didn't really exist. She feels ashamed, fooled, and she can't believe that she's been so stupid. Yet she can't quite deny the happy times they shared: driving in the car, walking Reggie, suppers in country pubs. She was so sure that he was in love with her. Yet he can simply walk away like this, without a word.

It was easy to tell from Al's face, when she spoke to him in the pub at Dad's party, that he hadn't known what excuse Cosmo had given for going away so suddenly. Al was covering for him. Earlier in the week she turned up at the barn conversion to ask where Cosmo was and why his phone was switched off, but whether Al was there or not, she got no answer to her knock.

Amy takes out her earphones, gets off the sofa and goes to prepare supper. Dad should be back any time now. She checks the fridge and decides to make a stir fry. Lots of vegetables and a few slices of chicken to make it tasty. As she chops and slices, her thoughts drift to Sam and her heart lifts a little. His friendship is giving her comfort, soothing her bruised pride. She is able to be open with him, to speak frankly about Cosmo and how she feels, and she likes the way that Sam stays calm, neither judging Cosmo nor taking any advantage of her weakness. He's just there. She's glad that he'll be back in Salcombe tomorrow and they've already made a plan to meet in the Coffee Shop.

Just as she looks up at the clock, she hears the front door open. Dad's home.

'You're very nearly late,' she tells him.

'Nearly but not quite,' he answers. 'Poor old Max is down in the dumps so I couldn't abandon him.'

'Course not,' she says, rolling her eyes. 'Any excuse. So what's his problem?'

There's a little silence and she glances round at him as she stirs the vegetables in the pan. He's frowning, looking serious.

'What?' she demands. 'What's wrong with Max?'

'It's Judith,' he answers. 'She's decided that they need to sell up and move to Oxford to be nearer their family.'

For a moment Amy forgets about her own heartache.

'Sell up? But they love it here. Oh, that's a big one, Dad. I hope they think very carefully about it. He's got a son at the university, hasn't he? I suppose it's because of the new baby.'

'And Judith is planning to ask Cara to buy the house.'

He has her complete attention.

'Why would she do that?'

'Because Cara seems to like being here and the family could come and visit her for holidays and Max could keep his boat.'

Amy turns back to her stirring. 'Got it all worked out, hasn't she?'

'It would seem so. Max's torn in two. He loves his family and he loves living here.'

Amy fetches plates and begins to serve up.

'Well, it might not work out quite so simply as Judith thinks,' she says. 'You know what they say. "It ain't over till the fat lady sings."'

Her father is laying the table but he still looks anxious. She knows that he's worrying about her, too, and the fact that Cosmo hasn't come back.

'By the way,' she says casually, 'I think I'm over Cosmo.'

He looks at her quickly, eyebrows raised, but resists making the teasing remark he might have made a few weeks back.

'Thought you might like to know,' she adds.

She doesn't tell him her plan for confronting Al but suddenly feels a little more confident.

'And has young Sam Chadwick got anything to do with this decision?' he asks.

She grins at him.

'None of your business,' she says, and they sit down companionably together and begin to eat.

As Sam drives away from The Keep after breakfast, he has a plan. It's a soft grey late autumn morning, berries burn brightly in the hedgerows, and the trees are beginning to show their winter shapes.

'Guess where we're going?' he asks Cara.

'Don't tell me you need another breakfast?' she asks.

He laughs and shakes his head. 'No, but we can have coffee and a walk along the beach.'

He is aware that Cara is still in an emotional state, coming to terms with yesterday's extraordinary events. Her story shocked him, and he feels very guilty for precipitating such a drama – Hal gave him quite a bollocking for that later – but Sam feels admiration for her; that she was able to tell them. How hard that must have been, after so many years. Once Cara went upstairs Fliss had a moment of inspiration and invited Susanna and Gus over for an impromptu supper, which diffused the tension and covered any embarrassment Cara might have felt when she came back downstairs. This morning she seems quietly happy, and he hopes that the diversion to Blackpool Sands will suit her mood and bring her further away from tragedy and into the light. As for himself, he knows why he is feeling happy. Amy's texts, treating him as confidant and friend, have brought a whole new aspect to his situation. Suddenly the uncertainty of his future, that weird sense of impending doom if he were to join the navy, even memories of Shanghai and those inspiring children and Ying-Yue – especially Ying-Yue – all these have reformed into a clear pattern, a template from which he can build, move forward. It's as if

Amy's trust, her need of him, has enabled him to throw off all his anxieties and tempting distractions, his looking back to the past, and to concentrate instead on the one true thing.

'I can see why everyone says you've been chosen to be a leader of men,' she said to him and, although it was said jokingly, he's begun to see where his strengths and loyalties lie and how he needs to stick with them. He laughs to himself, knowing that it would all sound rather fanciful if he tried to explain it to anyone else, but he doesn't have to. The crisis is over. He's back on track, following in his father's footsteps.

When they pass the Britannia Royal Naval College gates, on the way down the hill into Dartmouth, he gives a mental salute, and when Cara says, 'You must be very proud to be going there,' he is able to answer honestly, 'Yes, I am.'

Everything looks different today – no dazzling sea or brilliant skies – but the coast road retains its magic and Cara exclaims at this different aspect of the view across Start Bay.

'So are you any nearer to making a decision?' he asks her when they're seated with their coffee in the conservatory of the Venus Café. He's decided that it might be best not to mention anything she disclosed yesterday unless she does, but simply to go on as usual.

She shakes her head. 'I simply can't put my mind to it. Fliss and Hal have been kind enough to offer me sanctuary at The Keep when Judith and Max throw me out.'

'Why wait to be thrown out?' he asks. 'Why not just bite the bullet and go? After all, Salcombe isn't far away. You must believe Fliss and Hal when they say they'd love to have you. It's the way The Keep has always been, full of friends and relations, and I think they find it too quiet, especially now that Lizzie's gone.'

He doesn't add that he'll be going soon, too, but she nods as if she's understood what he's saying.

'Maybe you're right,' she says. 'Maybe I just need some extra little push.'

Sam is silent. He's received a text from Amy this morning. Breaking news. Max told Dad that Judith wants them to move to Oxford to be near family. She wants Cara to buy the house! It's a pity you can't warn her but better not say anything!

'I shan't stay with them much longer anyway,' Cara is saying. 'It puts too much strain on them. It's just making the final cut, isn't it? You sort of want the decision to be taken for you.'

'No,' he says at once. 'It's much better to jump than be pushed. What you do is, you walk in and say, "Hi, I'm back but only just to pack my things. It's been great and we'll be seeing each other, but it's time to move on." And then you do it.'

She's staring at him in admiration. 'Are you always so confident?' she asks.

'I haven't been just lately,' he answers honestly. 'But I'm working on it.'

Cara looks out at the beach and the placid sea. As he watches her she straightens her shoulders, lifts her chin a fraction, as if she's coming to a decision.

'Go for it,' he says quietly.

She looks at him. 'D'you know, I think I might do just that,' she answers.

She looks anxious, as if she is marshalling her resources, and suddenly he needs to reach out to her, to show her that he sympathizes with all that she has suffered rather than to behave as if the revelations yesterday hadn't happened.

'Cara,' he says, 'yesterday you talked of Philip's secrets. You used the plural, but you only told us one of them. What was the other one?'

Cara looks at him with surprise, almost with gratitude, as if she is glad that he has become so close to her that he noticed her deliberate omission, and that he cares enough to ask. She hesitates, as if she is searching for exactly the right words, and then she says simply: 'Philip was in love with Max.'

For a moment Sam can't take it in and Cara watches him sympathetically, accepting his astonishment.

'How difficult it is,' she says, 'to tell other people's secrets. But I shall be glad to be free of it all. I was in shock still, after Joe's death and the discovery that I was pregnant, when Philip first told me he was gay but I hadn't realized that he was in love with Max. He'd always loved him, of course, but in the early days I was too young to understand it. I just accepted that he and Max were like brothers. Philip was always so sweet to me. And ultimately, when I saw the truth, it made a bond between us. We needed each other. Ours was such a strange relationship, but it worked. We loved each other and we both loved Max. He never knew, of course. Max is a simple soul and accepted the fact of our marriage and was glad of it.'

'I'm sorry,' Sam says inadequately, trying to cover his embarrassment. 'Perhaps I shouldn't have asked.'

'Yes,' she says quickly. 'Yes, you should. I'm glad. It's not good, bottling things up.'

'No,' he says. 'No, it isn't,' and suddenly he finds that he is telling her about Shanghai, about the children that he taught, and even, finally, about Ying-Yue, and how he's been divided in his loyalties, unable to commit.

There is a silence when he finishes.

'And now?' Cara asks at last.

'I know now,' he says.

'Good,' she says. 'Go for it.'

He smiles and repeats her own words. 'D'you know, I think I might just do that.'

After Sam and Cara have gone, Hal and Fliss take Honey up on the hill.

'I think she'll come and stay, don't you?' Fliss asks. 'What a terrible tragedy and how awful to keep it a secret all these years. It was a shock when she just came out with it like that. Like a dam bursting.'

'I think it's just as much a tragedy that she and Philip married,' says Hal. 'I can see how it happened but it simply reinforced the awfulness of it all. Terribly claustrophobic. Never talking about it, never letting it achieve any kind of acceptance and then letting go, has simply kept it as a nightmare in her mind.'

Fliss thinks about this for a moment. Then she says, 'But whatever the shortcomings of the relationship, it's clear that Cara loved him.'

'What a mess,' Hal says. 'But then what do I know? I can't talk, can I? I made a mess of my first marriage and for a great deal of the time Maria and I were very unhappy. Cara and Philip probably were happier than most.'

'But now, I hope, she can begin to let it all go. Or at least put it into some perspective.'

They stand together on the top of the hill, looking out across the valley to the misty tors of the moor, and Hal slips an arm around Fliss's shoulders.

'We've been so bloody lucky,' he murmurs. 'It would be nice just to be able to pass some of it on. Share it around a little.'

She nods. 'I know what you mean. I feel the same. I have a feeling that she'll come and stay, I really do.'

His arm tightens suddenly and she feels him tense beside her.

'Look,' he says quietly, urgently. 'Look.'

His other hand shoots out and she turns, looking to see what he's pointing at. Honey is running down the hill at full tilt, uttering little excited barks as two crows fly up from the ground in front of her. They flap and croak above her head whilst she rushes in circles, tail waving. Hal is laughing, Fliss can feel it right up his arm as he holds her tightly against him.

'She did it,' he cries. 'Good old Honey.'

Fliss laughs too. It might be foolish but she sees it as an omen. If Honey can cast off a lifetime of habits and restrictions, to run free, then so can Cara. Fliss remembers how Mole overcame his fears and ran round the spinney alone, and she hugs Hal tightly. All shall be well. Hal bends to kiss her. Whistling to Honey, turning for home, they walk back arm in arm to The Keep.

Alistair spends the days after he met Amy in the pub avoiding the town. Each morning he takes Reggie off in the car to explore some of the coast. They go to Dartmouth and Kingsbridge, and up on to the moor. Cosmo phones him at intervals from Hackney. Though Becks has thrown him out he is keeping up a determined siege. Al tells him each time that he has to be back in London by Thursday at the latest, and on Tuesday evening Cosmo gives in and says that he's coming back to Salcombe.

'Have you seen Amy?' he asks Al.

Al has indeed seen Amy. This morning soon after breakfast he heard a car coming up the track. Watching from the window he saw Amy emerge from the car and, acting on instinct, he fled upstairs and stood listening, holding his breath. There was a sharp knock at the door, Reggie barked, another knock, then eventually he heard the car engine start into life and the sound of it driving away. He felt ashamed, and furious with Cosmo. Since then he's been on tenterhooks in case she comes again.

'She came out here,' he tells Cosmo, 'but I laid low. What am I supposed to tell her, for Chrissakes? Just get back here and sort it out yourself.'

'I'll be down tomorrow afternoon,' Cosmo says. 'Can you meet me?'

Al is swamped with relief. 'Definitely,' he says.

They agree times and then Al says curiously: 'What will you tell Amy?'

'I shall tell her the truth. That I've been finishing a long and difficult relationship so that she and I can be together.'

'And you call that the truth?'

'I'm all washed up with Becks,' Cosmo tells him. 'She's never going to take me back. I realize that now. So this has simply made up my mind for me. Sometimes you need that, don't you? A helping hand in the right direction. I'm sure Amy will understand once I get the chance to explain it to her.'

'*If* you get the chance,' Al reminds him. 'Do you really think she's waiting here for you with open arms?'

'It'll be fine,' replies Cosmo confidently.

'And when you finish here at the end of next week?'

'It's not that far from London. We'll sort something out.'

Al shakes his head in silent disbelief at Cosmo's supreme self-confidence and shrugs.

'Fine,' he says. 'I'll see you tomorrow. Be on that train.'

'He's crazy,' he says to Reggie, who is waiting patiently for his supper. 'Utterly loco. But I don't care. Tomorrow I'm out of here.'

CHAPTER TWENTY-TWO

Cosmo drives slowly in the steep, narrow lanes, although at least now he is used to driving on roads that have grass and moss growing along the centre of them. But he still can't resist those views beyond the gateways: those glimpses of estuary and creeks and little boats. As he drives, he remembers that very first visit with Al and how he was captivated by the magic of this place.

'Three months' paid holiday in a dream location, mate,' Al said. 'What's not to like?'

And now, all over again, the magic is working its spell and he lingers to look at the miracles of light and landscape. He thinks back to his last homecoming, when he walked Reggie out to the point and met Cara with her dog. He guessed that Cara knew that he was playing away, but he managed to avoid any difficulties then and he's praying that he can do it again now with Amy. There was no way he was able to pull it off with Becks but then she's trained to spot a lie at fifty paces. He grimaces a little as he recalls the way she reacted when she saw that text from Al. Up till then it had been so good, just like that first weekend when he went back to London to prevent her from coming to Salcombe. He was too slow when Al's text suddenly pinged in, and she was on it before he fully realized what was happening. Two large glasses of Shiraz dulled his reactions and Becks was grabbing his phone, reading the text, scrolling up to previous messages.

Cosmo pulls away from the gateway, instinctively shutting down on the scene that followed, trying not to remember the names she called him. He was unable to counter her razor-sharp interrogation and although he convinced himself she would change her mind, that he could talk her round, he was obliged at last to accept that it was completely and utterly over.

Now he has Amy to face; to explain away his sudden flight last Saturday and the phone silence he's maintained simply because he didn't know what to say to her. Even on his visits to Becks' flat, while he collected his things together and pleaded with her to be reasonable, he was still trying to think of some scenario that might satisfy Amy should Becks continue to refuse to relent.

He told Al that he would tell Amy the truth, and this is still his best plan: that, once he met Amy, the on-and-off relationship with his long-term girlfriend was simply no longer tenable and that he went to make an end to it. He can see that there are flaws in this story – that he has been deceiving both of them; that the day of the party was not the moment to rush away without explanation; that it's taken four days to break up with this girlfriend – but he is relying on Amy's feelings. She told him that she's in love with him, they've made love, he's come back to her. This is where he must start and he's pretty sure that he can bring it off. He remembers that Al asked what he would do when his house-sitting comes to an end next week, but he can't plan for that. He still has a romantic notion of handing in his notice and taking up photography, though, if he's honest, he knows that it's a crazy idea. Maybe he could sell the flat and fund himself through a training course.

Just for a moment there, at the station, it was uncomfortable with Al. His old friend was a bit cool; a bit off-hand. But the years of friendship won through. Al could see that things were tough, he gave him a one-arm hug and said: 'Try not to be more of a prat than you can help.' After that it was easier, and Al told him about the school reunion, and how some of them were planning more nights out together. He'd reeled off some names, including Melissa's. Cosmo remembered Melissa, a very pretty blonde girl. He had a massive crush on her when they were both in the sixth form, and they enjoyed a rather romantic interlude during the summer before they went off to different universities.

'Sounds fun. If I'm back in London by then, I might come along,' he said casually, and Al said, 'Great. I'll keep you posted.'

Now, Cosmo drives in through the gateway and bumps slowly up the drive. The first thing is to make a plan to meet up with Amy. He reaches for his phone, thinks for a moment and then texts.

```
Back at last. Can't wait to see you. Lots to tell
you. Can you come over this evening? Really
missed you. C XX
```

He waits for a moment but there's no reply, so he gets out and goes to release Reggie. Cosmo bends to stroke him and then straightens to look around him. He hears a strange noise, rather like the baying of hounds, and then he sees a skein of geese in perfect formation flying eastwards. He watches them out of sight, sighs with pleasure at being back again, and follows Reggie into the house.

Amy is home alone, waiting for Sam. She texted him as soon as she heard from Cosmo and asked him if he could come round. It's odd, this need to see him, to ask for his company and advice, but somehow he has become important to her. There's something stable about him; she feels that she can trust him. It's as if this whole Cosmo thing has been some kind of dream that is fading in the light of something more real, but she still feels angry and hurt, and, even worse, a fool for being taken in.

When she hears the knock at the door she hurries to open it. Sam stands outside and she resists the urge to fling her arms round him.

'It's the cavalry,' he says, grinning at her, stepping past her into the big kitchen. 'So. What's new?'

'I've had this text from Cosmo,' she says, without preamble. 'He's back. No explanation or anything. Just asking if we can meet up and can I go over to his for supper.'

'Well, you're not going to do that, are you?' says Sam firmly, then glances quickly at her to see if he's taking too much for granted.

She shakes her head, remembering the last time she was with Cosmo at the barn. 'No,' she says. 'No, I'm not. But I'm going to have to see him and I don't want to bump into him unexpectedly. I just don't know how to do it.'

'You suggest that you meet at the Coffee Shop,' says Sam. 'After all, that's what you often do, isn't it?'

'The Coffee Shop?' She stares at him. 'Seriously? In public?'

'Definitely in public,' answers Sam calmly. 'That way you're totally in control. He can't shout or get stroppy in the

Coffee Shop. You'll be able to listen to him and then tell him how you feel.'

Amy thinks about this plan. She can see that it has its merits.

'It's sounding,' says Sam rather tentatively, 'as if you're not expecting him to have any good excuse for dashing away.'

She shakes her head. 'I haven't. He's been out of touch for so long. And when I asked Al he just looked really embarrassed and ducked the question. I knew then that something's going on and . . . oh, I don't know. I don't want to be made a fool of, I suppose. Though it'll be interesting to hear what he has to say.'

'Well, either way, for you it's a win-win situation. If you think he's conning you then you just pick your moment and walk out, but if he's utterly convincing and you change your mind then you can take it from there.'

Amy watches him. She has a very strong feeling that Sam is hoping that it will be the first option, and she likes him even more for not trying to influence her against Cosmo.

'And if I walk out,' she says casually, 'will you be around somewhere? In case he follows me or something.'

'I think that could be arranged,' he says, imitating her casual tone. 'You could just come straight up to Buckley Street or you could text. What time will you arrange to meet him?'

'I'm working in Island Street this week,' she says, 'but I can take a coffee break. I'll say that I'll meet him at ten thirty before it gets too busy in the Coffee Shop.'

'OK,' says Sam. 'I'll be around. But just let me know if he convinces you he's on the level and you plan to stay there for a while.'

'I'll do that,' she says nonchalantly. 'Thanks.'

'You're welcome,' he says.

'By the way,' she adds, 'what did you think of Judith's idea of Cara buying their house? Has she mentioned it yet?'

'I don't know. I more or less dropped Cara off and came straight round here. I think it's a bit cheeky, actually. My people have invited Cara to stay for a little while and I hope she's going to take them up on it. I have a feeling there might be quite a ding-dong going on with Judith and Max. I was glad to keep out of the way, actually, so you're doing me a favour.'

She laughs. 'So would you like to stay to supper?'

'Well,' he hesitates. 'I wouldn't want to put you to any trouble. Can I buy you a drink? We could go to the pub.'

She shakes her head. 'I don't want to go out in case I bump into Cosmo, but you're welcome to stay for a bit if you'd like to. Dad'll be in soon.'

'Thanks,' he says. 'I'd like that.'

'Good,' she says. 'That's great. I'll send him a text and then we'll have a drink.'

She feels calmer, ready to face Cosmo. She takes out her phone and begins to text him.

By the time Cara and Sam arrive back in Salcombe, Max's nerves are stretched to snapping point. Judith has now fallen totally in love with her idea of selling the house to Cara and moving to Oxford. She's shortlisted three properties and has completely convinced herself that she and Max will be doing Cara a favour.

'She's in such a dither,' she said to him, 'that it's almost a kindness to make up her mind for her. And we'll be able to come back here for holidays. It's good for everyone.'

As she talked on, giving him no chance to put a point of view, Max grew angry and frustrated, and more depressed at the prospect of leaving his life here in Salcombe, in Buckley Street. When he suggested discussing the plan with Paul and Freya, Judith said that she wanted to make absolutely sure that Cara was in a position to pay the recommended price for the house so that they could buy what they wanted in Oxford.

'After all, we don't know what commitments she and Philip had,' she said, 'and though it's unlikely there would be a problem it's best to be clear. And Freya and Paul will be pleased,' she added confidently. 'Freya will want to go back to work before too long and she'll be very relieved to have child-care lined up.'

The more she talked, the more hopeless Max became. He was certain that Cara would believe that her agreement was key to this new plan: that she might feel obliged to go along with it to give them the opportunity to be near their family. Max knew he would have no chance to get her alone and tell her that she didn't have to buy the house if she didn't want it. He wondered how she'd feel at the prospect of him moving away just after she'd come to Salcombe to be near him. In an odd, irrational way he feels that he's letting Philip down.

And now here they are, waiting for Sam and Cara. Judith is alert, expectant. Max is nervous. But as soon as Sam and Cara come in he's aware of some indefinable change in both of them. Sam has a newly confident air, a kind of suppressed excitement. And no sooner have they arrived than he's off again to see Amy.

'Bit of a crisis,' he tells them airily. 'Not sure when I'll be back but don't wait supper.'

Max can see that Judith is irritated by this casual behaviour, but, before she can comment on it, Cara is speaking. She talks quickly, as if she fears that she might lose her nerve, yet there's a new determination about her.

'We've had a great time,' she says, 'and while I've been away I've come to a decision. It's been really great to be here but I know I'm crowding you a bit so I've accepted Fliss's invitation to stay with them while I continue to look around for a place to live.'

Cara looks from one to the other, almost as if she is expecting approval or, at the very least, relief. Max smiles at her, waiting for the blow to fall, but Judith stares at her sister-in-law with an almost indignant expression: this is not how she's planned the conversation. Just as Judith begins to speak, to protest, her phone rings. She hesitates, visibly irritated at the inconvenient timing, then snatches it up to see who's calling.

'It's Paul,' she tells them impatiently. 'I'll have to take this.'

She moves along the passage towards the bedroom but they can hear her responses: surprise, disbelief, shock. Max looks at Cara, raises his eyebrows, and she draws down the corners of her mouth. It doesn't sound like good news. Max wonders if he can manage to brief Cara whilst Judith is otherwise occupied but the call finishes abruptly and Judith comes back into the kitchen. She looks stunned and Max stares at her anxiously.

'What's happened? Are they OK?'

Judith sits down at the table without looking at them. She moves a mug aside, folds the newspaper.

'Paul's been offered a research post at Harvard,' she says at last. 'They'll be moving to Massachusetts early next year.'

They both stare at her. Cara is the first to speak.

'I know that it'll be tough for you with them so far away,' she begins tentatively, 'especially with Christopher in Dubai, but it's good for Paul, isn't it? And rather exciting for Freya and the children.'

It's too late now to explain the original plan to Cara, and Max experiences a moment of exquisite relief before he speaks.

'It'll take a bit of adjusting to, for us,' he says encouragingly to Judith, 'but remember how much you and the boys enjoyed Washington when I was posted there. It's a great opportunity for them all. We shall be able to visit them. To explore.'

Oscar gets out of his basket and goes to sit beside Judith, as if he senses her distress. He puts his head on her knee but she pushes him away.

'I wasn't expecting this,' she says crossly.

Max sees that there is going to be a great deal of talking and persuasion to bring Judith to a positive place and he glances at Cara, who immediately takes the hint.

'I thought I might take Oscar for a walk before it gets dark,' she suggests. 'If that's OK?'

'Yes,' Max says quickly, gratefully. 'You do that.'

As she goes downstairs with Oscar clattering behind her, Max sits down at the table and prepares to comfort his wife.

During the night a north-easterly breeze stirs the branches of the trees, shredding the mist that drifts in the valleys, and ruffling the waters of the estuary. In the east, the morning brightness swallows the dim stars and, as the sun rises, starlings begin to disperse from their roosts. The tide is on the turn and little boats swing at anchor, reflections shiver and break, and an egret, hunched against the cold breath of the wind, steps delicately along the shoreline. Up on the hill, a line of cows are making their way across the field towards the milking parlour, farm machinery is clanking into action, and a dog barks. A plane passes high overhead, its vapour trail slicing the sky in two, and a seagull, ghostly pale in the early

morning sunlight, floats low, skimming across the water. The
town stirs into life: a postman is walking along the quiet
streets, shopkeepers are unlocking their doors, schoolchildren
are gathering at the bus stop. In the church the priest is beginning Morning Prayer: '*The night has passed and the day lies
open before us . . .*'

Cara, sitting at the table in the corner of the Coffee Shop, is
trying to come to terms with this strange new sense of release;
of freedom. She can hardly believe that after all these years she
has broken the silence. This is how it must be when a boil is
lanced and the poison allowed to pour out. She feels guilty that
she told Philip's secrets, yet they were so much a part of the
whole, and nothing can harm him now. There has been so
much guilt. As she drinks her coffee, she sees Cosmo come in
and sit at the table by the door, which he watches anxiously.
Presently Amy arrives, goes to order coffee and sits opposite
him. Neither of them notices her and she continues with her
own thoughts.

The extraordinary thing was that Hal and Fliss, and Sam
too, were so calm that the reliving of her traumatic past was
almost anticlimactic. Afterwards she slept heavily for an hour
or so and when she woke she stayed curled up on her bed for a
while, coming to terms with this strange new sensation, wondering how they could all possibly go forward. She scraped up
her courage to go downstairs, to face them all, only to find that
Fliss's younger sister and her husband were there having a pre-
supper drink. It was clear that Gus and Susanna knew nothing
of what had gone before, the atmosphere was totally natural,
cheerful and relaxed, so that Cara was able to join the party
and allow their friendliness to embrace her.

Even as she remembers it all, Cara is watching Amy and Cosmo. They are totally absorbed in each other, but not in the way they once were. They no longer gaze at each other with faces alight with love. They are arguing in a quiet but furious way. Amy is flushed, her hands clenched into fists. Cosmo is gesticulating. His face wears an expression of disbelief that is almost comical. Cosmo is clearly trying to laugh Amy out of her anger, trying to persuade her that her fears are groundless, and not only that, rather foolish. To Cara it's as if the scene in Rome is being replayed. Cosmo won't fall to his death but she can see that he has already lost the battle. There is no sign of Reggie.

As people come and go, coffee is distributed and life goes on around them, it's clear that Amy isn't giving an inch. She leans forward, speaks softly but firmly, knocks away Cosmo's entreating hand, then she gets up and walks out. She looks strong and confident, and Cara feels comforted by that look. Amy is moving on.

After a moment Cara gets up and, carrying her coffee, makes her way to Cosmo's table. He's sitting with his head in his hands but he looks up quickly. The momentary hope in his eyes dies as he sees who is sitting down opposite. Cara sits in silence drinking her coffee and presently Cosmo leans back in his chair, pushing his fingers through his short black hair

'I completely misjudged that,' he says conversationally, almost as if Cara has been sitting there all the time, witnessing what has gone before. 'And now I've lost them both.'

A moment of silence whilst she thinks about that, then she says: 'In which case it would seem that neither of them was meant for you.'

He looks at her in surprise. He is so like Joe but, even though she still experiences the mixed emotions that the memory calls up, she knows that at last she, too, is moving on. Telling Fliss and Hal and Sam has freed her up and shown a way forward out of the darkness. Now that she's smashed the distorting mirror and seen her true reflection, she wants to break the pattern for Cosmo, too.

'Next time,' she suggests gently, 'be wholehearted in your love.'

Cosmo frowns, as if the idea is new to him.

'I was blown away by it all, you see,' he says, as if he is expecting her to understand how he feels, to empathize with him. 'There's a magic about this place. About Amy. It was like walking into a fairy tale.'

'Fairy tales rarely survive in the face of reality, and you'd have to go back to London soon, anyway, wouldn't you?' she asks.

He nods. 'At the end of next week. But it needn't have made any difference.'

'Needn't it?'

He stares at her and then smiles, acknowledging the real meaning behind the question.

'OK. It wouldn't have been easy . . .'

She watches him in silence and he goes quiet. After a moment he gives a little shrug as if he is accepting that he has lost. He pushes his empty cup aside.

'At least you have something to go back to,' she says. 'You have your work. Friends. Al, is it? The things you had before you were bewitched.'

Cosmo shakes his head at the word, as if he suspects her of teasing him, and then he begins to look thoughtful, as if he is remembering something, as if he has already been offered some kind of way forward. He smiles a little – already she sees his vitality is returning – then he gets up, gives her a little bow and makes his way out. She watches him go. Perhaps the pattern will be broken and he will get a second chance at life.

'You look miles away. OK if I join you?'

Jack is standing beside the table, smiling down at her, and she is filled with such delight at the sight of him that she is taken slightly by surprise. She realizes that, for the first time, she feels free to approach him on equal terms.

'Of course,' she says. 'Have you ordered?'

He nods, sitting down opposite. 'So what was the great thought for today?'

'Nothing. I've been watching Amy give Cosmo his marching orders and I'm planning a long visit to Sam's family at The Keep until I find a place to live.'

His look of surprise seems rather excessive and she raises her eyebrows at him.

'I thought you knew it was on the cards?'

'Yes.' He still looks perplexed. 'Yes, I did.' He hesitates. 'Do Judith and Max know you're going?'

She begins to laugh. 'It's odd that you should ask that. D'you know, it was really weird. I took Sam's advice and decided to announce it as soon as I got back. Well, when I got in there was a kind of atmosphere, as if they'd been having a row, but I decided to tell them anyway, and I have to say they both seemed rather taken aback by it.' She frowns, remembering. 'In fact Judith looked quite angry, which was odd because I thought she'd be pleased. Then her phone rang and she looked at it, and said, "It's Paul." So she answered it and then I thought she was actually going to pass out. Apparently he's been offered a research post at Harvard University, and he and Freya and the children are moving to the States in the new year. Poor Judith is gutted. Max stayed calm. He was trying to comfort her, saying they'd go and visit, trying to show the positive side of it. He was still behaving a bit oddly, though, so I decided to give them some time together to discuss it and took Oscar for a walk round the creek.'

By the time she's finished her recital Jack is laughing. He laughs and laughs, whilst she watches him, amused but baffled.

'So what's all that about?' she asks, when at last he is able to control himself.

'Nothing,' he says, taking out his handkerchief and wiping his face. 'It's just . . . nothing. So you're moving out?'

His coffee arrives and he sits back, smiles his thanks.

Cara nods. 'I think it's the right decision. When I got back from walking Oscar, Judith was already on the phone to Freya, trying to make a plan about them coming down for Christmas, and Max was still looking a tad stressed so I slipped away and came here. If Freya and Paul and the children are coming for Christmas there won't be room for me anyway. I'm just very fortunate that there's somewhere I can go for the time being. Fliss and Hal are incredibly kind and great fun.' She gives a little sigh of relief, almost disbelief, at her luck. 'I'm intending to embark on a life of pleasure.' She gestures towards the beam above their heads. 'That's my motto from now on.'

Jack looks up, reads the words chalked there and chuckles. '*Dolce far Niente*?'

Cara smiles at him. '"The sweetness of doing nothing." So. Any ideas?'

'Well,' he says thoughtfully, 'if you're not too taken up with your smart new friends we could begin with a night at the opera.'

'Sounds like a plan,' she agrees. 'What's on?'

'*Rigoletto*.'

She looks pleased. 'Oh, yes. Great fun. I'd like that.'

He smiles, and then quietly hums the opening bars of '*La Donna è Mobile*'. Cara bursts out laughing, aims a little blow at him.

'I must get back,' she says, and she gets up.

'So must I,' he says. 'I've got work to do.'

They part outside the Coffee Shop and Cara climbs the steps beside the Fortescue Inn and crosses the street. Max is standing on the balcony leaning on the balustrade. She waves to him and goes into the house and up the stairs. There is no sign of Judith or of Oscar, and Cara crosses the kitchen to the door leading to the balcony. She hesitates, holding the door jamb, remembering the night of the hunter's moon, and Max turns to smile at her. He looks cheerful, as if some burden has been lifted from him, and Cara smiles back at him. She takes a deep breath, lets go of the door jamb, and walks out on to the balcony to join him.

Turn the page to read the beginning of
Marcia Willett's new novel

THE GARDEN
HOUSE

Out now in hardback and ebook

PROLOGUE

T he church is full. The service has ended and the organist
plays quietly as friends and family file out of their pews to
follow the coffin into the churchyard. The nave is flooded with
bright slanting sunshine sliced by sharp black shadows, and
long-stemmed flowers, purple and blue, cast splashes of colour
across cold grey stone.

Half hidden behind a pillar at the back of the church, struggling to control her tears, not wishing to be seen, Julia watches
them. One or two she recognizes from photographs; most are
strangers to her. As she stands up, preparatory to slipping away,
she sees the tall young man that she noticed outside before the
service. Her sudden movement catches his attention as he
makes his slow progression down the aisle, and their eyes meet,
hold for a moment, before he is drawn into a group of friends
just inside the porch.

Julia quickly makes her way out of the church, skirting the
groups of people in the churchyard, hurrying away into the
little lane that leads into Duke Street, heading back to the car
park. Climbing into the car, casting her bag on to the passenger
seat, she takes a huge breath, slumping for a moment, giving

herself time to regroup. Martin is dead. Martin, who was so full of life, is dead because he stabbed his finger on some black-thorn and died of sepsis within forty-eight hours. Julia still doesn't know how to process this: the shock, disbelief, and the devastating loss.

Sitting quite still, staring unseeingly ahead, she recalls moments of their love. She remembers their first meeting at The Garden House, his first text to her:

Crosby, Stills, Nash & Young. Woodstock.

Suddenly she knows where she must go, as if he is showing her the way. The words sing in her head: 'We are stardust, we are golden . . . And we've got to get ourselves back to the garden.'

She switches on the engine, pulls out of the car park, and drives away into the warm, late summer sunshine.

CHAPTER ONE

O n this journey to claim her inheritance, El is filled with nervous anticipation. As she drives past familiar signposts and landmarks, she is wondering how it will feel to turn the key in the lock and walk in, knowing that this time it's not just for a holiday or a visit; knowing that the Pig Pen belongs to her. El remembers how Pa phoned her during her first term at Durham.

'I've found the perfect place to live, El,' he said. 'But you won't believe what it's called.'

Even as she remembers, she is seized with this new sense of grief that overwhelms her at unexpected moments. Pa is dead. How can that be true? She wasn't with him. She was celebrating with her university friends in Durham, having got a First in English. Thank God he'd known that; that she'd dashed down to see him as soon as she knew her results and that they'd celebrated in the Royal Oak at Meavy.

'I'm so proud of you, darling,' he said, raising his glass to her. 'So very, very proud.'

'You'll come to my graduation won't you?' she asked anxiously.

Her father hesitated, cutting up some food, pretending to think about it. Even now, five years after the divorce, events that might involve both her parents are fraught with difficulty. Her mother has never forgiven him for being unfaithful; never shifted from her position as the betrayed wife. Nor has she forgiven El for continuing to love him.

'I shall be furious with you if you don't come,' she told him fiercely.

Now, as she drives through the early autumn landscape, she wishes she hadn't said that. The graduation was hedged about with grief and shock. Her mother was there with Roger, El's stepfather, but the event was coloured with a terrible sadness that couldn't be dispelled. Roger was gentle and kind because it is his nature to be so, but her mother, even on such an occasion, was incapable of hiding her bitterness. El could see her consciously making the effort to hold back some blighting remark. She almost expected her to say, 'Serves him right.'

How awful, thinks El, pulling in to the Exeter motorway services for a pit stop – that's what Pa always called them: 'Time for a pit stop,' – how very sad, to be able to bear a grudge, to keep hatred and jealousy so vividly alive, for so long. She parks the car and reaches for her bag, checking her phone. There's a text from Angus. Angus has guided her through the mysteries of probate, kept her focused despite her grief, and now, as Pa's senior partner and closest friend, is welcoming her home.

Home. She needs some coffee and to concentrate on what lies ahead, to stay strong, but it's been difficult to remain positive in the face of her mother's opposition.

'You can't seriously be considering living there?' she asked incredulously. 'In a cottage with a ridiculous name in a small village in the middle of Dartmoor? What on earth will you do?'

Her mother has never seen the Pig Pen. After the separation, and as soon as the family home near Plymouth was sold, she moved back to Dorchester to be with her own father, taking sixteen-year-old El and her older brother, Freddie with her. Freddie is a peacemaker. He tries to be all things to all men; he arbitrates between their mother and El with inarticulate affection. She understands that her obstinate love for her father is seen as disloyalty by her mother, but how can you help loving? How can you simply switch off such an instinctive emotion? It doesn't help that deep down she can sympathize with the reasons why Pa might have been tempted by the offer of unconditional love, of warmth. Her mother is critical, touchy, driven.

'She just wants us to do well,' Freddie would say consolingly when there were tears over homework, or, 'She likes us to feel proud of ourselves,' when there were criticisms after the end-of-term concert. When Freddie went to Manchester to study medicine their mother was delighted. Freddie is her darling, her golden boy, and his loyalty to her is unquestioning. El loves him very much but, even at sixteen, she could see that it is sometimes necessary to take a stand, to choose a side, even if you might be on the losing team.

'I can't stop loving Pa,' she shouted crossly during those awful early days of separation, 'just because he's done something wrong. Everybody does a wrong thing sometimes but it doesn't mean you can just switch off everything you feel for them.'

Her mother tried to explain the values of faithfulness, of loyalty, the difference between right and wrong, whilst Freddie watched anxiously, willing them both to arrive at a manageable, peaceful conclusion.

Remembering, El smiles wryly. Even now, six years on from the initial parting, this is still a consummation devoutly to be wished. Barely two years later her mother married a boyfriend from her youth, Roger Bennett: a widower with a son, Will, six years older than Eleanor. Pa became a senior partner in the law firm in Plymouth where he'd worked all his life and then bought the Pig Pen from a farmer out on the moor not far from Tavistock. It was one of two conversions from old agricultural buildings: square stone buildings, slate roofed, separated from each other by an orchard and set about with dry-stone walls.

'He says he doesn't hold with all these fancy names for conversions like the Linhay or the Old Dairy,' Pa told her, laughing. 'He's called the other one the Hen House. Don't you just love it? I can't wait for you to see it. It's small but perfect for everything I need. Hope you approve.'

Now, El replies to Angus's text, shoulders her bag and locks the car. She loved the Pig Pen from the very first moment she saw it, and now it belongs to her. Despite her fears, her anxieties that she should follow her mother's advice to sell the Pig Pen and look for a job in London, El feels driven to take this opportunity: to try to make a life for herself where she has been so happy with Pa. Swallowing down tears, straightening her shoulders, she goes to find some coffee.

Over the moor in Tavistock, Angus emerges from the Pannier Market, pauses to buy a loaf of bread from the stall just outside, and heads across the square to the Bedford Hotel's car park. As he loads his shopping into the car his phone pings: it's a text from Eleanor. He reads it and then goes into the hotel and up the stairs. In the bar he glances round, and then smiles at the sight of two women sitting at the table by the window, laughing together over the coffee cups. Cass and Kate have been meeting here for more than forty years to discuss husbands, lovers, and, latterly, their grandchildren. Cass's daughter Gemma is married to Kate's son Guy, and their twins, just off to university, are the joint delight and concern of the two older women, as is their extended family who own and run a sailing school down on the Tamar. Angus orders his coffee from Lynn at the bar, catches Kate's eye and is warmed by the way both women wave, indicating that he must join them. Their friendship is all the more precious to him since his beloved Marina died nearly three years ago. She was very fond of Cass and Kate.

'They're such fun,' she'd say, after a coffee session in the Bedford. 'And yet they're so different. Cass is a hedonist and Kate is an idealist. It must be wonderful to have a shared past that goes back to your schooldays, and then all those years as naval wives, supporting each other.'

Angus agrees with that. Very old friends still see in each other their former selves. In this way, they never truly grow old.

'El's moving in today,' he tells them, as they transfer coats and bags to a spare chair to make space for him. 'She's stopped off for coffee at Exeter. Now tell me, would it be a good move to go over to the cottage to be waiting for her so as to welcome her, or is this something she should do alone?'

The two women look at each other. Cass, her fair hair silvery now, long and twisted into the back of her neck, is elegant, whilst Kate, dressed in jeans and a guernsey, still has an oddly youthful look.

'Alone,' suggests Kate. 'I think she needs to have time to take it all in. I know she's been there once or twice since Martin died but it's different this time, isn't it?'

Cass nods her agreement. 'Yes. If you're there she'll think she needs to concentrate on you rather than just being able to enter into the whole thing naturally.' She pushes aside her cafetiere to make space for Angus's coffee. 'But you could let her know that you're around?'

They glance at him, concerned, slightly wary, and he suspects that they're wondering if this is reminding him of Marina. He is touched but has no intention of allowing the conversation to become maudlin.

'Good,' he says cheerfully, pouring his coffee. 'That confirms my gut reaction. So what's the latest news? You were looking rather conspiratorial when I came in. How's Tom?'

Cass rolls her eyes. 'He's got his nephew staying with us. Dear fellow but he can't eat this and he can't tolerate that and he's given up booze. Utterly dire, darling.'

Kate grins and Angus bursts out laughing.

'Sounds like a fun visit,' he observes. 'How's old Tom dealing with that?'

'Not very well,' admits Cass. 'After all those years in submarines he doesn't have much patience with fads. It's lucky we've got Kate staying, too, so she and I can sneak off when the going gets tough.'

'He is rather too precious to live,' admits Kate. 'He asked us why our sixties generation was so degenerate. You know, drugs, sex and rock'n'roll? And Cass said, "FOMO, darling," and he just stared at her blankly.'

'No sense of humour,' says Cass bleakly.

'Hang on,' says Angus. 'What's FOMO?'

They look at him disbelievingly, then at each other and shrug at such ignorance.

Cass sighs. 'Fear of missing out,' she says slowly and patiently. 'Got it now? Do keep up, Angus.'

Angus laughs. 'I'll try. So, in that case, why don't I invite you both to lunch?'

He drinks his coffee, watching them as they look at one another, deciding, and he hopes that they will accept his offer. He's beginning to understand the ruthlessness of the really lonely but he fights against it, and so he waits, determined to say nothing else that might persuade them.

'I don't see why we shouldn't,' says Cass at last. 'Tom can manage lunch for them both but I'll have to phone him.'

Angus glances at his watch. 'Nearly midday. Why don't I finish my coffee and then get us a drink while we have a look at the menu?'

Cass beams at him. 'Sounds good to me,' she says. 'There's not a good enough signal to phone from here so I'll have to dash outside.'

She gets up and goes out. Kate smiles at Angus.

'This is very kind of you. I must admit that life at the old rectory is a bit stressed at the moment. Tom's irascibility hasn't improved with age. So do you think El's right to be moving in?'

He's slightly surprised by the change of direction and sips his coffee to give himself time to think.

'I don't know,' he says at last. 'I hope so. I know she loves the place but it's going to be very different without Martin and I'm not sure what she's considering career-wise. She says that her mother isn't very happy about it.'

'Well, I can understand that,' says Kate. 'It's been a very unhappy situation anyway, hasn't it? But this is a big step for a young girl. Quite a distance from her uni friends and her family. No job. I can imagine that Felicity would be anxious about her.'

'El's got friends here, too,' says Angus. 'I think she needs time to come to terms with things. After all, lots of young people take a year out after university, don't they? They don't all immediately start on a career. She needs a bit of space.' He shakes his head. 'I still can hardly take it in. It was so quick. Poor old Martin. He was so proud of her.'

Before Kate can answer, Cass is back.

'Tom's not pleased but he sends his regards, Angus, and says have a wet for him.'

Angus grins at the naval expression. 'I certainly will. We all will.'

He feels cheerful at the immediate prospect and meanwhile he'll wait to see if El needs any kind of support. As her lawyer, and as Martin's closest, oldest friend he feels a strong sense of responsibility for her.

'Let's have that drink,' he says.

As he moves to stand up his foot encounters something soft and there's a small yelp. He bends down to see a flat-coated retriever coming out from beneath the table, tail wagging, her whole bearing apologetic.

'I'm sorry, Floss,' exclaims Angus, bending to stroke her. 'I had no idea you were there.'

'It's OK,' says Kate, holding the lead. 'You know how much she loves coming into the Bedford so I didn't have the heart to leave her in the car. We've already taken her for a walk up around Burrator so she'd crashed out by the time you arrived. She'll be fine.'

She strokes Floss, settling her again.

'How long are you up from Cornwall for?'

'I'm decorating my cottage in Chapel Street in preparation for new tenants,' answers Kate. 'So I'm here for as long as it takes, unless Tom chucks me out. If he does, then I'll have to come and stay with you.'

Angus grins at her; he enjoys these little flirtatious moments with Kate.

'Open house,' he says. 'You know that.'

'I'll come and help you carry,' offers Cass, and they go to the bar together. Angus is still thinking about El and Martin, and Cass takes his arm for a moment as if to comfort him.

'Don't worry too much about El. She'll be OK,' she tells him. 'El's tough. We're not far away and Martin had a good network of friends. We'll be looking out for her.'

'I know,' he answers gratefully. 'It's only because she has such little family support. Now, what are you and Kate drinking? Let's get some menus and then you can tell me all the news.'

SUMMER ON THE RIVER
Marcia Willett

Evie loved the house. The bright rooms looking across the river. The fruit trees growing against the high stone walls. The scent of lavender at the end of a hot day. It was a family house.

As summer beckons, Evie's family gathers once more at the beautiful riverside house they all adore – especially stepson Charlie, escaping from an unhappy marriage in London. But when Evie discovers a secret, and a chance encounter changes everything for Charlie, a shadow falls over them all: this summer by the river could be their last together . . .

As Evie and Charlie struggle to keep their secrets safe, they long for the summer to never end . . .

Can the happiness of one summer last for ever?

'A beautifully woven tale of families and their secrets'
LIZ FENWICK

THE SONGBIRD

Marcia Willett

When Mattie invites her old friend Tim to stay in one of her family cottages on the edge of Dartmoor, she senses there is something he is not telling her.

But as he gets to know the rest of the warm jumble of family by the moor, Tim begins to relax again and he discovers that everyone there has their own secrets. There is Kat, a retired ballet dancer who longs for the stage again; William, who guards a dark past he cannot share with the others; and Mattie . . . who has loved Tim in silence for years.

As Tim begins to open up, Mattie falls deeper in love. And as summer warms the wild Dartmoor landscape, new hopes begin to bloom . . .

SEVEN DAYS IN SUMMER
Marcia Willett

Busy mum of twins Liv is looking forward to summer at the Beach Hut in Devon, even if she feels that something's not right between her and Matt. She's sure he's just too busy at work to join them on holiday, not that he wants time alone . . .

Baz loves having his family to stay by the sea, but when an unexpected guest arrives, he finds himself torn between the past and the future . . .

Still reeling from a break-up, all Sofia wants is a quiet summer – until she meets Baz and her plans are turned upside down. She knows she's rushing into things, but could this summer at the Beach Hut be the start of something new?

And back home, Matt might be missing Liv and the children, but when an old friend appears he finds himself distracted . . . What does she know about his family's past that she's not letting on?

As summer tensions rise, the holiday at the Beach Hut begins to take an unexpected turn . . .

HOMECOMINGS

Marcia Willett

At the end of the row of cottages by the harbour's edge, stands an old granite house.

First it belonged to Ned's parents; then Ned dropped anchor here after a life at sea and called it home. His nephew Hugo moved in too, swapping London for the small Cornish fishing village where he'd spent so many happy holidays.

It's a refuge — and now other friends and relations are drawn to the house by the sea.

Among them is Dossie, who's lonely after her parents died and her son remarried. And cousin Jamie, whose career as an RAF pilot was abruptly cut short. Both must adjust to a new way of life.

As newcomers arrive and old friends reunite, secrets are uncovered, relationships are tested and romance is kindled.

For those who come here find that the house by the harbour wall offers a warm welcome, and — despite its situation at the very end of the village — a new beginning . . .